Praise for *Yoga*

Featured in *Good Morning America*'s "33 Books to Heat Up Your July," *Us Weekly*'s "Us Musts" (7/19/21), and *Forbes*'s "The Books to Pack in Your Beach Bag When You're in the Hamptons This Summer"

"The third email-filled missive, full of capers, classrooms, and complications . . . *Yoga Pant Nation* is guiltily entertaining and pokes fun at the craziness of modern motherhood."

—*Good Morning America*

"Laurie Gelman's first two novels in the series were a hit—and it would be shocking if *Yoga Pant Nation* . . . didn't follow suit."

—*Us Weekly*

"A candid and engaging look at how a mom faces the challenges of daily living all while wearing a uniform of yoga pants."

—*Forbes*

"Dixon wields her power through snarky emails, spin classes, skilled matchmaking, and adroit parenting choices, all the while clad for exercise. . . . Ms. Gelman has an eye for the zeitgeist."

—*The East Hampton Star*

"PTA presidents, aging parents, fifth-grade sleepovers . . . Jen's struggles will be amusingly familiar to many women living in the sandwich generation, and fans of previous books in the series will be delighted to follow along with this latest outing of the mom who says the things they wish they could."

—*Booklist*

"Another home run for Laurie Gelman! *Yoga Pant Nation* is hilarious and warm, with sharp observations and unforgettable characters. When I wasn't laughing, I was cheering, rooting for a chaotic yet loving family that somehow manages to figure it all out."

—**Byron Lane, author of *A Star Is Bored***

"By page three, I had already laughed out loud five times. Jen Dixon, everyone's favorite class mom, is back and better than ever. Gelman's razor-sharp wit never falters in this page-turner. PTA-philes and -phobes alike will revel in this hysterical romp, which packs big feelings and genuine emotion while delivering a chuckle a minute."
—**Elyssa Friedland, author of** *Last Summer at the Golden Hotel*

"Hilarious mom, daughter, wife, and grandma . . . not to mention room mom and overachieving fundraiser—Jen Dixon is the friend we all need in the journey of life!"
—**Julie Chan, host of** *Beyond the Book with Julie*

"I started laughing (and crying) from the first page. Laurie Gelman's *Yoga Pant Nation* took me right back to my life navigating the treacherous world of overzealous parenting, negotiating with teachers, handling high-stakes snacks, and literally spinning. Let's just hope the kids are all in camp this summer, so we can enjoy the perfect beach read. Bravo, Laurie Gelman!"
—**Jane Ubell-Meyer, founder of Bedside Reading**

"Jen Dixon is back . . . [with her] typical sarcasm, funny threats, and a side of shaming for those parents who don't follow through with their duties. . . . Gelman packs it in yet again . . . with the irresistibly uproarious one-liners [and] the cast of characters whom readers have loved since *Class Mom*. . . . Readers will be changing from their 'house' yoga pants into their 'dressy' yoga pants."
—*Library Journal*

"Jen Dixon is now a caregiving grandma, a classroom parent, a PTA fundraiser, *and* a spin instructor—*Stay in the saddle, riders!* . . . The irresistibly snarky Jen . . . can still do jokes about spelt-spirulina pretzels and gluten-free cookies."
—*Kirkus Reviews*

Yoga Pant Nation

ALSO BY LAURIE GELMAN

Class Mom: A Novel

You've Been Volunteered: A Class Mom Novel

Yoga Pant Nation

A Novel

Laurie Gelman

A HOLT PAPERBACK

HENRY HOLT AND COMPANY

NEW YORK

Holt Paperbacks
Henry Holt and Company
Publishers since 1866
120 Broadway
New York, New York 10271
www.henryholt.com

A Holt Paperback® and Ⓗ® are registered trademarks of Macmillan
Publishing Group, LLC.

The Library of Congress has cataloged the hardcover edition as follows:

Names: Gelman, Laurie, author.
Title: Yoga pant nation : a novel / Laurie Gelman.
Description: First Edition. | New York : Henry Holt and Company, 2021. |
    Series: Class mom ; 3
Identifiers: LCCN 2020052631 (print) | LCCN 2020052632 (ebook) |
    ISBN 9781250777577 (hardcover) | ISBN 9781250777584 (ebook)
Classification: LCC PS3607.E465 Y64 2021 (print) | LCC PS3607.E465
    (ebook) | DDC 813/.6—dc23
LC record available at https://lccn.loc.gov/2020052631
LC ebook record available at https://lccn.loc.gov/2020052632

ISBN: 9781250838988

Our books may be purchased in bulk for promotional, educational, or
business use. Please contact your local bookseller or the Macmillan Corporate
and Premium Sales Department at (800) 221-7945, extension 5442, or by
e-mail at MacmillanSpecialMarkets@macmillan.com.

Originally published in hardcover in 2021 by Henry Holt and Company

First Holt Paperbacks Edition 2022

Designed by Meryl Sussman Levavi

Printed in the United States of America

10 9 8 7 6 5 4 3 2 1

This book is dedicated with love to my mother-in-law and father-in-law, Rhoda and Ron Gelman. Thank you for making me feel like I actually deserve your son.

Yoga Pant Nation

To: Caregivers of Ms. Stone's Fifth-Grade Class
From: Shirleen Cobb
Re: Welcome Back to School
Date: September 1

Well Hello!

My name is Shirleen Cobb and guess what? I'm your Class Mom this year! Many of you know me as the president of Not for Nuthin', the nut/dairy/gluten-free club for the environmentally challenged (new members are always welcome!), but this year I'm branching out (pun intended!).

Our fifth graders are facing their final year here at William Taft before they head off to middle school so let's make it a good one, okay?

That's it for now. You can click on the link below to see all the information the PTA president sent out.

I'm going to end this with an inspirational quote.

Zip-a-dee-doo-dah, zip-a-dee-ay

My oh my what a wonderful day!

Shirleen Cobb

PTA final.docx
13p clipping

1

"Well? What do you think?"

Shirleen Cobb is hovering behind me like Trump at a debate. Her presence makes my kitchen feel smaller for some reason.

"What's the pun?" I ask.

"What?"

"What's the pun? You wrote 'pun intended.' But I don't get what the pun is."

Shirleen folds her arms across her ample torso and arches one bushy eyebrow at me. I can tell she thinks I'm kidding.

"I'm serious!" I start laughing.

"'Branching out'! From the environmentally challenged club. Branch. Tree. Environment." She is exasperated. "Jennifer, I swear, I thought you were clever."

Aaaannd this is what I get for agreeing to help Shirleen write her first-ever Class Mom email.

"Okay, well, sure. Now I see it." I don't.

Hell must have frozen over, because Shirleen, after years of judging from the cheap seats, is now dipping her toe into the class mom swamp. This year is the first time her son Graydon and my son, Max, are not in the same class, and apparently no one else wanted the job in Graydon's class—shocking, I know, what with all the fame and fortune that come with it. So, I guess the PTA president, Sylvie Pike, started pulling names out of a hat until she found someone who caved to her wily intimidation. I should know—she snagged me again with a combination of flattery and threats. That woman could talk a virgin into a threesome. I'm hoping Shirleen leaves soon so I can get my own email out to my class before the end of the day.

"Why did you address it to caregivers?" I ask her.

"The PTA sent out a note saying we shouldn't use the word 'parents' anymore."

This is news to me. I really shouldn't delete every PTA email sight unseen. It's just habit at this point.

"Why not?" I ask her.

"I guess not everyone is a parent." She shrugs. "They don't want to offend anyone."

In my mind I wonder just how far this PC thing is going to go before we all just give up talking. But then I'm cheered up thinking about all the things I can call my class besides parents.

"The inspirational thought is a nice touch," I say to Shirleen.

She beams. "Well, I thought so too. I just hope I can keep it up. I really started with my best one."

"Are they all going to be Disney themed?" I ask this because "Hakuna Matata" seems like low-hanging fruit to me.

"I'm really going to try." She says this as though it's the most important task she's taken on since motherhood.

I get up from the kitchen counter office and walk to the fridge to grab a LaCroix lime seltzer water—my new crack.

"Want one?" I ask my guest.

"No thanks. I don't drink anything I can't pronounce. But I was hoping to see that baby before I go."

Ah yes, "that baby"—also known as the light of my life and the bane of my existence, all rolled into one perfect almost-two-year-old package.

"I don't think she's going to be up for another half hour. Italian for Toddlers really took it out of her this morning."

Shirleen nods solemnly. "I get it. Learning a new language is hard." She has clearly missed the sarcasm in my voice. "Well, I'll just have to see her some other time." She grabs her bright-red purse and slings it over her shoulder. "Thanks for the help. See you at the PTA breakfast."

Oh no you won't, I think as I watch her lumber out my back door and onto the streets of Overland Park, Kansas. As luck would have it, I have my annual Pap smear that morning, so I won't be able to make it yet again, much to the annoyance of PTA president Sylvie Pike. I think it speaks volumes that I'd rather have my vagina scraped than break bread with my fellow class parents.

Just as I sit back down at my computer, fully intending to start my own class email, I hear Maude on the monitor. Yes, you read that right: Maude. The name my eldest daughter, Vivs, decided to saddle her baby with despite pleas from just about everyone not to (except my mother, whose middle name is—you guessed it!—Maude).

"Sweetie, please think about what you're setting her up for," I said to her more than once in the last month of her pregnancy. "'Maude smells like a cod,' 'Maude is odd'—plus, she's going to have a lifetime of people singing 'And then there's Maude' to her."

"Mom, only people your age remember that show, and you'll all be dead soon. I love the name, and I want to do it for Nana. End of discussion."

I really thought she'd have an eleventh-hour turnaround, but I was proven wrong when she took her newborn into her arms for the first time, smiled exhaustedly, and said, "Hi, Maude."

So Maude she is, and Maude she will remain until she asks a judge to legally change it, which I really think is just a matter of time. As I run up to get her, I can't help but sing the TV theme song to the rhythm of my feet hitting the steps. "Uncompromising, enterprising, anything but tranquilizing. Right on, Maude!"

I open the door to Vivs's old bedroom, and Maude is standing in her Pack 'n Play, her dark curls damp with sweat and a smile on her face that I'm sure will be the death of me.

"Who's that? Who's that girl?" I needlessly ask. I have become a complete parody of a doting grandmother. I can't help myself—something about this kid turns me to mush. I pick her up and take her to the changing table for a much-needed diaper swap.

"Did you have a good sleepy-bye, bunny?" I blow raspberries on her stomach, and she giggles. "My little Maudey mush!"

"Mom, please stop talking baby talk to her" is how Vivs announces her presence in the doorway. She is in her work attire of a blue shirt and black pants, and her long, dark hair is in a loose braid.

"She *is* a baby," I mumble as I do up the snaps on Maude's green onesie.

Vivs comes to the changing table and scoops her daughter into her arms. "*Ciao, amore mio. Hai fame?*"

I roll my eyes. "I see your Babbel lessons are coming along."

Vivs sticks out her tongue, then marches downstairs to the kitchen. "Do you have any mango-carrot-cauliflower puffs?" she asks over her shoulder, her butt sticking out of the snack cupboard.

"Yes, they're right beside the spelt-and-spirulina pretzels," I say dryly. Vivs and I are in a constant tug of war about what is considered appropriate snack food for Maude because, apparently, I don't understand her definition of eating clean. "There should be some Cheerios," I offer.

"Cheerios are why I have asthma."

Oh God, I can't have this conversation again. According to my eldest daughter, everything I did for her as child has caused adult-onset you-name-it.

I sigh. "How about some homemade applesauce?"

She smiles. "Now you're talking!" She tickles Maude. "*Nonna è così divertente a volte!*" To me she says, "I just told her how funny you are sometimes."

Yes, I'm hilarious. In fact, these past two years have been a yuk a minute as I have endeavored to understand Vivs's unique parenting style, which can best be described as a cross between Mary Poppins and the surgeon general.

I wasn't supposed to be this involved. The plan was for Vivs and her younger sister, Laura, to live together and raise the baby. I, on the other hand, had planned to sashay in a few times a week and turn their chaos into order with my vast knowledge of parenting and life skills.

But three very unexpected things happened after Maude was born. The first was that Laura followed her culinary aspirations and took a job as a chef at a nursing home. Unfortunately, this forced her to renege on her promise to be home during the day to help Vivs raise her baby.

The second was that Maude came out looking so much like Raj, Vivs's on-again, off-again boyfriend and one of four potential baby daddies, that there was absolutely no question who the father was.

And the third was that Vivs decided to let Raj know he had a daughter. She made it clear this was an FYI situation and she wasn't looking for support of any kind. She was the only one who was surprised when Raj jumped in with both feet and now comes from Brooklyn every weekend to see her.

"Well, what did you expect?" I wanted to know. "*Of course* he wants to be involved. You're lucky he's even civil to you after you kept this from him."

Vivs resisted the visits at first, but it's been over a year now, and I think she is resigned to Raj being a part of Maude's life. There is no sign they will rekindle their own romance, but at least they are united in their love for their daughter.

But with Laura working all day, Vivs needed someone to watch Maude. Before she was born, I would have been all for just putting the kid in full-time day care, but that changed as soon as I laid eyes on her. Have I mentioned the smile? She's with me three days a week, and although it's freaking exhausting, I love every minute of it. Thus my constant battle with Vivs over what is good for the baby.

"How was work?" I ask.

"Slow. We spent most of the day cleaning out the storage room."

A few months ago, Vivs was appointed temporary manager of the Jenny Craig where she works when her boss, Caroline, took a job at the corporate office. Since she took over, new enrollment has slowed down a bit, and Vivs seems to be taking it personally.

"You'll pick up in the new year."

"Tell me something I don't know," she grumbles as she spoons applesauce into Maude's mouth and then some into her own. "Mmmm. This is good. *È buono, Nonna!*"

"Your grandmother made it," I inform her. "Something she never did for me—or for you, I might add."

"Well, you should have named me Maude. How's she doing, anyway?"

I shrug. "The same."

The back door opens, and my husband, Ron, storms in—soccer cleats in hand—looks at me, and says, "You deal with him."

By "him" he means our ten-year-old son, Max, who comes skulking in about ten seconds later, also carrying his cleats.

"What happened?" Vivs and I ask at the same time.

Max comes over and buries his face in my chest. I look at Ron.

"We were having a great time, playing soccer with all his friends and their dads, and all of a sudden he took a swing at Zach."

"Which Zach?" I ask, for clarification. Max is best friends with Zach T. and Zach B. but not so much with Zach E.

"Zach E."

I figured as much. I gently pull Max's head away from my chest and cup his cheeks in my hands.

"Why, sweetie?" I ask kindly. Ron's look tells me he doesn't approve of the velvet-glove approach.

"I don't want to talk about it right now," Max says quietly. "Can I go to my room?"

I furrow my brow. "Okay. But we're not done with this."

Max kisses Maude's head, then tramps up the stairs. I give Ron a curious look. "Were you trying to be Coach Ron again?" Ron has been pushing Max toward sports since the day he came out of my womb, with little success. God knows what he had to promise him to get him to play soccer today.

"No! I wasn't even on the field. I was talking to Buddy when it happened."

"Buddy was there?" I'm surprised. My friend Peetsa's ex-husband doesn't come around much anymore—not since he knocked up his twenty-four-year-old girlfriend and announced he's getting married again.

"I was surprised too."

"Anything newsworthy to report?"

"He got an earring."

"Douche," Vivs chimes in. She isn't a fan.

"So, what did Max say happened?"

"He told me Zach E. said something to him that made him mad, but he wouldn't tell me what."

"Was Dean there?" That's Zach E.'s father.

Ron shakes his head. "I guess he got deployed again. It's his third tour." He sniffs himself—"I'm going to take a shower"—and heads for the stairs.

"Don't use my razor!" I yell after him.

As I'm finishing my sentence Laura glides in the back door, carrying a shopping bag. I can't help but smile. I really am happiest when all my chicks are home . . . even for a few minutes.

"Free Vaseline samples, courtesy of Chateau Geezer." She plops the bag on the kitchen table.

Vivs lunges for it and looks inside. "Really? What's wrong with them?"

"Nothing! Bianca gave them to me 'cause they're kind of a useless size for her." Bianca is the head nurse at Riverview Assisted Living, the retirement home where Laura works.

Laura grabs a coconut water from the fridge and sits beside Maude and Vivs. "Hello, Maude Squad!" Maude squeals with delight as Laura loudly kisses her cheek.

"Why don't you all stay for dinner?"

They look at each other. "What are you making?" Vivs asks.

"Bees' knees and snake eyebrows." It's the answer I always gave them when they were little.

"I'm in," Laura chirps. "It can't be any worse than the crap I had to feed my old people today."

"I thought they were going to let you create your own menu?"

"They are. But I'm still working through all the dietary restrictions. Until then, it's creamed beef on toast."

✦ ✦ ✦

When the girls have gone home, I join Max in the living room, where he has scattered dozens of Pokémon cards all over the carpet.

"I didn't know you still traded these." I take a seat on the sofa.

He scowls at me. "I don't! I'm organizing them for Crystal's son." Crystal works as a receptionist at one of Ron's yoga studios.

"You're giving them to him?"

"Ya."

"Well, that's nice of you."

"Dad told me to."

"It's still a nice thing to do."

He gives me the one-shoulder shrug.

"Can you tell me what happened with Zach E.?"

Max sighs and shakes his head. "It was no big deal."

"What was?"

"I think he was just joking."

"What did he say?" I lean forward.

"He just called me a stupid name. It doesn't matter."

"Well, it mattered enough for you to hit him. I'm amazed his mom hasn't called me." The thought of getting on the phone with uptight Trudy Elder makes my head hurt.

Max chuffs. "She won't. There's no way Zach E. would let her."

"What did he call you, sweetie?"

Max glares at me. "That's it. He called me sweetie."

"No, really."

"*Really.* When I missed the goal, he said, 'Nice shot, sweetie.'"

I frown. "That was it?"

"Ya. It made me mad." Max had finished with his Pokémon cards but was still looking down at the carpet.

"No matter how mad you are, you know you shouldn't hit anyone."

"I know."

"Next time someone makes you mad, take a deep breath and walk away, okay?"

"I will." He wipes his nose on his shirt sleeve.

"Okay. When you're finished here please take a shower. You smell like the inside of Dad's gym bag."

Max jumps up and heads past me to the stairs. I stare at the stack of Pokémon cards and realize the old adage "Bigger kids, bigger problems" has caught up with me once again.

2

To: *The Bill Payers of Mr. Green's Fifth-Grade Class*
From: *Jennifer Dixon*
Re: *The most excruciating night of the year!*
Date: *September 20*

Greetings, gang!

Two weeks in, and how is everyone feeling? That's a rhetorical question, so please don't clog my inbox with answers to it.

Let's talk Curriculum Night, shall we? That most wonderfully horrendous train wreck of an opportunity to judge your fellow parents will be fast upon us! Who forgot to touch up her roots? Who is still drying out from a summer of rosé all day? Whose kids are getting on their last damned nerve? Spoiler alert: They are all me!

To make Curriculum Night as tolerable as possible, I have decided to use my unilateral power and unmatched wisdom as class mom to assign what everyone is bringing. Resistance is futile, so please, no complaints. And if you're thinking about not showing up, I'd think twice. Word has it that our teacher, Mr. Green, actually does a little stand-up routine that is hi-LARIOUS.

> *So, here are your assignments, and I will see you October 3 in Room 252, at 6:00 p.m. Be there or be . . . really, really, REALLY sorry.*
>
> *Dixons—shrimp*
>
> *Burgesses—chips and salsa*
>
> *Changs—water*
>
> *Alexanders—cheese plate and crackers*
>
> *Westmans—cups and plates (Jackie, I'm upgrading you)*
>
> *Batons—wine*
>
> *Wolffs—wine*
>
> *Zalises—wine*
>
> *Lodys—wine*
>
> *I'd say response times will be noted, but there is no need for any of you to respond. You have your assignments. So, go! Do! Thanks in advance for your cheery cooperation.*
>
> *As always,*
>
> *Jen, the bitter class mom*

I hit Send and immediately check *Write curriculum night email* off my long to-do list. Right underneath it says *Call Nina*, but I think I'll save that for later. I'm going to need more than ten minutes to catch up with my best friend, who has lived in Memphis for the past three years. She and my former trainer, Garth, just got back from their honeymoon, and I want to hear all the gritty details. I'm assuming there was actual grit involved, because they spent two weeks helping to build a school in southern Mexico. Not exactly my idea of romance, but then again, their wedding song was "Build Me Up Buttercup," so . . .

I scan the rest of the list and grimace. Since I have Maude three days a week, I need to jam all my errands into the other two, and believe me, it's like packing ten pounds of potatoes into a five-pound bag, as my mom, Kay, is so fond of saying.

Groceries
Gas
Goodwill
Call cable
Make dentist appointments for all
Return curtains
Spin party—2PM

The last item is the only one I'm looking forward to. The spin party is the final stop on my journey to becoming an instructor. It was Ron's idea, and I'm so glad I listened to him for once.

I was taking at least four classes a week at Fusion Fitness and loving every minute of it. But tragedy struck when the love of my life, my favorite instructor, Carmen, took a job at Peloton. I was devastated. I immediately wanted to add a Peloton bike to Ron's Gym and Tan (the special name I have for the workout area by the washing machine), but when I found out how much they cost, I decided to try other classes at Fusion instead. It was the equivalent of starting your drinking with Chateau Margaux and switching to Two-Buck Chuck. I either hated the music or didn't enjoy the teacher's style. I was bereft, until Ron suggested that I become an instructor myself so that I would be able to teach my own classes and play all the corny music I liked.

The three-day training, over the weekend, was challenging but totally doable. The cardio wasn't a problem, but I was surprised by the amount of written work we had. I needed to actually study for the first time since college, and let's face it, that was last century. As you can imagine, I am the oldest one in the class. I know it's mystifying that no other fifty-three-year-olds are launching careers in fitness, but then again, I'm nothing if not a trailblazer.

Today the group is meeting to get our written exams back and celebrate getting through it. I can't freakin' wait 'til I can play any music I want and have a class full of people whooping and hollering for *me*!

I run upstairs to change into the latest iteration of the mom uniform—yoga pants, a T-shirt, and a cardigan. I don't even bother with jeans anymore. Yoga pants are so comfortable, and I pretty much have a pair for every occasion—cropped, flared, high waisted, even ones that look like dress pants but are stretchy and forgiving. Yoga pants just might be the world's most perfect piece of clothing.

I grab the large bag of clothes I had set aside for Goodwill and jump in the minivan. I still have the white Chrysler Pacifica, but the lease is just about up, so I need to start thinking about my next vehicle. Maybe a small SUV? We don't seem to need the space of the minivan as much now that Max is getting older and all Ron's plans for hauling around Max's sports equipment never really materialized.

I dash off the first half of my to-do list with a song in my heart (not really) and get back to the house within two hours. I figure I can call Nina during lunch and kill two birds with one stone.

"How was it?" I blurt out when she answers the phone.

"Amazing." She sighs. "Just really amazing."

"Did you get any beach time?"

She laughs. "No! I wish! We worked the whole time, and oh my God was it hot, but it was . . ."

"Amazing?" I interject.

"Ha-ha. Yes, exactly. I couldn't have said it better myself."

"Did you get the school built?" I take a bite of my turkey-and-mayo sandwich.

"No. But we're going back over Christmas to help finish it up."

"Wow! You guys are committed. My mother will be thrilled when I tell her."

"I'm like the daughter she never had!"

I know Nina's teasing, but many a true word is spoken in jest. No matter how many times I do a good deed or volunteer my services, I will always be in the red column of Kay's charity spreadsheet. It's just never going to be enough. "Tell me about the people you met."

"One couple was there celebrating their fortieth birthdays—Carrie and John Something-or-other. They were from Vermont. And there were two guys from Southern California vacationing together—Chet and Al. Apparently, their wives went to Houston to shop and they went to Hidalgo to build."

"Sounds like the wives had the right idea."

"I think you might actually like it if you tried it," Nina admonishes me, and I realize I'm starting to miss the friend who was as snarky as I am. She's been under Saint Garth's influence for too long. Time to remind her who she's talking to.

"How was the sex?" I ask bluntly. "Did that book help you?" I gave Nina—oh, let's call it an "adult novel," about a handsome Viking and the wild woman he tries to tame. Not for nothing, but she's been with Garth for almost five years, so I thought she could use something to grease the wheels.

"Ah yes, *The Runaway Wench.* Thanks for that. It definitely took us up a level."

"Well, there's a whole series if you need it." I can hear her rolling her eyes.

"How's baby Maude?"

"Delightful and delicious! Thanks for asking."

"What are you doing for her birthday?" Maude is turning two next week.

"If it were up to me, I'd throw a parade, but Vivs is only letting me have a small family party."

"Killjoy."

"I know, right? She's driving me nuts."

"Tell me the latest." Nina sighs. She loves hearing about Vivs's off-the-charts parenting because she totally feels my pain.

"Last week she went through my fridge and threw out everything that she deemed expired, like Maude is going to wander over to the fridge and help herself to some past-its-prime Activia."

Nina's laughing. "Well, not yet, anyway."

"How's Chyna?" I ask, referring to her teenage daughter.

"A bit shell-shocked from spending two weeks with Yvette."

Yvette is Garth's very eccentric eighty-year-old mother. I met her at their wedding, and may I say she makes quite an impression. As Nina likes to say, she's quite lovely and perfectly normal until she starts talking to two imaginary people she calls her "spirit guides." It's a bit disconcerting until you get used to it.

"What happened?"

Nina sighs. "According to Chyna, one night they were discussing movies, and Chyna brought up *The Sixth Sense*, which they had both seen at some point."

"Right." I encourage her along.

"I guess Yvette started yelling for Chyna to be quiet and not ruin the ending."

"But I thought she'd seen it."

"She had, but one of her *spirit guides* hadn't."

There's a moment of silence while I absorb this little nugget, and then I burst out laughing.

"It's funny for you," Nina cries, "but poor Chyna got ripped a new asshole for it!"

"Why did you leave her with Yvette in the first place?"

"The idea was they'd look after each other while we were away. Yvette's fully functional except for this one little glitch. And I've told you before, those guides of hers have said some pretty interesting things."

"I know, I know—they told you where to find your keys, blah blah blah." I'm not big on the whole psychic thing.

"Do *not* 'blah blah blah' me. There was no way she could have known those keys were in the bathroom trash can."

Not wanting to get into this argument again, I change the subject.

"Hey, are you guys still coming for Thanksgiving?"

"Of course. I love your mom's way-too-salty gravy."

"You'll have to learn to live without it. Kay has hung up her apron."

"You're kidding! When did that happen?"

"Over the summer. She realized my dad didn't care what the hell he ate, and she was tired of knocking herself out."

"Good for her. How's Ray?"

"He's fine, but my mother says he never wants to do anything.

I swear, if it weren't for my mother making him get dressed and go out every day, he would just stay in his pajamas and sleep."

"That's not good. I'm sorry."

"What can you do?" I sigh as I put my plate in the dishwasher. "Anyway, I've gotta run. I get my written test results back from the spin instructor course today."

"I'm so proud of you for doing that. I can't wait to see you in action!" Nina enthuses.

"You and Garth are required to come to at least one class over Thanksgiving, if I find a place that will let me teach."

"You will. I have no doubt. Say hi to everyone for me. I'll call you in a few days."

"Okay. And tell Yvette I lost my virginity about forty years ago, so if her guides know where it is, let me know."

✦ ✦ ✦

An hour later I'm pulling into the parking lot of the Jewish community center, aka "the JKC." I'm so happy that my spin training has been held here, otherwise I don't think I would have known what an insane sports facility they have. The J literally has everything you could want, including a pool and childcare. At first I thought, "Lucky Jewish people!" but then I found out that anyone can join, so I just might. I'm hoping I can teach here and Maude can enroll in the day care. Of course, I'll have to run it by my germ-obsessed daughter, and get an earful yet again on the evils of publicly shared toys.

I head to the room with the spin bikes and see the young, nubile millennials I have been learning alongside: Sugar, a bleached-blonde female body builder, Tai Tai, a petite Asian girl with a British accent, and Bronx, who looks like he jumped off the pages of some manly outdoor-living magazine, are hanging out by the instructor bike, taking selfies. They greet me warmly with the unfortunate nickname I have been given.

"Grandma Jen!"

I wince. "Hey there. Is Todd here yet?"

As I say it, our instructor, Todd, strides in with purpose, his messenger bag slung over his shoulder. He's built like a linebacker but is surprisingly flexible, as he has shown us during our pre- and post-class stretches.

"What's up, spin bitches?" he asks affectionately. I really love this guy, in a completely non-creepy, older-woman way. I would set up either of my daughters with him in a heartbeat if he wasn't gay. I think he would be the perfect antidote to Vivs's bitchy firstborn demeanor.

Todd pulls a stack of papers out of his man bag and fans them dramatically.

"Who first? Grandma Jen?"

"Uh, sure." I hold out my hand and try not to scream with delight when I see I got a perfect score.

"Good goin'." He winks at me.

Tai Tai, Bronx, and Sugar are also smiling, so I assume everyone passed.

"So, what's next?" Bronx asks the question we are all thinking.

"Well, you need about ten hours of practice, so I encourage you to hit up your local spin gyms and see if they'll let you hold some freebie classes."

"Do they do that?" Tai Tai asks.

"Some do, some don't." Todd shrugs.

"What about this place?" Sugar is reading my mind.

"I honestly don't know. It's worth asking."

As I contemplate the logistics of kneecapping Sugar so I can get to the manager's office first, Todd cleverly suggests we head to a pizza joint called Spin! (how perfect!) to celebrate our success and toast our future. I really can't wait to get this next phase going.

3

To: Jennifer Dixon

From: Sylvie Pike

Re: Let's meet up!

Date: September 25

Jen,

Great to see you today. I hope everything with Max is okay.

I didn't get a chance to mention it earlier, but I'd like to talk to you about a special project I have in mind for you.

How about lunch Wednesday?

Thanks,

Sylvie

Sylvie Pike

PTA president

William Taft Elementary School

Note to self: Never *ever* stand around at school looking like you have nothing to do while you're waiting for your son.

I was excited to get to school at pickup today because it was Max's first time doing safety patrol. My plan was to show up early and watch the fun from the sidelines.

I pulled up in time to see No Longer Homeless Mitch leading vest-clad Max and Suni Chang out the back of the school. Mitch is a war veteran who used to be homeless and hung out at the park near school, but two years ago, at my urging, the school hired him to supervise the safety patrol and to do odd jobs around the campus. He now has an apartment, a salary, and even a girlfriend, I think. It's a great happy-ending kind of story.

Safety patrol really takes on a whole new dimension when it's your kid doing it instead of you. A mixture of pride and relief swelled in my chest as I watched my little man march out to his assigned position, looking serious and responsible. It's seldom we as parents get to observe our kids without them knowing it, so I was really hoping Max wouldn't see me.

I said a quick hello to my usual pickup gang—Ravi Brown, Alison Lody, Asami Chang, Shirleen Cobb, and sometimes Peetsa Tucci if it's her day to pick up her son—then headed to a nearby tree with a good view of the corner. As I settled in, a familiar voice startled me.

"Hey, stranger. Are you hiding from me?"

PTA president Sylvie Pike had no idea how right she was. If I hadn't been distracted by my Max mission, I totally would have been on the lookout to avoid her.

"Hey there!" I said cheerily. "Of course not! I just don't want Max to see me. How was your summer?"

"Like a true vacation. All five kids went to the church camp—two of them were counselors!"

"Nice!"

"Ya, it was great, but I constantly felt like I was forgetting something. Hey, you missed the PTA breakfast again. What do I have to do to get you there?"

"Nothing anymore. This is my last year!" I glanced over to check on Max and saw Zach E. lingering nearby. It looked like they were having a conversation.

"Well, let me catch you up on what you missed."

I was only half listening to Sylvie, because I was studying the dynamic between the two boys. There was a lot of back-and-forth but no smiling or laughing. Suddenly, and much to my surprise, Max threw down his stop sign and walked away. *What the*?? I was about to walk over, but I saw No Longer Homeless Mitch was already on the case.

"What are you looking at?" Sylvie wanted to know. It was clear I wasn't listening to her.

"Something is going on with Max. Excuse me for a minute."

I crept toward Max's corner and saw him pick up his discarded sign. Mitch patted him on the back and gave me a salute hello.

Before I said anything, Max turned on me.

"I did what you said! I walked away!" He was practically shouting.

"I know you did. I saw you. Are you okay?"

"I'm fine! Can you please not stand here?"

I knew he was taking his anger out on me, and I let him. "I'll be in the car when you're done," I told him calmly. I turned toward the parking lot and saw a small group of parents and kids watching. I really wanted to scream "Are you not entertained?" like Russell Crowe in *Gladiator*, but even I knew that was a little much. Instead I avoided all eye contact and jogged to the minivan.

About fifteen minutes later, Max slipped into the car without a word. I let the silence last about twenty seconds, then asked him what happened.

"Same sh—crap." He looked up after he said it, not sure if I was going to object to the word. How could I, when he's heard me say it daily since he was born?

He continued. "He talks to me for no reason and says sh—crap he knows will get me mad."

"Maybe I should call his mother."

"NO! Mom, please. Promise me you won't. Please, please don't."

"So, is that a maybe?" I turned quickly to wink at him.

He shook his head but didn't give me a smile.

"Okay, I won't. Does he ever get physical with you?"

"You mean like hit me?"

"Or shove you or bump you in the halls at school."

"No. He just says sh—crap."

"All right, that's enough with the 'sh—crap.' I let it slide twice, but don't push me."

And now he sits at the kitchen table, allegedly doing his homework. I send a quick note back to Sylvie Pike telling her Wednesday lunch will be great, then get up to start dinner. It's going to be quick and dirty tonight, like most Mondays, because Ron and I go to a six-thirty yoga class at the studio. It's our new version of date night. I have discovered that yoga is a great counter-workout to spinning, which has a tendency to tighten up my legs and hip flexors. And how convenient that we now own three yoga studios in the greater Kansas City area, thanks to the money my aunt Barbara left us when she died two years ago.

Ron downsized his sporting goods store to make room for a real yoga studio—not just a place in the back of the store with a bunch of mats—and that's how Om Sweet Om was born. In the past year we've opened two more, one in Leawood and one in River Market, and so far, so good.

As I scan the fridge for something quick and easy, the phone rings. It's probably Ron telling me he doesn't have time to come home and wants me to meet him at the studio. This happens every other week. But when I look at the call display, I see it's my mother.

"Hi, Mom."

"Jennifer, I'm so glad I caught you."

"What's up?"

"I can't get your father out of the bathroom. He locked the door, and the knob fell off."

"Is he okay?"

"He's fine. Why wouldn't he be?"

I have no response to that.

"Have you called anyone?"

"Yes, I called *you*, Jennifer! Can you come and get him out?"

"Let me call Ron. He can get there quicker." I hang up and call my husband's cell.

"Hi." He answers on the first ring.

"Hi. I need you to go to my parents' place. My dad is locked in the bathroom."

"He's *what*?"

"Locked in the bathroom. The doorknob fell off, and my mom doesn't know what to do."

"Okay. On my way." I can hear he's on the move. "I'll call you from their house."

"Thanks, babe."

I hang up and turn to Max. "How about mac and cheese for dinner?"

Normally this prospect would elicit an ecstatic "*Yes!*" but he just looks up from his homework and nods. I debate trying to get him to open up about this afternoon but decide against it. Instead I pull out his frozen dinner and pop it in the microwave.

I'm relieved to see that although Max seems down in the dumps, there's nothing wrong with his appetite. He scarfs down his dinner in record time and helps himself to four chocolate chip cookies.

Ron hasn't called me yet, so I try my parents' house. My mother picks up on the third ring.

"Jennifer, your husband is a miracle worker! It only took him two minutes to get your father out."

"Is Dad upset at all?"

"Oh, he's fine. He got a bit dizzy, so he sat on the toilet and read a magazine while he waited." My mother has always kept a current issue of *Good Housekeeping* in a basket along with the extra rolls of toilet paper.

"Okay. Tell Ron I'll meet him at yoga."

"I will. Bye, sweetheart."

I sigh and look at Max. "Is your homework done?"

He nods. "Except math. I'm waiting for Brinda."

Thank God for Brinda, our babysitter/math tutor. We started using her last year when Max was having trouble with long division. She's currently a high school senior, but I hope life will steer her in the direction of teaching and away from her current ambition, which is to become a TikTok influencer. I still can't believe that's even a thing.

Once Brinda arrives I hightail it to the studio. I always feel like a bit of a rock star when I walk in—not because I'm even remotely good at yoga but because I helped build this place. Om Sweet Om has become the go-to Zen place in Overland Park thanks to its mix of old-school practice and modern space. The overall décor is light and contemporary—lots of white and wood and glass, plus pops of rusty orange. Plenty of sofas for hanging out in the open-concept reception area, free Wi-Fi, water, and tea. But the actual classes are definitely old school. None of that goat yoga crap for Ron. He's a purist, and so far, his vision is paying off.

After an hour of Jivamukti with Andrea—pronounced "Ahn-*dray*-ah"—Ron and I head home together in the minivan, but not before he goes to the back parking lot and lovingly covers up Bruce Willis, his beloved BMW. I swear I don't get that kind of treatment when he's leaving me for the night.

"So, tell me what happened at my parents'."

"It was fine. Your dad was totally calm." He starts to laugh. "Kay is such a character."

"What else is new?"

"No, I mean really funny. She kept telling me that the doorknob fell off because the people in the basement loosened it."

"Who are the people in the basement?"

He shrugs. "I think she was joking."

"Let's hope so. Unless she's taking in boarders that I don't know about."

✦ ✦ ✦

"Hey there!" I smile and greet Sylvie Pike as she slides into our booth at Chili's. She is decked out in her usual hippielike attire of a peasant blouse and skirt in two shades of autumnal orange. Her long black hair is blow-dried straight and hangs behind her shoulders.

"Hi. Thanks for meeting me here. I know I should change it up, try some other place for lunch, but I just love their fajitas."

I make a mental note to go straight home and burn my clothes, because her steaming fajitas will inevitably make me smell like the wallpaper in a Mexican restaurant.

"No worries at all. I love the chicken Caesar."

"Everything okay with Max?" she asks.

"I'm not sure." I pause and consider her for a moment. "Have any of your kids ever been bullied?"

"He's being bullied?" Her eyes nearly pop out of her head. "Have you told Principal Jackowski?"

"No, I'm not sure he's actually being bullied. I know he's having some trouble with Zach Elder, but I don't know what's going on."

"My oldest was bullied in fourth grade." She shakes her head. "It was awful."

Our waitress, Debbie, interrupts us with water and a relatively unenthusiastic "Do you know what you want?" I can imagine that at one time Debbie did this job with a skip in her step, but those days are long gone. We order our lunch, and she departs with a nod. I lean into the table.

"What kind of bullying was it?" I ask, because as we all know, it comes in many forms.

"He was small for his age, so they called him Frodo and a few other choice names and shoved him around in a circle every day. But they would only do it at recess, and they made it look like a game, so the teacher never noticed. Kids can be so freakin' sneaky."

"Was Matt upset?"

"He never even said anything! I finally found out through Jani Kyo. Her daughter told her one day after school that everyone was being mean to Matty Pike, so she called and let me know."

"So, he never said anything to you?"

She shakes her head. "No, but I should have known something was up. He was in a perpetually bad mood that year."

I think of Max's relentless crabbiness and nod my understanding.

"I went to see the principal—it wasn't Jackowski back then—and he handled it pretty quickly."

"I can't imagine Matt being small!" I chuckle. Her son is a six-foot-two junior in high school.

She laughs. "I know! That growth spurt he had in seventh grade was his best revenge."

After Debbie unceremoniously plunks our drinks on the table, I can tell Sylvie is ready to get down to business.

"So," she starts, "the reason I wanted to talk to you is that I think you're the perfect person to lead this year's PTA fundraiser."

Diet Coke shoots out of my nose like a geyser and burns my nostrils. I knew something was coming, but not this. God, not *this*.

Unfazed, she hands me a paper napkin and keeps talking. "We're trying to raise ten thousand dollars to get new tablets for the fourth and fifth grades, and we need some fresh ideas."

Let me explain. Every year the PTA raises money to assist with some kind of school initiative. It is notoriously the worst task to be handed. I know I've said this about both class mom and safety patrol, but running the fundraiser wins the golden turd award, hands down. Last year they asked Paulina Pruitt (PP to her friends) to raise two thousand dollars toward resurfacing the school's playground. She and her crew sold cookie dough and colorful sheet sets until their feet bled and still came up two hundred dollars shy of their goal. Legend has it that PP's husband had to send her to her mother's house in Florida for two weeks to recover and she came back with a permanent eye twitch, but I think that's just a suburban myth. I mean, I've never actually *seen* PP's eye twitch. But for Sylvie to want me to somehow raise *ten thousand dollars* makes me wonder what she's smoking.

"I feel like we need to think bigger than just selling to our own community. You and your team could really shake things up."

I'm barely listening, but the phrase "you and your team" stands out. "Sorry, what? My 'team'?"

Sylvie nods. "Uh-huh. People have already volunteered to help out."

"Why can't one of them take the lead?"

Sylvie scowls at me. "You know, you really need to drop this"— she puts on an annoyingly whiny voice—"'Oh God, I hate volunteering, don't put me in charge of anything' act you've got going on. It's getting old."

Ouch. That kind of hurt. Plus, I really don't think I sound like that. Just to add insult to injury, here comes Debbie with the big tray of fajitas blowing that stinky steam—and as predicted, I'm downwind.

We don't say anything while we take the first few bites of our lunch. I'm stewing over Sylvie's impersonation of me but also considering the message behind it. I really feel like I've been getting better about graciously volunteering for things and not making such a big deal about it. But this is different.

"Here's the thing," I begin. "Of all the things I'm not very good at, raising money is probably at the top of the list. Don't you remember when I had to sell chances to get out of safety patrol just to raise money for my mother's cancer walk?"

"What I remember is that you came up with a really clever way to raise money."

"No, I did that because I have no ability to ask people for money."

"You don't have to ask people for money. You just need to think of a way to get them to want to give it to you. And *that* I've seen you do." Sylvie sighs. "I know it's a big ask. I can take you off class mom duties if you like. Trudy Elder said she might be interested."

I chew on that suggestion. I'm not sure I want to give up my class when this is Max's final year. Next year, in middle school, they don't have class moms. "So, you said there's a committee?"

Sylvie nods enthusiastically. "Yes! I'll email you their names. There are about seven moms, including the three Cathy Reids."

I frown. "The three Cathy Reids?"

Sylvie looks surprised. "You do know that we have three moms named Cathy Reid in our school, don't you?"

"I don't even know one Cathy Reid."

"Well, all three have volunteered for the fundraiser, so you'll get to meet them en masse."

"That won't be confusing at all," I grumble.

"One of them refuses to use a cell phone or computer."

"Excuse me?"

"Ya." Sylvie rolls her eyes and starts stacking her fajita plates. "It's kind of a pain in the ass, but if you can track her down, she gets stuff done. Want anything else?"

"No, I'm good, thanks." I look around for Debbie and signal for the check.

"So, this is a yes?" Sylvie realizes I haven't really agreed yet.

"It's a yes." I give her a half smile.

"Okay. I'll leave it to you to set up a meeting with your team. And Jen"—she looks directly at me—"I wouldn't have asked you if I didn't think you would hit it out of the park. You've got this."

I smile and thank her for her faith in me. But as I walk to the minivan, I realize that I have once again let myself sip from Sylvie Pike's Kool-Aid.

4

To: The former diaper changers of Mr. Green's Fifth-Grade Class
From: Jennifer Dixon
Re: A victory lap
Date: October 5

Hi, everyone!

And may I say, well done! I believe we just had the best Curriculum Night since second grade.

Not only did everyone bring what they were supposed to, we ended up with so much wine that we were able to contribute to Ms. Stone's class party, which, according to Shirleen Cobb, was drier than Utah on a Sunday.

A special shout-out to our comedian-in-residence, Mr. Green, whose story about the first time he ever got drunk had us all rolling in the aisles. I'm assuming he doesn't share that one with our kids! I'm not a prude, but that would really be crossing a line.

Big, big news! (For me, not you.) I have been asked to run the PTA's fundraiser this year, so don't expect too many sparkling classroom updates from me, because I'll be otherwise occupied. Please stay calm and don't freak out. You're big kids now. You don't need me holding your hands through everything like I did in kindergarten. I'll still give you updates on what you need to know, and if you have any pressing questions, try asking each other! Who knows? One of you may have the answer.

Now move along. I'm very busy.

Jen Dixon

"O-kay, Maude! That's done. Want to go to the park?" I look at my granddaughter, sitting in her high chair, and laugh. She has been eating bits of organic chicken beside me as I type my class email and has managed to get one stuck on her nose. We're spending the morning together, and then Raj, who is in town for a long weekend, is taking over this afternoon, because I'm going to teach my first spin class! I'm in a ridiculously good mood.

After my training finished, I went back to Fusion Fitness, where it all started for me, and asked if I could teach some free classes. The manager, Jodi, whom I've known for three years, said I could teach one class and we would see how it went. I've been hyping it up on my social media (such as it is) and working on my playlist for a week.

Today I've stuffed my workout clothes and spin shoes into Maude's diaper bag by the door, and now I have two hours to kill until Raj meets me to pick her up.

"C'mere, you big goof." I pick her up, run a wet paper towel across her mouth, and dash upstairs to change her diaper and dress her warmly before we head to the park. The sun is shining, but it's a brisk October day, so it's sweaters and hats for both of us.

My minivan has turned into Maude's activity center. She doesn't really like being strapped into a car seat, so we have tried all manner of things to keep her entertained. My last resort used to be putting on a video, but now it's the first thing I do. Vivs would have a fit if she knew, but who's going to tell her?

"Not my Maudey-body, that's for sure," I say aloud and look at my granddaughter in the rearview mirror. Maude isn't a big talker. She babbles a lot, but very few clear words come out. Vivs, of course, is panicking and wants to bring her to a speech therapist, but I've convinced her to wait at least six months. She doesn't remember, but Laura didn't talk until she was three. I feel like this child will talk when she is good and ready.

I have a newfound appreciation for the playground now that I'm a grandmother. I used to dread it when my kids were little. It was . . . boring. There, I said it. I was never able to embrace the whole culture of hanging out with other mothers and trading tips. Now I go, and it's like I'm holding office hours while I push Maude on the swing. I get questions about sleep training, first foods, teething, you name it. I find it funny, for a couple of reasons. First, my own daughter sees me as more of a hindrance than a help when it comes to parenting advice, and second, it's not like I'm such a great mother, it's just that this is my fourth trip to the rodeo, so I can't help but have a few tools in my belt.

After the swings (Maude's favorite), it's over to the jungle gym for some assisted climbing. This is where I get my upper-body workout. She loves to climb but isn't very proficient yet. I have no doubt she will scale Everest one day, but for now GG (which is what she calls me—we were trying for "Grandma," but this is what stuck) will be there to help her go upsy-daisy.

I've just checked the time when I notice Raj sprinting into the playground. When Maude sees him, she practically does a backflip trying to get out of my arms so she can get to him. He scoops her up and twirls her around. I've always liked Raj, and I'm sorry he and Vivs couldn't make a go of it, because he has proven to be an outstanding father even though he lives twelve hundred miles away.

"Sorry I'm late. I got hung up on a work call." He leans in to give me a kiss on the cheek.

"It's okay. But I have to dash. My class starts in fifteen minutes." I give Maude a kiss on the head. "Bye, sweetie. GG loves you!" I turn to Raj. "She probably needs a change."

"Okay. Where's the diaper bag?"

"It's right . . ." I stop and look around, but I don't see it. "It must be in the car."

We walk to the minivan, but it isn't in there either. I try to remember if I've used it in the past two hours, but I don't think I needed anything. And then it hits me.

"Shit! I think I left it at home." I also realize I put my spin shoes and workout clothes in her bag *so I wouldn't forget them.* A look at my phone tells me I now have ten minutes to get to Fusion for my first spin class. I look at Raj and try to problem-solve.

"Look, you're going to have to go to the house and get it." I hand him my house keys. "You may as well stay there for her nap, too. I've got to run."

✦ ✦ ✦

By breaking many, many traffic laws, I get myself to Fusion with about thirty seconds to spare. I grab a pair of shoes from the front desk, ignore Jodi's scowl, and dash to the spin room. I'm pleasantly surprised to see about ten people already on their bikes. Not bad for a Thursday at 2:00 p.m.—not exactly a high-traffic time at the gym. I'm wearing sweatpants and a T-shirt, which will have to do. As I put my shoes on, I'm mourning the loss of the super-cute outfit I had planned to wear.

I glance out at the class, and the first people I see are Vivs and Laura.

"Hi, girls!" I greet them from the podium. Then I notice Ravi, Alison, and Peetsa are also there. I'm really touched.

"I can't believe you guys came!" I gush.

"Mom, some of us have to get back to work, so can you get this going?" Vivs is her usual effervescent self.

"Yes, right. Sorry. Hi, everyone. I'm Jen Dixon, and this is my first class as a teacher, so please take it easy on me!"

"Oh great," says a voice in the back. I look up in time to see (*oh my God!*) Ron's ex-wife, Cindy, say, to the person beside her, "No wonder this is a free class."

My heart leaps into my throat and practically chokes me. My

hands start to shake, and immediately I'm at DEFCON 1. Crazy Cindy! In my spin class! I look at my daughters with what I can only imagine is sheer panic in my eyes. They look back at me curiously, and I realize that although they've heard many stories about Crazy Cindy, they have never seen her in person. She has cut her hair and muted the red down to a strawberry blond, but her big blue eyes and big, big boobs are unmistakable. Why is she here? We haven't heard from her in at least five years.

I must look like a nutjob to the other people in the class, so I take a breath, put on my microphone, and plug my phone into the mega receiver.

"Okay, let's get to it!" I say with as much positivity as I can muster in the moment. "Take all the resistance off, then put three turns back on."

Just then, the first song kicks.

"Awwwwww, FREAK OUT!" Chic starts to blare on the speakers. I was *so* excited to start my class with a kick-ass, fun song that I figured everyone would know and sing along to. I was expecting some whooping and hollering in reaction, but when I look out at the class, you'd think they were on a death ride. Even my best friends are looking down.

"Alright, let's get warmed up," I yell. The microphone is much too close to my mouth, so I immediately get screeching feedback from the speakers.

"Sorry." I adjust the mic and take a breath to steady my nerves. I peek out at the riders, and everyone is still looking down at their handlebars.

"One, two, one, two, one, two." I yell out the beat and am glad to see people start to speed up. I keep quiet for the rest of the song, and as the second one—"The Climb," by Miley Cyrus—starts, I tell everyone to turn it up for our first steep hill. "Stay in the saddle for now," I instruct them. Why does everything I say sound so lame? I've dreamed of teaching this class for months. I never thought I would be a rock star from the moment I took the instructor bike, but this lead balloon of a class isn't what I expected either. Everything that comes out of my mouth sounds false and weak.

As the next song comes on ("Seasons of Love," from the *Rent* soundtrack), I ask my riders how they're feeling.

"Great!" yells Ravi enthusiastically, and Peetsa gives me a "woohoo." Everyone else keeps their head down and pedals. I sneak a look at Crazy Cindy, and she's texting—her legs barely moving.

I think of Carmen, my spin goddess. I never once saw anyone take their phone out in her class. I realize I need to do something, to say something, to get the energy up. Unfortunately, as I'm deciding between "Get off your butt" and "Get off your tush," I yell out, "Get off your *bush*!"

I'm immediately mortified. Vivs and my friends look up in stunned silence. The rest of the class have confused looks on their faces, like they're wondering whether to take me seriously. In that moment, I do the only thing I can think of: I double down.

"You heard me! Get up! Even you, sir," I say to the lone male in the studio. We finish the song at a fast jog and ease into the next one, and the one after that, and before I know it, we're stretching to Rihanna's "Take a Bow." The first line of the song is, "How 'bout a round of applause?" Once, when Carmen played it, the entire class gave her a deafening cheer. Not so much for me. I halfheartedly lead the stretch and thank everyone for coming. My friends come up to the front bike to tell me how fun it was, but I can tell they're a bit disappointed. I guess I've been talking a big game about what a great teacher I was going to be.

"Good job, Mom!" Laura stands beside me.

"I have to get back to work." Vivs gives me a super sweaty hug. "I assume Raj has Maude?"

"Yup. They're at my house, I think."

"Okay, thanks. I'll call you later. We can talk about your playlist."

I'm putting my shoes on and still smarting from Vivs's remark when I hear, "Of all the gym joints in all the world, huh?"

Crazy Cindy is standing in front of me with a smirk on her face. I'm gratified to see she's as sweaty as I am.

"Good one." I smirk back. "I didn't know you were a member here."

"I joined a few weeks ago. Are you teaching here now?"

"Not sure. This was my first class. I'm here on a trial basis."

She nods. "How's Ron? I see he has yoga studios now."

"Yeah. He got into it a few years ago, and now we have three." I'm hoping she catches the "we" I threw in. There's a pause, and I brace myself for whatever crazy thing she's going to do or say next, because let's face it—we don't call her Crazy Cindy for nothing. But then she utterly surprises me.

"Well, let me know where you end up teaching. Your class was good."

"You were on your phone for half of it," I point out before I can stop myself.

"I was texting people how good you are. I'd take your class again."

"Uh, well, thanks. I'll let you know."

My head is spinning as she walks to the door, but I have the presence of mind to yell out, "Hey, can you let Jodi know you liked it?" The door swings closed, so I'm not sure if she heard me.

✦ ✦ ✦

On the way home from the gym I go over every minute of the class in my head. There wasn't one song on my playlist that Carmen hadn't played in her class at some point. I was upbeat and supportive. I think the class was challenging enough for the riders, but the energy was like mud—even my friends couldn't muster much excitement. What the hell did I do wrong? I'm so disappointed in myself.

It starts to rain, so I turn on my wipers. I realize I need to talk to someone who understands. I wish I had Carmen's phone number. Maybe I'll reach out to her on Facebook.

"Or I could call Todd," I say out loud, and chastise myself for not thinking of it sooner. "Call Todd," I say to my onboard computer, and within seconds his phone is ringing.

"Grandma Jen!" Todd answers, and I want to scream, "Don't kick me when I'm down!" Instead I laugh and ask how he's doing.

"Doing great, thanks. Just having a quick snack before I teach tonight."

"I just taught my first class," I blurt out, and then it's as though the proverbial Dutch boy took his finger out of the dike. I tell him how excited I was, how long I worked on my playlist, how many people were there, how Crazy Cindy was on her phone half the time, and how the whole thing was a complete train wreck. When I finish, all I hear is laughing.

"It really wasn't funny," I mutter.

"Oh my God, Grandma Jen, by first-class standards you hit it out of the park. When I taught my first class—first of all, I only had three riders, and halfway through, one of them yelled out, 'I want my money back.'"

I gasp. "Oh my God, that would have killed me." I pull into my driveway, put the minivan in Park, and start to giggle. "What did you say?"

"Nothing! I was too scared I wouldn't be allowed to teach again if I mouthed off at a client. But you know what? He was probably right. I did suck—for him."

"Did you change anything?"

"Nope. And after a few practically empty classes, people started finding me."

"And look at you now," I marvel.

"Look at me now. Keep your chin up, Grandma. You're going to find your people."

"Thanks, Todd."

"You bet."

✦ ✦ ✦

"That's what she said?"

Ron and I are cleaning up after a dinner of lamb chops and broccoli, and now that Max is in the living room finishing homework, I'm telling him about my encounter with his not-so-beloved ex.

"Yup. She wants to take my class again."

"Well, whatever you do, don't tell her where you're teaching."

"I have to say, she seemed a little less crazy than usual."

"That's one of her tricks. She seems fine, and then, *whack!*" He hits himself on the back of the head for emphasis.

"I don't think I need to worry." I shrug.

Ron shakes his head. "I'm going to remind you of this conversation in six months."

"Be my guest."

"Hey, did you ask about teaching other classes?"

"Jodi wasn't around when I left. I'll try her tomorrow."

"You gotta strike while the iron's hot, babe."

"Yes, well, this particular iron is only lukewarm, so I figure, no rush."

Ron yawns and stretches his arms over his head, exposing his toned abs, and I'm once again reminded of the cruel inequity that life has handed women. I could do crunches for six months straight and never achieve what he gets by simply doing yoga and running on the treadmill—three babies and perimenopause have sufficiently put the nail in that coffin. Of course, Ron doesn't drink a lot of wine or eat chocolate, which I most certainly do. Oh, well—if he wants a woman who only eats salad and seltzer, he's welcome to sign up for eHarmony.

5

To: Delia Cramer, Alison Lody, Terry DiLorento, Liana Jones, Cathy Reid, Cathy Reid

From Jennifer DIxon

Re: Wake up, we need to make money!

Date: October 19

Hello, moms!

First of all, congratulations on volunteering for that most prestigious of all PTA committees, the We Fundraise Until Kingdom Come Team (WeFUKCT)! Our elite squad will be the talk of the school once we get together and decide on a team uniform and mascot.

So, who's free to meet in the cafeteria this Thursday morning after drop-off?

Thanks,

Your fearless leader, Jen Dixon

P.S. If anyone sees the Cathy Reid who doesn't use a computer, can you mention this to her? I have no idea what she looks like.

With that out of the way, I grab my phone and call Fusion. When I talked to Jodi the day after my class, she said she didn't have anything to offer me at the time, but to call in a couple of weeks. Today is two weeks exactly, so I'm hoping she sees how committed I am.

It goes to voice mail, so I leave a message. I really hope Fusion comes through. I've taught three other classes in the past weeks, all at a community center near city hall that had just invested in six spin bikes in the hopes of bringing in a younger crowd. Imagine their surprise when fifty-three-year-old me showed up to teach! There were two riders in my first class— Bruce and Trudy Morrow, a husband and wife, both in their sixties. So much for attracting a younger crowd. My early-1970s playlist was perfect for them. They seemed to know every song, and when James Taylor started singing "Fire and Rain," Bruce actually belted out the chorus. It was such a rush! Not exactly Carmen's level, but I definitely got a taste of it.

I went back a few days later, but Bruce and Trudy were a no-show. The David Bowie retrospective I had planned for the class wasn't going to cut it with the three millennial girls who showed up on their lunch break, so I pulled up the top ten songs on Apple Music instead. They loved the tunes, but I didn't know half of what was playing, so it was challenging to teach properly. I ended up babbling on and on about the time Harry Styles dated Taylor Swift and she wrote a song about him called "Style," just to prove how down I am with the 411. News flash: no one says "411" anymore.

When I went to teach a third class at the community center, I brought a variety of playlists to suit whatever crowd showed up, but sadly, no one did. I taught the class anyway, complete with yelling encouragements and singing along to the music. Anyone watching would have thought I'd just escaped from Dr. Jordan's private asylum.

The good news is I'm feeling more and more comfortable as a teacher. I mean, I still make a lot of mistakes (although nothing as egregious as "Get off your bush"), but no one seems to care, so I don't either. I thought I was so ready to blow the roof off as a spin teacher, but these past few weeks have shown me what an arrogant idiot I was. I mean, just because you like to drink doesn't mean you'd make a good bartender.

I head upstairs to check on Maude, who is having her afternoon siesta. She's still zonked out from all her exploits at My Gym this morning. I sneak back out just in time to hear my cell phone buzz. It's Peetsa. I haven't had a chance to catch up with her in ages. Her life has changed so much in the past few years: I met Peetsa when Max started kindergarten, and back then she was a married, stay-at-home mother of three. Now she's divorced and is kicking ass selling cars for a living. I didn't know what her life would turn into after Buddy left, but after a six-month pity party she got herself up off the floor and took charge. Now she's a successful Hyundai salesperson and a frequenter of online dating sites.

The dating is what she's calling about. I don't think I've ever known anyone to go out on so many *first* dates. Her stories make me thank God I'm not out there trying to find a new man. You always hear about how crazy women are, but Peetsa has informed me that men are even worse.

"Tell me" is how I answer my phone.

"Oh God." She sighs. "I mean, why me?"

"What did he do?"

"It's more what he didn't do. Everything seemed fine. He was normal looking and interesting enough to talk to."

"Which one was this again?"

"Greg. He works in marketing at Hallmark."

"Uh huh . . ." I'm making my way back down to the kitchen. "So?"

"So, we had dinner."

"Where did you go?"

"Garazzo's."

"Nice."

"Right? That's what I thought. We ordered wine and pasta, and I'm thinking this is going pretty well."

"Okay . . ."

"But then he's eating his fettuccine Alfredo, and the cream sauce is getting all over his face and dripping down his chin."

"Didn't he have a napkin?"

"Yes, he had a napkin! But he didn't pick it up. And his food was just all over his face."

I sit down at the kitchen counter office and try to get a mental picture of what she's describing.

"Did you say anything?"

"Finally, I said, 'Greg, you have Alfredo sauce all over your face.' And you won't believe what he said."

"What?"

"He said, 'I know. That's how I eat. I just do one big wipe at the end.'"

"Shut your damn mouth!" I yell and keel over laughing. "Come on!"

"I swear it on Zach's life. Seriously, where has this guy been his whole life that he thinks this is acceptable restaurant behavior?"

"Did you have dessert?" I laugh.

"Oh sure. He just stuck his face in a key lime pie, and we called it a night."

"Oh, P, I'm sorry. How many does this make?"

"Six. I hate men."

"No, you don't. You just need a different pool to choose from. What are you on now?"

"Still on Match."

"Have you tried maybe one of the sites for . . . mature people?"

"You think I'll have better luck finding a guy who can feed himself on a geezer dating site?"

"It's fifty-plus. Not all of them are on feeding tubes."

"Wanna bet?"

"How's work?" I can hear Maude starting to stir, so I know I'll have to cut this short.

"Good, thank God. Made my monthly quota, no problem."

"What about the guys?" Peetsa's been having a little trouble with the male energy at the Hyundai dealership.

"Whatever. They don't bother me anymore."

"Gee Gee!" Maude yells. I want to talk to P some more, but I hate to keep my little love waiting.

"Whoops! Maude is up—gotta go."

"Kiss her for me! And girls' night out soon!"

"Definitely." I place the phone on the counter and run upstairs. Maude is overheated from her nap, but she isn't crying. She starts to jump up and down when she sees me, and really, who needs anything more than that?

"Hello, little love. How was your nap?" I ask Alexa to play "Baby Shark" (God help me!) and change her entire outfit. I give her a sippy cup of water and force myself to sing along while I attempt to trim her nails. Then we go down to the kitchen for a snack, and while I'm cleaning up the mess Maude made eating her squash, Raj comes in the back door. He's been spending more and more time in KC lately, and I'd be worried about his job security, but he claims his boss doesn't mind that he works remotely.

"Dada!" Maude screams, and my heart melts. She just loves her father. Raj gives me a quick hug, then scoops his daughter out of her high chair and kisses her chubby cheeks.

"Hi, ladies!" Raj is beaming.

"You're early," I say but I'm secretly glad. It's so much easier to pick up Max without Maude—although I do love the swirl of oohs and ahhs I get from my friends when I have her with me.

"Yeah, I finished work early. I get so much more done when I'm not in the office. No distractions unless I have this one." He kisses Maude's head. "Hey, I wanted to give you a heads-up about something."

"What's up?" I take a seat at the kitchen counter office.

"My mother is coming to visit."

"Varsha's coming? That's great! I've always wanted to meet her. When?"

"For Christmas. Is that okay? I know you always have a houseful."

"There's always room for one more. I bet she can't wait to meet her granddaughter. I can't believe she's waited all this time."

"I know. But she hates leaving home."

"Well, I'm really glad she's coming. Will she stay in a hotel?"

He scratches his head and sighs. "I'm not sure yet. There's a lot to figure out."

"Well, let me know if I can help in any way."

"Thanks. I will. Do you mind if we hang out here for a while?"

"Of course. I'll be back in half an hour."

✦ ✦ ✦

"That's exciting!"

This is the reaction I get from Ravital Brown when I go to pick up Max at school. Ravi is the mother of Zach B. and a good friend. It was touch-and-go for us in kindergarten because, at first, she really didn't get my class-mom emails. She was pretty horrified until her husband, Rob, schooled her on the finer points of being snarky. Once she got it, she was all in, and we've been friends ever since.

I've just told the pickup squad that Raj's mother is coming for Christmas and how excited I am.

"I know. I can't wait to meet her. We've known Raj for so long, and it's weird that we've never met his mother."

"Mothers-in-law." Alison Lody gives a visible shiver.

"I'm with you," Shirleen chimes in. "My mother-in-law is the worst."

"She can't be any worse than mine was," Alison Lody grumbles. "My house was never clean enough for her—even if I had the frickin' professionals come in and do it." She crosses her arms and shakes her head.

"Buddy's mother hated me," Peetsa says. "One of the best things about the divorce is I never have to sit through another dinner where she talks about all the great girls he dated that got away." She rolls her eyes. "I overheard her say to my father-in-law once that when Buddy met me he gave up on his dreams."

"Wow—that's harsh. But she's not my mother-in-law. She's a fellow grandparent," I remind all of them. And technically she isn't Vivs's mother-in-law either, since she and Raj aren't married.

"That doesn't mean she's going to be nice." Alison still has a sour expression on her face. "I mean, who here likes their mother-in-law?" Ravi raises her hand, and the pickup crew stares at her like she just admitted to drunk driving.

"Seriously?" Peetsa says. "You *like* your mother-in-law?"

"I love her! She thanks me all the time for being so good to Rob."

This sits like a bad smell in our little circle, which is kind of sad considering we're probably all going to be mothers-in-law someday. I really can't relate. Ron's mother died when he was in his twenties, long before I met him. I tell them as much.

"Well, consider yourself blessed." Shirleen nods with authority. "Bud's mom is *so* passive-aggressive. She'll say things like, 'I'm sure you meant to put clean sheets on my bed, but you just forgot.' And for years, every time she saw me, she asked if I was pregnant." Shirleen pats her stomach for emphasis.

This leads to a free-for-all of complaining until the bell rings and the kids come running out of school like someone just yelled, "Free ice cream!"

I love watching the little ones amble out. It makes me nostalgic for the days when Max was that young. My little man is now in the top grade at school, and when he walks out with Zach B. and Zach T. flanking him, I can't believe how tall he's getting. He used to run up and hug me, but now all I get is a nod and maybe a "hey." I debate smothering him with hugs and kisses and decide the fallout wouldn't be worth the moment of joy.

While I'm driving home and trying to get absolutely anything out of my son about his day, my phone rings.

"Hello? You're on speakerphone!" I answer.

"Jen, is that you? It's Jodi from Fusion."

I sit up a bit straighter and try to sound casual. "Hey, Jodi, what's up?"

"Josiah just canceled. Could you sub in for the four o'clock class?"

A quick glance at the clock tells me I'd have about thirty minutes to get home, get changed, and get to Fusion. Totally doable.

"Absolutely! Thanks for thinking of me."

"Well, you're my fourth call. It was actually helpful that you left me a message this morning. I had completely forgotten about you."

That's flattering, I think to myself. "I'll see you by four," I tell her and hang up. "Yes!" I take a peek at Max in the rearview mirror and panic for about ten seconds, thinking I don't have anyone to look after him, but then I remember Raj is at the house. I'm sure he won't mind staying a bit longer.

When we get home, Raj is sitting on the floor in the living room playing Elefun with Maude. The butterflies are shooting out of the blue elephant's trunk for what I'm sure is the twentieth time, and she's jumping around trying to catch them with her net.

"Do you mind staying a bit longer and watching Max while I teach a spin class?" I'm trying my hardest to sound casual, like this happens every day, but I can tell I'm not pulling it off because of the grin Raj gives me.

"It'll cost you dinner," he says playfully.

"Seems like a fair trade, although in this house you eat at your own risk."

✦ ✦ ✦

When I get back home ninety minutes later, I feel like I've been ridden hard and put away wet. Subbing for a popular teacher isn't for the faint of heart . . . or ego. I expected a lot of things, but not for someone to yell out, in the middle of class, "Your music sucks!" I mean, it's not like I was playing an Andy Gibb retrospective. But Josiah's regulars are used to a hard-rock class, and I didn't have time to put together anything even remotely resembling that.

The hardest rock I have downloaded is INXS, so I played "Suicide Blonde" to kick things off and prayed that the ghost of Vivs's maybe daddy, Michael Hutchence, would get me through this. Little did I know that Josiah's riders' idea of hard rock is more Judas Priest and Megadeth, so no matter what I played (granted, there was a lot of Toto and Journey, and the only Guns N' Roses song I had was a ballad) people kept walking out. By the end of the once-full class only four riders were left, and I'm counting myself in that number.

I thanked those who stayed and made a joke about the *Titanic*, which went over about as well as you'd expect. As the last guy was leaving, he helpfully informed me that I was trying too hard—the perfect end to a perfect class. I felt like a fraud and a failure and a million other things, fears that I thought I'd put to rest in the last few weeks. On my way out I saw Jodi at the front desk.

"Was that a test?" I asked her.

"Kind of." She shrugged.

"Because it felt more like a hazing. I didn't realize it was Hell Week."

She just looked at me.

"Well, did I pass? Because I feel like shit."

"You definitely passed the 'Can I rely on you?' test. The fact that you were able to teach with thirty minutes' notice is great."

"Okay, well, that's something." I don't know what I expected her to say—maybe an acknowledgment of what a tough class she had handed me?

"You have my number," I said as I walked out the door.

"And maybe I'll use it," Jodi called after me.

6

To: WeFUKCT
From: Jennifer Dixon
Re: Today's meeting
Date: October 23

Hello Fellow Fundraisers,

After this morning's meeting I feel there are a few basic rules I need to lay out.

First, a fundraising meeting is just that. We meet to talk about how we are going to raise money for good old William Taft. It is not, I repeat, not an opportunity to get caught up on school gossip or to debate the merits of washing your hair every other day versus two times a week.

Second, show up with ideas. Unlike some of the other committees you may have served on, this isn't a social club. We've been given the Hindenburg of assignments, and I want to make sure we deliver.

So, let's try this again on Monday. Same time, same place, different attitude.

Thanks (but really, for what?)

Jen

P.S. If anyone bumps into No-Tech Cathy, please let her know.

I know this is a bit dictatorial, and it's really not directed at *everyone* who was there, but it needs to be said. This morning's meeting was a colossal waste of time. I was afraid this would happen. There are moms who are great volunteers and really work hard on their committees. However, certain moms volunteer just so they can talk about how busy they are—when it comes time to actually get some work done, they're useless. They would rather drink coffee and chit-chat than get anything of substance done. Well, not on my watch, ladies. I have no intention of being the sole worker on this. For the first time ever, I want input! I want to delegate! I want to say yes and no to ideas that are brought to me. Is that too much to ask?

Thank God for Alison Lody, my former nemesis turned good friend, who actually tried to help me steer the conversation back to the subject at hand. Unfortunately, even she got sucked into the all-important discussion about what happened on *The Bachelor*.

On the bright side, I did finally get to meet the three Cathy Reids, whom I now call Cathy Funfair (because she told me no fewer than six times that she is head of her church's spring funfair and she will be very busy doing that), Cathy Red Nails (for obvious reasons), and No-Tech Cathy. Of the three, I believe No-Tech is going to be my hardest worker. She informed me the best way to contact her is on her landline. I thought about asking why she rejects twenty-first-century technology but decided I don't really care. To each her own.

So, we'll see what they come up with for Monday. Right now, I have to head over and make dinner at my mother's house. She wants everyone over for a visit, but she doesn't cook anymore, as she kindly reminded me earlier today.

"Well, why doesn't everyone come here?" I asked her. "I'll cook, and you can just relax."

"I really don't think I can get your father dressed and out of the house, sweetheart. He's become such a homebody. He doesn't even have lunch at the club anymore."

By "the club," my mother of course meant the Kiwanis club, of which he has been a member all his adult life. He used to love the monthly lunch meetings with his friends.

"When did he stop going?"

"Oh, I don't know. The summer? Anyhoo, why don't you just cook dinner here, and I'll set the table."

I sighed. "Okay. I'll be over around four." I hung up.

✦ ✦ ✦

"Max, I'm heading to Nana's. Will you be okay until Dad gets home?" I yell up the back stairs from the kitchen.

"Ya," he yells back.

"I'm on my cell if you need anything or you feel scared," I call out as I bag up the ingredients for one-pan Mexican chicken quinoa.

"'Kay."

"I'm locking the door behind me, and the front door is locked too."

"'Kay."

This is the first time I'm leaving Max at home alone. I was informed last week that all his friends get to stay home alone, so why was I being such a pain about it? After conferring with Ron, I figured he should be able to handle a couple of hours on his own. But his mood has been so down this fall, and I'm worried about him. When I get in the minivan, I immediately call Ron.

"I'm on my way to my mother's. Can you please get home as soon as possible? Max is alone."

"Yup. Just finishing some paperwork and I'll be right there. What time do we need to be there?"

"Six. Can you call the girls and remind them?"

"You got it."

While Maroon 5 tells me they got the moves like Jagger, I mull over the implications of my dad not wanting to leave the house. I'm no expert, but that doesn't sound like a good thing. I definitely need to pay more attention to what's going on over there.

When I get to the house the first thing I notice is that the lawn is covered in a colorful blanket of leaves. This is only noteworthy because I have never seen as much as a stray dandelion on my father's lawn. It's his pride and joy.

"I'm here!" I yell loudly as I open the front door.

"We're in the kitchen!" my mother yells back.

I deposit my grocery bag on the counter and notice an impressive number of dishes in the sink. I kiss them both, then start loading the dishwasher.

"Sweetheart, don't worry about that. We get to it eventually." My mother is rubbing her temples.

"What's wrong with your head?"

"Nothing. Just a little headache."

"You had a headache the last time I was here."

"Really? I don't remember. Anyway, leave the dishes."

"I can't. I need room to cook."

"Suit yourself." My mother turns back to the newspaper she and my dad are sharing.

"What did you guys do today?" I'm a little afraid of the answer.

"Oh, what did we do, Ray?"

"Not much." My dad utters his first words of the conversation.

"Well, after breakfast I took a look at the Trader Joe's flyer and made some notes." She pauses. "I put a load of laundry in. It should probably go in the dryer." She doesn't move an inch after that realization.

"I can do it once I get dinner going."

As I chop onions, I notice the dirt on the counter in front of me. There are toast crumbs and what looks like the remainder of spilled coffee, and a glance at my feet shows more crumbs and smudges on the floor.

"Was Amelia here today?" I casually ask about their longtime cleaning lady.

"I don't think so," my mother replies. "Ray, when was Amelia here?"

My dad shrugs and turns the page of his newspaper.

"We only have her once every few weeks now," my mother continues. "We just don't need her. We barely make a mess."

When do old people stop seeing the dirt? Is it their eyesight, or is it a lack of caring anymore? My mother was a fastidious housekeeper, but nothing here indicates she has so much as wiped the counter in days. I remind myself again to keep a better eye on these two. My Maude obsession has caused me to take my eye off the ball.

While I throw together the ingredients for dinner and put it to simmer on the stove, I regale my parents with stories about Maude and Max and my terrible career as a spin instructor. They listen amiably and toss in a few questions, but the level of engagement is definitely less than I'd like. I ask a few times if they're okay, but then my mother complains that I'm repeating myself, so I stop.

Once dinner is simmering, I go to the mudroom at the back of the house to put the laundry in the dryer. You know the smell that damp clothes have when they've been sitting for a while? Well multiply that by a hundred and you'll get an idea of what the washing machine smelled like. Think wet dog that rolled around in its own crap. This load has been in there for at least three days. I throw in some laundry soap and wash it again.

On my way back to the kitchen, I notice the dining room table isn't set yet, so I pull out placemats, plates, and cutlery and lay them out quickly.

"Hey, why don't we go for a walk around the block?" I ask my parents. I feel like I need to get them up and moving. From the looks of them you'd think they just rolled out of bed.

My mother frowns. "Jennifer, why would we do that? I know what our neighborhood looks like. I don't need to walk the block like a tourist."

I decide not to ask why a tourist would be walking around their neighborhood and just keep pressing.

"Just to get some fresh air, Mom. Come on. It'll be fun. Dad? What do you say?"

My dad looks up from the paper. "Say about what?"

"Want to take a nice walk around the block?"

"Sure. Let me get my shoes." He gets up slowly and weaves a bit. I take his arm to steady him.

"Are you okay?" I put my arm around him.

"I stood up too fast." He shrugs off my embrace and walks to the door.

"Mom?"

She sighs. "Oh, all right. I guess it couldn't hurt to blow the stink off."

My thoughts exactly. I turn the stove to Low, and once we have shoes and jackets on, we head out. I take three deep breaths as a way of encouraging my parents to do the same.

"Sweetheart, you shouldn't breathe so deeply. God knows what's floating around in the air. You don't want to give the flu an open invitation to infect your lungs."

I decide not to attack her logic and instead turn the conversation to observations about the neighborhood.

"When did the Newberrys paint their house blue?" I ask, expecting my father to launch into a tirade about the "radical" colors people are choosing for their houses. But he doesn't take the bait. What he does notice is that his own lawn is a mess.

"What the hell is this?" he asks. "Kay, do you see the lawn?" It's nice to see him get animated about something.

"You know I never notice," my mom says with an eye roll toward me. "Really, Ray, nobody cares what our lawn looks like."

"Well, I sure as hell care. You two go walk. I'm going to grab my rake."

This is the Ray Howard I know and love. That guy sitting in the kitchen was a stranger. I tell my mom we'll just walk up and down the block so we're not too far from my dad, in case something happens.

"I'll tell you what's going to happen—the neighbors are going to think we're spying on them," she retorts.

"Why would you even think that?" I ask her.

"Because that's what I would think if I saw someone walking up and down the street."

I loop my arm though hers and lead her to the sidewalk. "Isn't this nice?" I say.

"Well, it's always nice when I can spend time with my daughter. I can't remember the last time I saw you! Wait, yes, I do. It was just before Max's first day of school."

Ouch. I really have been an absentee daughter. "I'm sorry, Mom. I've volunteered for a school project, and it has me preoccupied." A little white lie never hurt anyone.

"What's the project?"

"I'm in charge of raising ten thousand dollars for the school so we can buy new tablets for the kids," I say proudly.

My mother lets out an exasperated huff. "Whatever happened to good old-fashioned books?"

"Well, the schools are all trying to cut down on unnecessary paper use, and the iPads help with that. Any ideas of how we can raise that money?"

"When you were young the school would send you door-to-door selling chocolate bars, remember?"

"I remember that I hated it," I grumble.

The days of asking kids to do anything door-to-door without supervision are long gone, and thank God for that. I mean, what the hell were our parents thinking?

We reach the end of the block and turn around.

"How is my great-granddaughter?"

"She's wonderful." I sigh.

My mother smirks. "Easier than raising your own kids, isn't it?"

"Well, it is and it isn't. Vivs has such crazy rules about what Maude can eat, and watch, and play with. It's exhausting."

"Oh, and you didn't? Remember when I wasn't allowed to use the word 'no' with the girls because you didn't like the negativity it put on them?"

"I remember it lasted a hot minute. Just like my ban on soda."

"Oh, well, how can you deny little girls a soda?"

"By saying no," I mumble. "Anyway, besides the crazy Vivs stuff, I'm loving being a grandmother."

"It just gets better." Kay smiles.

"How's your headache?"

"Better, thanks." I can tell the fresh air has done her a world of good.

We're back in front of the house, and I see that about a quarter of the lawn is raked as my dad slowly turns his attention to a new area.

"Is Dad okay?"

"He's fine. He just has little moments every now and then."

"What do you mean by 'little moments'?"

She shrugs. "Sometimes he just sort of stares off in the distance. And sometimes he loses his balance."

"Has he fallen?" I ask, a bit alarmed.

"Once, but he got right back up."

She walks toward the lawn and raises her voice. "Ray! How's the raking going?"

My father looks at us with a cloudy gaze that slowly clears, like the fog on a damp morning.

"I'm raking!" he yells back and continues to pull more leaves toward him.

At this point I'm happy to see Bruce Willis making its way down the street, and delighted when it's followed closely by Vivs's blue Jetta. There are a round of hellos, and kisses for Maude, then we all head inside except for my dad and Ron, who have committed to finishing the front lawn.

"Dinner in fifteen!" I yell behind me.

Thankfully the Mexican chicken quinoa I've thrown together hasn't burned, and we all settle in the dining room for a long-overdue family dinner.

"So, what's new at work?" I ask Laura.

"Well, my menu finally got approved."

The whole table gives a chorus of congratulations.

"They're letting me start next week. I really hope my old people like it."

"I really hope you don't poison anyone," Vivs jokes as she puts more chicken on Maude's plate.

Throughout dinner we cover the latest in the girls' jobs, Max's

Halloween costume (a gangster), Maude's Halloween costume (a sunflower), the yoga studios, and finally the upcoming holidays.

"Mom, did Raj tell you Varsha is coming?"

I nod. "Do you know where she's staying?"

"I'm hoping with you. It'll be too tight at my place."

"With us? Oh God, Vivs, don't you think she's going to want to be with Maude?"

"Who's coming?" my mother asks in her now-habitual loud voice.

"Raj's mother, Varsha, is coming for Christmas," I yell back, meeting her decibel level. "Ron"—I turn to my husband—"what do you think?"

Mr. Easy Like Sunday Morning shrugs and utters those three magic words: "Whatever you want."

"I mean, Vivs, I really think you should let her stay with you. She'll want to spend Christmas morning with her son and grand-daughter. She can stay in Laura's room, and Laura can stay with us." Laura nods and shrugs, her mouth full of food. Vivs looks unhappy, but she doesn't disagree.

My parents have been mostly quiet through dinner. Their ennui has returned, and I'm worried but decide not to share it with anyone just yet. I need to spend some more time with them.

After dinner, I step out to put the laundry in the dryer, and Max follows me.

"Mom."

"That's me."

"I may want to change my Halloween costume."

"Why?" I don't even try to keep the annoyance out of my voice.

"Zach T. told me that Zach E. is going to be a gangster too, and I don't want to dress like him."

"Is he still giving you a hard time?" Max has been silent on the matter since the safety patrol incident.

He shrugs and looks at the floor.

Hmmm. If I say yes, I'll be breaking my own rule of "No

costume rethinks after October 10." And believe me, that rule is in place for a reason. I try a different tactic.

"I thought you loved your costume."

"I did, but Zach T. and I kind of want to do a group costume with Suni and Isabel."

Well, *this* is new. The prevailing wind regarding girls has been pretty stinky his whole life. Now he wants to invite two girls into the hallowed grounds of Halloween. Who is this child?

"What do you guys want to dress up as?"

"Football players and cheerleaders. I think Suni's mom is making our costumes."

I wonder if Asami knows she's been volunteered for this little task.

"Why don't you just wear one of your jerseys and use Dad's helmet?"

Max gives me a devilish grin. "'Cause I'm not going to be a football player. Zach T. and I are the cheerleaders, and Suni and Isabel are the football players." He can't help laughing at the sheer genius of this idea. I mean, no boys have *ever* dressed up like girls before!

"That's a cute idea," I enthuse. "And Mrs. Chang is *making* your costume?"

"Well, I know she's making the pom-poms. What else do I need?"

I sigh because I now realize I have somehow been suckered into agreeing to a new costume.

"A skirt and a top would be my guess. Let me call Peetsa and see if she kept any of Stephanie's old outfits."

While Max smiles with relief, I wonder which one of us is going to have to break this news to Ron.

Back in the kitchen, the girls are cleaning up the dinner mess and talking to my parents, who are sitting at the table. They seem very tired.

"Nana, why is the basement door locked?" Laura asks loudly.

"Because if I don't lock it, the people come up here."

"Who's in the basement?" Vivs asks.

"Well, I don't know their names, but they've been down there for a while."

All activity stops while we absorb her answer.

"Do they pay rent?" I ask, figuring I may as well see how far this delusion has gone.

"No, and they'll steal our food if I don't lock the basement door."

I have no idea how to go forward with this. Ron comes to my rescue.

"Kay, I told you before—there's no one in the basement. I went down and looked, remember?"

"Well, I still hear them, and so does Ray, don't you, Ray?"

"Don't I what?" My father looks up from the kitchen table when he hears his name.

"You hear the people in the basement too," Kay repeats.

"Oh—well, sometimes."

I am now on high alert. When Ron mentioned my mother alluding to the people in the basement, we both thought it was a joke. I had no idea Kay had made this part of her reality.

"Well, I'm going to see who's down there." I walk to the basement door and unlock it. "Anyone want to join me?"

"I'll go," Vivs offers, and I'll admit I'm a bit relieved. I mean, I know there's no one down there but, you know . . . what if there is?

We turn the light on at the top of the stairs and head down.

"Hello?" I yell.

"Oh, please." Vivs pushes past me on the stairs.

The basement has a dank smell and feels like it hasn't been visited in a long time. Remnants of my daughters' childhoods can be seen stacked in corners—a baby stroller, stuffed animals, and a few board games, plus books and an Easy-Bake oven.

"You should go through this stuff for Maude," I suggest.

"Why do they still have it all?" she wonders.

"They're from the generation that never throws anything out. If I look hard enough, I bet I'll find all my grade-school report cards."

We walk through the rec room and utility room, and the only thing we see is a dead mouse.

"Is Nana losing it?" Vivs asks me.

"I don't know, sweetie. I thought I had more to worry about with Poppy, but now I see I need to keep an eye on both of them."

"Or hire someone to help out."

I laugh to myself. I can guess Kay's response to a suggestion of having full-time help. And when we head back upstairs and I bring it up to her, I'm right on the money.

"Jennifer, I know you enjoy spending our money for us, but I'm not the Queen of England and I don't need a maid."

"I said you might want to think about an *aide*, not a maid."

"Well, I won't thank you for either," she assures me.

I realize it probably wasn't the best time to bring this up, so I decide to discuss it with her tomorrow. We pack up our things, and Ron makes a big show of locking the basement door before we head home.

7

"How do we look?"

I look up from the kitchen counter office to see Max and his friends standing in front of me—Suni and Isabel dressed as cute little football players and Zach T. and Max as cheerleaders. They have scraped together outfits by begging and borrowing but hopefully not stealing anything, and they look hilarious. The boys are loving wearing skirts and wigs and shaking their pom-poms, but I had to put the kibosh on the socks they secretly stuffed into a couple of old bras from Zach's sister. I'm now known as the killer of all things fun. Tell me something I don't know.

"You look fantastic!" I assure them. "Best costumes ever."

"Are you guys ready?" Asami asks as she comes out of the bathroom by the front hallway.

"Yup." Suni giggles and puts her football helmet on.

The kids are going to a Halloween party at the school in lieu of trick-or-treating. The whole door-to-door thing is really just for little kids and parents, as far as I'm concerned, and I'm thrilled the PTA decided to sponsor this party to keep the older kids from getting into trouble. I'm still wondering how I didn't get roped into chaperoning but I'm not looking a gift horse in the mouth. Asami is taking this particular bullet tonight, so Ron and I get to stay home and terrorize Halloween fun-seekers, as is my wont.

"Max, Mrs. Chang is in charge, so please listen to her. That goes for all of you," I address the kids.

"Oh, please, Jennifer. They know how to behave," Asami sniffs. "And they know what will happen if they don't," she adds for effect. "Okay, everybody out to the car." She turns to me. "It's over at eight thirty, so I'll have him back right after."

"Thanks. Who else is chaperoning?" I ask as we all walk toward the front door.

She shrugs. "Does it matter? It's not a social event for me."

Yes, God forbid Asami has fun at something.

"Bye, Mom!" Max dashes out the front door and makes his skirt flip up as he bounces down the steps. He passes two little boys dressed as Peter Pan and Captain Hook coming toward our door, with their mom dressed as Wendy trailing behind them.

"Ron! We're on!" I yell to my husband. He comes out of the kitchen carrying our Halloween candy bowl.

"Trick or treat!" the boys say and hold up their bags in anticipation.

"What's your trick?" I ask them. They stare in confusion, so I say it again.

"They don't have a trick," their mother says through tight lips.

"Well then they can't get candy." I shrug. "Come on, you guys must have some cool pirate moves."

"Arrrr!" The Captain Hook growls and points his plastic sword at me.

"Nice one!" Ron says and holds out the candy bowl.

"Arrr!" Peter Pan copies his brother, but I let it pass and let him pick as well.

"Have a good night!" I say to Wendy. She leans toward me and says in a low voice, "I see everything I've heard about you is true."

"Well, I certainly hope so!" I give her the smile I save for people who really don't get me.

I close the door and grimace at my husband. "God, I hate Halloween."

"And yet you hide it so well. I hope you've noticed that we get fewer and fewer trick-or-treaters every year. Your reputation is everywhere."

"Good. My master plan is to put an end to door-to-door candy begging by the time Max is in high school."

"Why don't we just turn our lights off and pretend we're not home? Why put the whole neighborhood through the torture of a trip to our house?"

"Like I've never thought of that," I scoff. "I'm only open for business this year because Vivs promised to bring Maude by."

"Of all the holidays to have a hate-on for." Ron shakes his head in dismay. He takes a seat in the living room, but the doorbell rings, so he's up again in an instant, saying, "Let me do this one. Why don't you grab us some wine?"

I take the suggestion and head to the kitchen to find a bottle and glasses. A little Oregon pinot noir should do the trick.

While I open the wine, I yawn and realize how tired I am these days. Dealing with Maude, my parents, my kids, and my school obligations, I can't seem to catch my breath.

Back in the living room I hand Ron his glass and sink into the sofa with a groan.

"When was the last time you worked out?" It's an innocent enough question, but in my current mood he may as well have asked me if I was getting my period or if I was really going to eat that donut.

"Why, do I look fat?"

"Yes, that's exactly why I asked." He gives me a good-natured shove. "No, you just seem a bit on edge, and I know spin class is a good stress reliever."

"It's been a while." I take a big gulp of wine. It's been crickets from Jodi at Fusion, and I haven't been in the mood to take anyone else's class. On a positive note, the second meeting of WeFUKCT went very well. I left feeling very hopeful about our mission.

✦ ✦ ✦

We met this past Monday morning in the school's cafeteria, and I was all business from the get-go. I made everyone sit in a circle of chairs and asked them to shout out their ideas, one at a time, lightning-round style—no judgment (except by me in my head).

"Sell candles!" *Meh.*

"Sell bedsheets!" *Double meh.*

"Sell wrapping paper!" *Meh, meh, meh.*

"Sell chocolate!" *Over my dead body.*

"A 5K run!" *I like that.*

"Have a party!" *That actually costs money.*

"Do a GoFundMe page!" *Really?*

"Do an auction!" *Maybe . . .*

"Have a golf tournament!" *That sounds like a lot of work.*

"Ask Hallmark for a donation!" *What?*

That last one came courtesy of Cathy Funfair.

"Do they do that?" I asked.

"I don't know. But it never hurts to ask. They do a lot of philanthropic things."

I doubted very much that their generosity extended to a local school in an upper-middle-class neighborhood trying to buy tablets, but I kept that thought to myself.

"Well, this is a good start. No-Tech, tell me about the golf tournament. How do you make money?"

She looked very pleased to have been singled out. "We did it once when my older one was in preschool. You basically find a golf club that will donate their facilities and let you throw a tournament. You have to pay to play, and it's a great way to get the dads involved. They tend to be big spenders when it's an activity they can get into."

"Do any of you golf?" I asked my team.

Cathy Red Nails raised her hand. "Does mini golf count? We could do a mini golf tournament."

"Or a poker tournament, like a casino night," Alison Lody suggested.

I liked a lot of these ideas, I just couldn't yet see a way to make big money from them. I said as much to the group.

"Maybe we should do a bunch of the ideas," Delia Cramer, parent of twin first graders, suggested. "You know, sell wrapping paper at Christmas, chocolate for Valentine's Day, sheets in April."

The rest of the group hummed their approval of this idea, so I asked someone to do the math based on what had been raised in previous years. Luckily, Liana Jones, mother of fourth grader Jasmine and second grader Brian, has been on the committee for three years, so she came up with an answer pretty quickly.

"Six thousand three hundred and change, all in!" she announced like a contestant on a game show.

"Over three years," I confirmed.

She nodded. "So, it's perfect. Easy peasy lemon squeezy."

I winced. God, I hate that expression.

"Do we want to do a silent auction?" Alison tossed out. I thought about that for a moment. It's definitely a good way to raise money, and the community generally gets behind the donations.

"Let's let these ideas marinate and figure out a way to expand on them. Are we all good to meet next Monday?"

They all nodded except Cathy Funfair, who let me know she has other commitments that day.

"We'll have to soldier on without you," I told her, and we adjourned the meeting.

I take a sip of wine and close my eyes. I like the idea of a few smaller fundraisers. Maybe start with something I've had huge success with: a bake sale. If I play it right, I'm thinking we could pull in four hundred dollars just from that.

The doorbell rings again. A little more torturing of children is in order, so I beeline it to the door before Ron can even get off the couch. But my plan to make misery is happily foiled when I open the door to see a pretty little sunflower jumping in front of me.

"Gee Gee!" Maude squeaks, and I bend down to her level and fuss over her costume.

"What do you say?" Vivs, dressed as a gardener, prompts her.

"Twee twee!" she shouts, and I clap. Ron comes over with the candy bowl and murmurs, "Aren't you going to make her do a trick?"

"Oh shush." I elbow him. "Maudey . . . do you want some candy?"

"Say no thank you," Vivs quickly steps in.

"No tan to," Maude repeats.

"You must be joking." I give my daughter a look, which she of course ignores.

"Nope. Too much candy when I was a kid is why I have adult-onset anxiety."

I ignore her and sweep Maude into my arms and carry her into the kitchen.

"Come here, my baby. Let me get you a snack." I turn to Vivs. "Is Raj around?"

"He's up in Brooklyn for a week or so. He's so bummed to miss Halloween."

"I'm sure he is." I take a tube of organic yogurt from the fridge and hand it to Maude before my daughter can object.

Vivs sits at the kitchen table. "If I tell you something, can you promise you won't freak out?"

"I would never promise that, but I'll keep my reaction to a minimum," I assure her.

"Raj is trying to sell his apartment and move here permanently."

My eyes bug out, but I don't say anything except, "How do you feel about that?"

"Honestly, I'm kind of relieved. I don't know what the hell I was thinking trying to raise a kid on my own." I wait for her to say, "I don't know how you did it, Mom. You are Superwoman." But that doesn't happen. Instead she says, "He's really helpful. I'd never really thought about him as a father, but if I had I probably wouldn't have expected much."

"He's a gem," I agree. "Would he live with you?" Right now, Raj stays with Vivs and Laura but sleeps on the sofa.

She makes a sour face. "God, no! There's no room for him. I'm pretty sure he wants his own place."

"Sounds like something you should talk about instead of speculate on."

"On what?" asks Ron, coming in for more wine.

"Can I tell him?" I ask Vivs purely out of courtesy, because I know I'll tell him as soon as she leaves anyway. She shrugs, which I take as a yes.

"Raj is selling Brooklyn and moving back here full-time."

"That's great!" Ron's smile is genuine. "Where's he going to live?"

"That's what I was asking."

Vivs sighs. "I'm sure we'll talk about it when he comes back."

"Any chance of rekindling the old—"

Vivs stops Ron with one of her death glares.

"That looks like a maybe!" he singsongs and heads back out to the living room.

"Did you ever find someone to work with Nana and Poppy?" Vivs asks.

I nod. "Kind of. They've let me rehire Amelia. She goes there three times a week. They think she's there to clean the house, but she runs errands and keeps an eye on them."

"Do you think that's enough?"

"For now. It's all they'd agree to. Nana keeps talking about this headache she's had for weeks, but she refuses to go to the doctor."

"I don't blame her. Last time she went to the doctor for a skin irritation, she found out she had breast cancer."

"That was hardly the last time she went to the doctor." As I say it, I wonder if I'm right.

"I forgot to tell you—Raj says he'd be happy to help out with them if they need stuff done around the house."

"That is so sweet of him."

"Well, he loves them. He and Nana have some weird connection."

"It's not weird," I tell her. "They both have very giving souls." The look Vivs gives me tells me we should switch topics.

"Hey, do you have any ideas on how I could raise ten thousand dollars for Max's school?"

"Have you considered organ donation?" she says dryly.

"Oh, right! How much did you get for your heart again?"

Our sparring is interrupted by Max tramping in the back door. He looks happy and exhausted. Vivs laughs at his costume.

"Max-a-zillion! I love it!"

He beams. "Thanks! I was part of a group."

"How was the party?" I ask.

"It was great! We played games and ate pizza and our costume won second prize!"

"What did you win?" we ask together.

"Key chain." He holds it up. It has a Kansas City Chiefs logo on it.

"Nice! How was Zach E.'s gangster costume?"

"He wasn't there." Max can't help but smile, and I'm guessing that's why he had such a good time. It's really hard when one person's presence can so completely derail your good mood. I think back to when I first met Alison Lody and thought she was the most miserable person I'd ever encountered. I couldn't stand her. It's so much better now that we're friends.

Unbeknownst to us, the little sunflower with the yogurt has fallen asleep in her booster seat, resting her head on the kitchen table.

"Time to go!" Vivs smiles and goes to pick up her daughter.

"Oh, why don't you let her sleep here? It'll save you having to drop her off in the morning."

"Really? That would be great." She hands a sleeping Maude to me and gives me a rare kiss on the cheek.

"Thanks, Mom. I love you."

I smile. Sometimes Vivs can really surprise me.

8

To: The Chauffeurs of Mr. Green's Fifth-Grade Class
From: Jennifer Dixon
Re: A friendly reminder
Date: November 18

Hello, fellow sufferers!

Just a quick reminder about parent-teacher conferences tomorrow. Contrary to popular belief, Mr. Green is not open to bribes for better grades. However, I do find if you laugh at his jokes, he tends to have a more favorable opinion of your kid. I included your conference times in my last email, so I hope for your sake you didn't delete it.

And in case you've forgotten, or the turkeys aren't enough of a hint, Thanksgiving is next week. We will be celebrating with a party in the classroom on the Wednesday before, so I will be needing a few fixins for the soiree. See below for your assignments, and if you don't like what you were given, be sure to tell someone who gives a royal rip. As I've said many times, resistance is futile, so let's hop to it like little bunnies. All goodies should be dropped off on that Wednesday morning.

And with that, I wish you all a drama-free conference and a happy Thanksgiving.

With all the love in my heart (not really),

Jen

Dixons—donuts

Burgesses—water

Browns—cupcakes

Elders—tortilla chips and guacamole

Alexanders—gluten-free treats

Westmans—cups and plates

Changs—apple juice

Batons—wine

And with that little gem off my plate, I scoop up my gym bag and dash to the minivan. I got a call from Jodi at Fusion yesterday to fill in for a morning class, and I'm allowing myself to be hopeful. These are my kind of people—middle-aged moms who want to work out after dropping their kids at school!

As I'm driving, I make a hands-free call to Peetsa.

"What's up?" she answers.

"Hey, are you busy? I just wanted to know how your date went."

"Hang on." I can hear shuffling and muted voices, and then she's back.

"Okay, I told my boss I was having a small female emergency, so I've got like five minutes."

"Does he think you're changing your tampon?"

"I left it to his imagination."

"Okay, so what happened?"

"We had dinner, he was charming, he told funny stories about working as an accountant, and he gave me a really nice kiss goodnight."

"Sounds promising."

"I know. I felt really good about this one. So, I checked my phone before I went to bed just to see if he had reached out."

"And had he?"

"Oh, he most certainly had! He texted me a picture of his erect penis and the words 'Missing you already.'"

"Oh my God! What is wrong with him?"

"I couldn't believe it. He was so normal at dinner. Honestly, I don't even know what warning signs to look for anymore. I think the Internet has turned everyone into a pervert."

"Did you respond?"

"I sent a throw-up emoji. I hope he gets the hint."

I start to laugh. "Ugh. I'm sorry. It's like someone put a curse on your dating life."

"It's probably Buddy's mother, damning me from the afterlife."

"You'd think she'd be picking on the new one," I say as I pull into the parking lot of Fusion Fitness.

"I know, right?" Peetsa laughs. "Okay, I've got to get back on the floor. Talk to you later?"

"You bet. Wish me luck! I'm teaching a spin class in like ten minutes."

"Give 'em hell."

"Bye."

✦ ✦ ✦

"Take one last deep breath, raise your hands over your head, clasp them together, and bring them to your heart. Have a great day, everybody."

And with that, and the help of Bette Midler's "The Rose," I end what is probably the best class I have taught so far to enthusiastic applause. I was right about the crowd. These are the people I should be teaching—mostly women around my age who appreciate music from another generation. Only one thing knocked me off my game: a, shall we say, "rotund" guy in the second row who started class in a sweatshirt and sweatpants, then gradually disrobed until by the end of class he was only wearing a wrestling-style unitard. It was gross and fascinating all at the same time, kind of like watching the Kardashians.

On my way out I see people lined up for the next class, among them Ron's crazy ex-wife, Cindy. She gives me a big smile and waves.

"I would have taken your class if I'd known you were teaching!"

I'm still not used to this new and improved Cindy, so I keep my guard up despite her compliment. "I'm still not on the schedule, so

I never know when I'll be teaching," I explain as I wipe the sweat still running down my face.

"Text me next time!" She waves and heads into the spin room.

I give her a thumbs-up, but I'm not sure I actually mean it. Ron really doesn't want me engaging with her, even though I believe she's turned a corner in her life. People change, don't they?

I grab my gym bag and run into the elusive Jodi as I'm heading out.

"Thanks for thinking of me again." I nod to her.

"Oh, Jen, hang on. Can you do the nine-thirty for the rest of the week? Kiki has the flu."

I know I have conflicts just about every day this week—my teacher conference, a badly needed WeFUKCT meeting, and grocery shopping with my mother—so I surprise myself when I say "Sure! No problem. See you tomorrow!"

I get to the minivan and immediately start to rework my schedule to fit in my spin classes. I'm sorry Kiki has the flu, but I plan to make hay while the sun shines. This could be my only opportunity to show Fusion how much I belong there.

✦ ✦ ✦

"Thanks again for coming out today instead of tomorrow," I say to my mom as we pull into the parking lot of Aldi. I picked her up after I showered and grabbed a snack at home.

"It's fine. I'm glad you got me out. I'm so lethargic lately. But I don't like to leave your father alone for too long." I realize I have switched my outing with Kay to a non-Amelia day.

"Why, do you think he'll harm himself in some way?" I want my mother to be as frank as possible about what the hell is going on in their house.

Kay does a double take. "What do you mean?"

"Like would he lock himself in the bathroom again, or turn on the stove and forget about it?"

"Why would he turn on the stove?"

"Do you still worry about the people in the basement?"

"What? Oh, no. They're gone."

"Really? What happened?"

She shrugs. "They just left."

I really hope they don't come back, I think but don't say. The only thing worse than a delusion is one that comes and goes.

"So, why don't you like to leave him alone?"

"He misses me when I'm gone."

"He said that? That's so sweet."

"No, you know your father isn't a gusher, but I can always tell."

I leave that alone and focus on getting us a couple of shopping carts.

As we roll through the aisles, I stock up on Thanksgiving dinner supplies, and my mom looks for anything that can be heated up in the microwave. We run into Asami in the poultry section.

"Jennifer, I'm glad I bumped into you."

"Hi! Asami, do you know my mother, Kay Howard? Mom, Asami Chang. Her daughter is in Max's class."

Asami looks my mom up and down. "I think I saw you at the airport once."

"I don't think so," my mom answers and wanders down the aisle. I don't have the heart to tell her that she did indeed meet Asami when her nephew, Jeen, and Laura were coming back from Europe together a couple of years ago.

"Are you getting a turkey too?" I ask as I heave a twenty-nine-pound frozen bird into my cart.

"No. I like mine fresh—the fresher the better. Anyway, I've been wanting to talk to you about Max and Suni."

"What about them?" I frown as I see my mom turn the corner and disappear from my sight.

"Do you think there's something going on between them?"

"They're ten. What could be going on?"

"Well . . ." She moves her cart closer to mine. "I hear Suni talking to her friends sometimes, and all they seem to talk about is Max."

"What about Max?"

"I don't know, I just hear his name all the time."

I shrug. "Well, they're friends and have known each other since kindergarten." I don't want to tell her that I have never heard Max, or his friends, mention Suni at all except when they were talking about their joint Halloween costume. "You know, it's probably a little girl crush. Boys at this age are clueless. All they care about is who brought the ball to play with."

"So, you don't think they're dating," Asami says with relief.

"No, I don't." I silently congratulate myself for not bursting out laughing.

"Good," she says with her trademark nod. "Do you remember what I was assigned to bring for the class party next week?"

"Yes, it's tattooed on my brain, just give me a second to access it."

"You can just say no." She's annoyed.

"Sorry, I think you have orange juice." I pause. "I have a lot on my plate."

She shakes her head. "I can't believe you agreed to do the fund-raiser. I wouldn't touch that with a ten-foot pole."

This gives me a moment of concern, because Asami is not one to shy away from a challenge.

"I wasn't sure at first, but we have some great ideas. I think it's going to be fun."

Asami looks at me like I'm nuts.

"I do!" I give a nervous laugh.

"You know what happened to PP, don't you?"

"Oh, come on, that's just school gossip."

"I've seen the twitch." She looks at me for a reaction, and I give her my best impression of someone with an eye twitch.

"No idea what you're talking about," I say with six winks.

She rolls her eyes and walks toward the dairy section, and I take off in search of the roaming Kay. I find her picking out bread.

"Your father just loves raisin toast," she informs me. "He has it twice a day sometimes."

"What else does he eat?" I'm hoping raisin toast isn't the sum total of his diet.

"He likes the Lean Cuisines." She points to her cart, which has about ten of them.

"Are you guys getting enough protein and fresh vegetables?"

"Of course we are!" She sounds a bit too defensive.

"What did you have for dinner last night?"

My mother waves my question away. "Oh, who remembers? Do I look like I'm missing meals?" She motions toward her stomach, which, truthfully, has been getting bigger since she finished chemotherapy a few years ago.

"You look fine. I just want to make sure you're not only eating Lean Cuisine and toast, that's all. Why don't we get you some things to make a salad?" I turn toward the produce section and make a mental note to have both Vivs and Laura stop by to check on them. They say it takes a village to raise a child, but I'm thinking it takes an even bigger one to parent your parents.

+ + +

As Ron and I head down the now way-too-familiar halls of William Taft, we play our annual game of What's Max's Teacher's Name?

"Mrs. Randazzo?"

"Nope. That was second grade."

"Uh . . . Mr. McKutchen?"

"He's our dry cleaner."

"Uh . . ."

"Mr. Green," I inform him.

"You didn't give me enough time!" he grouses.

The classroom door is open, and Mr. Green is sitting at his desk, looking very casual in jeans and a red, long-sleeved polo shirt.

"Come on in, guys!" He looks up and smiles.

The classroom is decorated like the PG version of a freshman boy's dorm room. Along with the obligatory maps and charts, Mr. Green apparently enjoys the humor of *The Far Side* and *Garfield* cartoons, as well as surfing posters. We take our seats at two desks placed side by side in front of the teacher's.

"Thank you so much for switching times at the last minute," I say. We were supposed to have our conference at nine this morning, but I changed it so I could teach Kiki's nine-thirty class.

"No problem at all." He smiles at us. "So, let's talk about Max."

He goes through the fifth-grade curriculum, including an intro to sex education planned for the second semester. This is news to me, so I ask if it isn't a little too soon to start talking about this with the kids.

"Well, it's called sex education, but it's mostly about hygiene and getting to know your bodies, although kids have been known to ask some pretty explicit questions." He starts to laugh. "The kicker is, I don't teach it—they bring in a specialist. Guess what her name is."

"No idea."

"Mrs. Seamen."

He and Ron burst out laughing.

"When she says she's coming to class, you'd better listen!" Ron adds to the reverie.

I'm thinking this is about as appropriate as a stripper at a church social, so I try to get things back on track by asking how Max is doing gradewise. Mr. Green assures us that academically, Max is working at grade-level expectations, and even excelling in some cases. We smile at each other with relief. I'm so glad to hear Max's hard work is paying off.

"How do *you* think he's doing?" he asks us.

I think we're both surprised by the question.

"I'm just curious what you've been observing at home," he adds.

"Well . . ." I start slowly. "He gets his homework done without too much drama. We have a tutor to help with math . . ." I'm not sure what he's looking for.

"Is he happy?"

Ron and I look at each other.

"I think so," Ron says. "He hasn't said anything."

"Why do you ask?" I turn the tables on the teacher.

"Let's just say he's not the happy-go-lucky kid I used to see in the halls last year."

We look at each other again.

"Well, I know he's had some issues with Zach Elder this year . . ." I offer timidly.

"Exactly!" Mr. Green slaps his desk. "He seems to avoid any contact with Zach. He will physically move if Zach is nearby. And if he's with a group of friends, and Zach joins, Max walks away. Any idea what's going on there? I've asked them both and they, of course, just say 'nothing.'"

I sigh. "I hate to say this, but I think we have a bit of a bullying situation going on." It's a relief to talk about it.

Mr. Green nods. "That's what Zach's mother said too."

This surprises me. "Trudy said that?"

"She's pretty upset about it. Her husband is in Afghanistan, so she doesn't have a lot of support at home."

I nod my empathy for her tough situation.

"Do you have any idea why Max would choose to pick on him?"

There's silence while my brain processes this question. Ron decides to fill the void.

"I think it's just boys being boys—"

I interrupt him immediately. "Max isn't bullying Zach! *Zach* is bullying *Max*!"

Mr. Green gives me a sympathetic look. "I know it's hard to find out that your child is being a bully. But it's important to take off the rose-colored glasses for a minute."

My heart is beating like a hummingbird's wings, and I'm about to jump out of my chair, but Ron holds my arm.

"You know, let us have a talk with him and see if we can get to the bottom of this." He stands, his firm grip on my arm telling me not to blow a gasket until we're in the parking lot. "Thanks so much." He shakes Mr. Green's hand. "We're happy to hear he's doing so well academically, and we'll talk to him about this thing with Zach."

"That would be great. They just need to find a way to get along." Mr. Green waves us out of the room.

We're near the car when Ron finally releases my arm.

"What the actual fuck?" I explode. "Are you kidding me? *Max* bullying *Zach*? It's ridiculous."

"Is it?" Ron asks.

"What do you mean, 'is it'? Have you met our son? He's not a bully."

"Jen, I did see him hit Zach at the soccer field that day."

"He told me he only did that because Zach was calling him names."

Ron frowns. "What names?"

I pause, because I know this is going to sound ridiculous. "Sweetie."

"What?"

"Sweetie. He called him 'sweetie.'"

"Zach called Max sweetie," Ron confirms. I nod.

He starts to laugh.

"It's not funny. Why are you laughing?"

"It's such a stupid thing to get upset about." He shrugs. "I mean, come on—sticks and stones."

"Names hurt too." I open the minivan door.

"Let's talk to him tonight at dinner. He needs to toughen up if he's letting a little name-calling get the better of him."

9

To: WeFUKCT
From: Jennifer Dixon
Re: My bad!
Date: December 1

Dear team,

   I owe you all an apology for the apocalypse that was yesterday's bake sale. I take full responsibility for the carnage that occurred when the baked goods and the animals collided. I had failed to read the most recent PTA blast about upcoming events so didn't know about the petting zoo that was scheduled to come, but in my defense, the zoo should have packed up and left when it started raining.

   Obviously, we didn't make any money from the bake sale, but I'm hopeful our next effort won't be the tsunami that this one was.

   Let's meet on Friday to regroup. Eight thirty, in the cafeteria.
   Onward,

                                                              Jen

I mean. Who the hell could have seen that one coming? I thought a bake sale right before Thanksgiving was the perfect way to launch our fundraising efforts. All the WeFUKCT moms contributed things, as did many other parents. I made six whole pumpkin pies! It was an impressive spread, and we had it all set up in the gym by noon. Everything would have been fine if it hadn't started raining, forcing the petting zoo people to move inside very quickly. They obviously didn't know about the bounty of baked goods just sitting there like a smorgasbord for the animals.

If you ask me, the goats were the worst. They jumped up on the table and attacked Shirleen Cobb's gluten-, nut-, and dairy-free cookies like it was the last meal they were ever going to have, and then they started in on the plastic tablecloths. While the zookeepers tried to wrangle the goats, the alpacas tore into cupcakes and the pigs grabbed anything that fell on the floor. Thank God none of the students were in the gym. The screaming from the adults was bad enough. It was mayhem and panic for about ten minutes as the zoo people tried to restrain the menagerie. As someone who is known as not much of an animal person, I was zero help. I could only watch as tables full of cupcakes and pies were upended and bottles of water that had been lined up like soldiers toppled to the ground and started rolling around, creating an obstacle course of tripping hazards. The three Cathys tried to salvage whatever they could, but in the end the zoo animals got to all of it. Once they were corralled back onto their trucks, we took in the destruction they left in their wake in stunned silence. It was like looking at a table at Chuck E. Cheese after fifteen toddlers were done eating.

"I'll get some trash bags," Delia Cramer said meekly.

"I'll find a mop." Alison Lody followed her out of the gym.

Cathy Funfair immediately told me she had a dentist appointment and left before I could say anything.

I think the smell was the worst part of the cleanup. Baked goods mixed with wet animal smell and poop made for quite a pungent odor. Thank God the custodial team came to our rescue, and among all of us, we had the gym back to normal within a couple of hours.

But the damage was done to my psyche. I don't think I'll ever eat Rice Krispies treats again after seeing them chewed up and spat out by a miniature horse.

Of course, I had to have the obligatory meeting with PTA general Sylvie Pike. She also brought in Selina Ford, who had made the unfortunate decision to relocate the petting zoo to the gym without checking first.

"Do you know what synergy is?" Sylvie asked us, clearly not expecting a definition. "It means one hand lets the other hand know what it's doing."

I'm pretty sure that's not what synergy is, but I decided it wasn't the time to be a know-it-all.

WeFUKCT met yesterday to lick our wounds and talk about our next move. Could we whip something together before Christmas to make up our loss?

"Could we do something with pizza?" I asked the team.

"Like what?" Alison asked me.

"Make Your Own Pizza Night?" I offer. I get blank stares from my crew and silently reprimand myself for taking Garth's mother seriously.

They were all here for Thanksgiving: Nina, Garth, and Chyna. Garth's mother, Yvette, was a last-minute surprise, but I always say, the more the merrier for Thanksgiving (and Thanksgiving only).

They stayed with us, crammed into Vivs and Laura's old bedrooms, with Chyna sleeping on the couch in the basement, and I'm happy to report that Yvette and her spirit guides did not disappoint.

While we were looking at pictures from their honeymoon on Garth and Nina's iPad, Yvette pointed to a guy in the background of a group photo and said, "My guides tell me that man has herpes."

She and my mother got along like macaroni and cheese. Kay just couldn't get enough of talking to her.

"When did they start talking to you?" "What do they sound like?" "Do they like us?" And, most prominently, "What are they saying now?" She would ask this at least ten times a day, and Yvette always had a little nugget to feed her.

"They're saying the family that lived in this house before you left something valuable in the basement."

My mother looks at me. "Did they, Jennifer? What did they leave?"

I think for a minute. "The washer and dryer?"

"Yes, that was it!" Yvette clapped her hands like she had just won something. I'd like to think I hid my eye roll, but I know better.

Over the obligatory leftover dinner on the Saturday after Thanksgiving, my mother asked me how my fundraising was going. I gave everyone the broad strokes of the bake sale fiasco and admitted I wasn't sure what we were going to do next.

"Pizza," Yvette yelled out of nowhere.

"What was that, Mom? You want pizza?" Garth asked her.

"Can we have pizza?" Max asked. "I don't want turkey anymore."

Yvette turned and looked directly at me. "The guides are saying the answer to your problem is pizza."

"What about pizza?" I asked Yvette.

She looked up and to the right, which I've learned means she's listening to her spirit guides. After a minute she shook her head.

"Nothing else. Just pizza."

I'm now really embarrassed that I even brought pizza up to WeFUKCT.

"Why don't we sell candles for the holiday season?" Terry DiLorento suggested. It wasn't lost on me that this was her suggestion at our second meeting.

"How much could we make?" I'm all about the money now.

"Five hundred to a thousand dollars," Delia says confidently.

I sigh. "Let's do it."

"The rep from the candle place goes to my church, so I'll talk to her Sunday," Terry offered.

"Okay, thanks." And with that, my dream of doing something out of the box and extraordinary to raise money floated out the window.

✦ ✦ ✦

It's Saturday, so the girls and I are going to drop in on my parents and get them out of the house. Max is hanging at Zach T.'s, working on their dialogue for a Spanish class project, and Ron is taking a rare boys' weekend trip to Snow Creek.

We talked with Max after our conference with Mr. Green. At dinner that night we asked if he really was actively avoiding Zach E. At first, he denied it, but after a while he admitted that he just didn't want to get in any more arguments with him. We talked about conflict resolution and shaking hands and how agreeing to disagree is the best way forward. He wasn't thrilled with the whole conversation, but he said he'd try.

As I turn the minivan into my parents' driveway, I'm happy to see it has been thoroughly cleared of the recent snowfall thanks to Josh, the industrious kid down the street who I'm convinced is going to be a millionaire by the time he graduates college. His mother told me that all he wanted for his thirteenth birthday was a snowblower. His friends thought he was nuts, but over the past four years, every time it snows, Josh looks less and less like a weirdo. He charges everyone on the block twenty dollars to do their driveway, which my mother considers price gouging, but he does a very good job, so I won't let her complain.

"I'm here!" I yell in full voice. Not surprisingly, my parents are in the kitchen. It's become like their assigned workspace. They don't even switch up their seats. Mom likes to face the fridge, and Dad sits across from her, facing the window. Not that he ever looks at the view outside.

"There's coffee if you want it, sweetheart."

"I'm good, thanks." I'd truly rather drink my own urine than the stuff my parents pass off as "coffee." It's freeze-dried swill as far as I'm concerned. I join them at the table.

"So, when the girls get here, any thoughts on where you'd like to go?"

"Do we have to go out? Dad and I are feeling a bit tired today."

"Today"?? How about every *day.*

"Oh, come on. The girls are coming, and you said you wanted to do some errands."

My mother sighs. "It's only one errand," she corrects me.

"What's the one errand?

"We need to go to Target to get something."

"What?" I ask.

She looks at my father, then back at me. "You don't need to know our personal business."

Now I do, I think but don't say. I'm about to ask what's so personal, but I hear a commotion by the front door, and suddenly a two-foot-something bundle of cuteness comes running into the kitchen.

"Gee Gee!" Maude sings, and I scoop her up for a hug.

"Say hi to Nana and Poppy!" I turn her toward my parents. She gives them a shy wave. My father, who has said nothing this entire time, suddenly comes to life.

"Well, how are you, little girl?" He reaches out and touches Maude's head.

"Hi," Vivs and Laura say in unison. He looks up and waves.

"So, what's the plan today?" Vivs obviously wants to get this show on the road. "If we're going for lunch it has to be someplace kid friendly and healthy."

We all look at her.

"McDonald's it is!" Laura declares.

+ + +

After lunch at Grimaldi's Pizza, which was Vivs's big compromise, we head to Target. But before we do, I have a halfhearted chat with the manager of our favorite pizza joint about their philanthropic endeavors. He tells me they send food to events, contribute to a range of not-for-profit organizations, and respond to local community needs. I keep that information in my back pocket just in case.

At Target we all go our separate ways. Vivs takes Maude to the toy aisle to keep her amused while Laura shops for them. I pick up some groceries and head to the electronics department to get Max his main Christmas gift—wireless Beats headphones—and, for Ron, a high-speed blender for his morning protein shakes.

As I'm checking out, I see my mother and father at the next cashier. The most notable thing in their basket is adult diapers. This is news to me, and I can't help but wonder who is using them.

Heading out to the minivan, Kay and Ray are pushing Maude in their shopping cart and singing "The Wheels on the Bus." The girls and I take our time loading the minivan in order to put things in sections, which will make for easier unloading. When we're done, I turn to tell my parents to get in the car, but they are nowhere in sight.

"Where are they?" I ask Vivs.

"I don't know!" she says, suddenly realizing that wherever they are, they have Maude. She starts running through the busy parking lot yelling for them, with Laura right behind her.

"They couldn't have gone far," I yell after them, but I'm secretly frantic as well. What the hell could they be thinking?

Vivs has stopped a security guard and is wildly gesturing at him, but I can't hear what she's saying. Laura runs back to me. "They aren't anywhere on the street, so that's good. I'm going to check the store."

Just as she's getting to the door, Kay and Ray come strolling out with Maude and what appears to be a toy drum. A wave of relief comes over me that is so strong I have to steady myself on the car door. Vivs leaves the security guard, who I'm sure has just received an earful from my bossiest offspring, and runs to hug her daughter.

As they all make their way to the car, I can't stop myself from laying into my parents.

"What the hell, you guys?" I yell. "Why would you leave and not tell us?"

"Jennifer, please, I can only handle one hysterical person at a time. As I told this one"—she jerks her thumb toward Vivs—"the baby wanted to get a drum, so we went back in to get her one."

I scowl. "She said that? She said, 'I want a drum'?"

"Well, of course not, but she kept saying 'bum bum' and clapping her hands." My mother shrugs.

Laura swoops in to bring calm to the turmoil. "Nana," she says gently, "when Maude says 'bum bum,' it means she has poop in her diaper."

"Oh, that's what that smell is. I thought for a minute it was your father." She cackles.

Well, at least I now know who needs the Depends. My father hasn't said one word through this whole drama, so I ask if he's okay.

"Oh, sure. Why wouldn't I be? Can we go home now? I'm tired."

Vivs has taken Maude back into Target to change her, so we all get into the minivan and wait in silence for them to return. My dad starts whistling "The Wheels on the Bus," and my mom hums along. I turn to her.

"You get why we're upset, right? We had no idea where you were, and we were worried sick."

"Well, where would we have gone, Jennifer? Honestly, you'd think we kidnapped Marge!"

"Maude," I correct her.

"That's what I said. She was fine."

Laura is sitting by herself in the third row of seats. Her eyes meet mine in the rearview mirror, and she raises her brows as if to say, *Do we need to find A Place for Mom?* à la the TV commercials with Joan Lunden. And I'm thinking we just might.

10

To: WeFUKCT

From: Jennifer Dixon

Re: A Pyrrhic victory

Date: December 21

Hey gang,

Never let it be said that we didn't try. You all did an amazing job selling candles these past few weeks. Almost too good a job, as we just found out!

I know you sold to the parents on the promise the candles would be delivered before Christmas. But according to Terry DiLorento, the candle company didn't expect such a robust order (way to go, overachievers!). We have been informed the candles should arrive in late January or early February. Maybe tell the parents they'll make great Valentine's gifts . . . well, except for the pine-scented ones.

The silver lining is we made almost two thousand dollars—well on our way to the ten thousand we need. So, please go into the holiday season knowing we are on the fast track to success!

See you at the Christmas concert!

Jen

PS If anyone sees No-Tech Cathy, can you let her know about this little pep talk? Thanks.

Yes, you read that right. I'm rallying the troops. I'm not much of a cheerleader when it comes to my school duties—I'm more of a tell-it-like-it-is bitch. After hearing that our Christmas candles wouldn't be arriving until a month after Christmas, my first instinct was to send WeFUKCT a blistering tome about our cursed quest to make money for this stupid school, but PTA prez Sylvie Pike strongly suggested I pivot and send a more encouraging message. Not nearly as satisfying for me, but I'm told it will be much better for morale.

This final week before Christmas is always when the rubber hits the road for me. Organizing the class holiday party, last-minute gift and food shopping, finishing the house decorations, and keeping WeFUKCT's spirits up has been taking more than enough of my time. Add to that a daily visit with my parents, sometimes with Maude in tow, and I'm busier than usual. Not to mention Varsha's impending visit has me caring a little more about my house decorations and the food I'm serving. I don't want her thinking we're a bunch of hillbillies.

I'm on my way to the school for Max's final Christmas concert of his primary-school life. It's one of the most significant "lasts" in a year of lasts that this school year keeps bringing, and I'm finding myself getting a little sentimental. What will my life be like when I don't have to go to William Taft every day? I really thought I'd be more excited at the prospect of kissing this place good-bye, but since I know this is truly my last lap around the parenting track (unless the universe has a cruel joke planned for my uterus), I'm trying to soak it all in.

I take a seat in the back of the auditorium, having been instructed by my son that I shouldn't sit anywhere he can see me. Apparently, I make weird faces when I'm recording on my phone. This year his class is singing "Merry Christmas, Darling," and Max has been belting it out for two weeks. He's been in a much better mood since our talk about Zach E., and I'm hoping it's because they've figured out a way to coexist.

Shirleen plops down beside me with a sigh. "Are you as sick of the song as I am?" is her greeting.

"I'm just happy they gave them enough time to learn it this year," I tell her. Last year their music teacher sort of dropped the ball, and they ended up completely botching "The Twelve Days of Christmas," which I didn't think was possible. They were each given a specific part, and no one could remember when they were supposed to sing except the two girls who were given "two turtle doves" and Draper Lody (Alison's son), who was given "and a partridge in a pear tree." Somewhere along the way he decided it would be funny to sing the Bob and Doug McKenzie version, which replaces the word "partridge" with "beer." It actually was funny, and the music teacher's reaction is now a meme. Good times in fourth grade.

"How's it going as class mom? Any better?" I ask Shirleen. She has periodically sent me her emails to her class, which pretty much followed the pattern of her first one—information, then inspirational quote—but she's had mixed responses all year, and she's been very frustrated.

"Meh. It's really a thankless job. You never said anything."

"Shirleen, are you kidding? I mentioned how much I hated it in every email I ever sent to the class!"

"Really? I never noticed."

I'm truly shocked at this revelation. Where did I go wrong?

"Anyway, I got all the food for this morning, and I got the teacher's gift done, so I don't have to worry about anything else until February."

I decide to let her live with that fantasy through the Christmas holidays. She doesn't need to know that the second half of the year is the most brutal for class moms. And anyway, the concert is starting.

After the cuteness of the kindergarten through third-grade children, this year's fourth grade comes out and gives an interesting interpretation of "O Christmas Tree." Someone—I'm guessing the music teacher—decided to rewrite the words, so it threw me off a bit when I went to sing along. But the kids all knew it, and that's what's important. I've been known to rewrite a Christmas ditty or two myself, so no judgment.

Ron slips in the back door of the auditorium just as the fifth grade is taking the stage.

"Sorry I'm late," he whispers and kisses my cheek.

"You're just in time."

The whole grade is wearing red scarves thrown haphazardly around their necks, and they're divided on stage by gender. I'm ready for "Merry Christmas, Darling," so you can imagine my surprise when they all start singing "Baby, It's Cold Outside." I guess no one got the memo that this song has been causing some controversy over its undertones of sexual harassment, but I'm not offended. And if anyone is, it will be Sylvie Pike's problem, not mine. After they finish, I'm about to dash up to the classroom to make sure everything is ready for the breakfast party when Max steps forward and starts to sing "Merry Christmas, Darling" by himself!! Ron and I look at each other as though we're watching a Christmas miracle unfold.

Max is singing. In public. Of his own free will. And he's good! I'm mesmerized by the sight of my son standing so confidently in front of all his peers and their parents. I can't stop the tears from falling—a mixture of pride and surprise and love.

I scan the cluster of classmates behind him and spot Suni Chang looking adoringly at him. So sweet.

When he finishes there's a huge round of applause. Max smiles impishly and bows. Principal Jackowski then gets onstage for his final remarks, and everyone is dismissed to their classrooms for holiday parties.

That's my cue to dash upstairs to the classroom. Thankfully one of Hunter's two moms—Carol, I think—volunteered to be my advance team, and everything looks great.

The rest of the parents and kids are fast on my heels, so the party is rocking in no time. I find my son loitering by the donuts with his friends. They're like dogs waiting to be told it's okay to eat the treat that was placed on their noses. I give him a huge hug, not caring who I'm embarrassing.

"That was amazing! I can't believe you didn't tell us you were going to sing a solo!"

He blushes and wiggles out of my embrace. "It was Mr. Green's idea."

Ron joins us. "Great job, buddy!" He gives him a one-armed shoulder hug.

"It was such a surprise!" I can't stop gushing. "I mean, I hear you sing around the house, but I had no idea you would ever sing in front of people!"

"Neither did I!" Max laughs.

I take a victory lap around the classroom and accept congratulations for my son's performance before settling with Ravi and a cup of coffee.

The piercing sound of a DJ's air horn stops all the chatter and Mr. Green welcomes everyone to Room 252.

"Merry Christmas, everyone! Happy holidays! We hope you enjoyed the concert. Weren't the kids great?"

We all applaud loudly.

"Jen, would you like to say a few words?"

I step to the front of the classroom with the class gift for Mr. Green.

"Well, I just want to thank you all for coming. Participation this year has been great, which makes my job a lot easier. Mr. Green, our kids are loving being in your class. And this"—I hold up a wrapped present—"is just a little something to thank you."

Everyone claps, and Mr. Green opens his gift—a book of jokes made by the kids. Making it was quite the adventure, much like sifting through trash is an adventure. I asked the parents to have their kids submit two jokes each and some kind of artwork to go with them. And is anyone surprised that 99 percent of the jokes were bathroom- or dick-related? Some of the highlights include:

Why can't you hear a pterodactyl go to the bathroom? Because the pee is silent.

An old married couple are in church one Sunday when the woman turns to her husband and whispers, "I've just let out a

*really long, silent fart. What should I do?" The husband says,
"You should change the batteries in your hearing aid."*

*What did the elephant say to the naked man? "How can
you breathe through that thing?"*

*Why did the chipmunk swim on his back? To keep his nuts
dry.*

And Max's contribution:

*What's the difference between a snowman and a snow woman?
Snowballs!*

"This is just perfect!" Mr. Green seems genuinely tickled.
"Thank you, everyone. I hope you all have a wonderful Christmas.
And—let's party!!" He blows the DJ horn again, and I can't help
but wonder how hearing impaired these poor kids are going to be
by the end of the year.

With the party in full swing, I slip into a corner with Peetsa and
get caught up. Another day, another bad date. This poor woman
must have stepped on a crack, broken a mirror, and walked under
a ladder all at the same time to be on the receiving end of this kind
of luck.

As she's telling me what she got Zach for Christmas, I see her
eyes shift to the classroom door and remain there. I turn and see her
ex-husband, Buddy, walk in with his pregnant fiancée on his arm.

"Did you know he was coming?" she whispers.

"No! I mean, he gets the class emails, but he didn't RSVP."

"Who the hell does?" she snaps, and I feel a bit chastened, like
she thinks I should have prevented this.

"P, he's allowed to come to school functions."

"But he's not allowed to bring *her*."

Buddy's fiancée isn't what I would have thought he'd choose
after his midlife crisis. He left Peetsa, a tall, beautiful Italian woman
with dark hair and dark eyes, for Patrice, who is basically a younger,

shorter version of her. I mean, the similarity is shocking. It's impossible not to see it.

Zach runs to his dad and gives both of them a hug.

"It's okay." I rest my hand on her arm. But I know it isn't. If *I'm* feeling weird, I can't imagine how she's feeling.

But P is nothing if not resilient. She squares her shoulders and walks over to the three of them. I'm not 100 percent sure, but I think she's standing a bit taller than usual, which makes her tower over Patrice. I can't hear what's being said, but it all seems very civil until Patrice bursts into tears and runs out of the classroom.

Holy shit show. I start to make my way across the room when I notice that everyone has stopped talking. The silence is cringeworthy. I need a distraction, so I grab Mr. Green's DJ horn and just start blowing it over and over again. The kids start whooping and hollering.

"Hey hey! These donuts aren't going to eat themselves," I yell. "Come on, you guys. I don't want any leftovers."

It's at this primo moment that PTA president Sylvie Pike walks in and immediately motions for me to come to her.

"There's a pregnant teenager crying in the hallway," she informs me.

"I know. I'm handling it," I say evenly.

She shrugs. "Okay. Just thought I'd mention it. Do you have any fruit left?"

I've known Sylvie for three years now and I still don't have a handle on what's going to upset her. I would have thought this would be a five-alarm fire, but she obviously just wanted some melon.

"What did you say to her?" I ask Peetsa when I join her. Buddy has followed Patrice into the hallway.

"Nothing bad. She apologized for being here, which I thought was nice."

I give her an expectant look because I know there's more to the story.

"Sooo, then Buddy said, 'It was my idea.' And I said to her, 'This can't be the first bad idea he's had. You have to learn to ignore him.' And then she started crying and ran out." She shrugs and takes a sip of coffee.

I don't really know what to say. In my world that's considered friendly banter between exes. But Patrice is pregnant, and I know from experience there isn't a set list of things that make you cry when you're in the family way. It can really be anything. I remember breaking down in a Babies "R" Us because I couldn't find the perfect going-home-from-the-hospital outfit for Max.

Mr. Green blowing the air horn gets everyone's attention once again, and he signals it's time to wrap things up. After a quick cleanup, thanks to everyone helping, we say our good-byes and head home. Winter break has officially begun!

✦ ✦ ✦

"Max!" I yell, a little louder than intended.

"What?" he answers from the living room.

"Excuse me, what did you say?"

Suddenly he's in the doorway to the kitchen. "Mom." He's using the tone of a mother talking to a five-year-old. "You know I'm polite. I'm the only person I know who says, 'Pardon me?' when I didn't hear something. My friends give me sh—crap about it all the time!"

"Well, you'll only get sh—crap from me if you don't say it," I inform him. "Now please clean up the mess you've been making in the living room. Our guests will be here in an hour."

He turns without a word, and I get back to work. We have a big crowd coming tonight for Christmas Eve dinner—my parents (making a rare evening appearance outside of their house), Laura, Vivs, Maude, Raj, and of course the guest of honor, Raj's mother, Varsha.

She arrived from Mumbai this afternoon, and I've been trying to get Vivs on the phone to find out what she's like.

Lasagna is on the menu—our traditional night-before-Christmas dinner—along with Caesar salad and garlic bread, and everything is just about done. The cheese on the lasagna is bubbling in the oven and the table is set for ten—decked with candles, holly, and small red poinsettia leaves. Christmas crackers are placed on plates, ready to be popped, and Ron has opened three bottles of Chianti. I'm as ready as I'll ever be.

I dash upstairs to finish getting myself ready—well, "dash" is an exaggeration. "Hobble" would be more like it. My hip flexors are ridiculously tight because of how many spin classes I've been teaching. Yup, you heard me. I've been covering shifts at Fusion for the past week, and I'm on the schedule for all the days between Christmas and New Year's—sometimes twice a day. It's been a great ego boost, but I need to spend more time stretching.

The mom uniform for tonight is dressy black yoga pants and a red J.Crew sweater—a nice, comfortable outfit for what may or may not be a nice, comfortable evening. I try Vivs again and still get voice mail, so I try Laura.

"What's up? Do you need something before I come over?" she asks.

"Are you with Vivs?"

"No, I told you, there's a holiday party at Riverview, and then I'm picking up Nana and Poppy. We probably won't be there till like six thirty."

"Did you meet Raj's mother?"

"No, Mom, and stop obsessing."

"I'm not obsessing!"

"Did Nana tell you she has a surprise for you?" She changes the subject.

"Yes, she did. Any idea what it is?"

"Nope. But you may want to set another place at the table in case she's bringing the people from the basement." This has become a running joke in our family, even though it really shouldn't be. My parents' possible dementia is nothing to laugh about, but the people in the basement have become a scapegoat for everything from who ate the last cookie to who killed JonBenét Ramsey.

When I get back downstairs, Ron has put on some Christmas music and lit a fire. I look around my living room, satisfied that no matter who Varsha turns out to be, she won't be able to resist being charmed by the magic of the season.

"You look festive," he says as he kisses me on the cheek. "Ooh, are those your *dressy* yoga pants?"

"Why, yes they are! Aren't you sweet to notice." I smile at his obvious sarcasm.

When the doorbell rings I get a kind of diarrhea feeling in my stomach. *This is it!* All will be revealed when I open the front door, which I do after taking a huge breath.

"Gee Gee!" Maude runs to my legs and gives them a hug. I bend down to pick her up and come face-to-face with a stunning woman. She is about my height, five foot four, with large brown eyes and a very defined nose and chin. She is so chic she could easily have stepped off the cover of *AARP the Magazine*. Varsha is wearing a black cashmere coat, which covers a tailored pantsuit in charcoal gray and a red shirt that nicely matches the spirit of the season. Her blackish-gray hair is in a low chignon, and her makeup is understated and tasteful. Half an hour ago I thought I looked great, but after seeing this woman, I have to downgrade myself to so-so.

Raj steps forward and hugs me. "Jen, this is my mother."

"Varsha Basak," she says, with a slight British accent, and holds out her hand, which I clasp with both of mine.

"Please come in! It's so lovely to finally meet you." I move aside and let them pass. I feel like royalty has just stepped through my door.

Ron steps in like a maître d' to introduce himself and take Varsha's coat. She smiles and displays a perfect set of white teeth.

"What a beautiful home you have," she says while taking inventory of our front hallway.

"Thank you. Please come see the rest of it." I gesture toward the living room.

I realize I still have Maude in my arms, so I put her down, and we all settle in our seats.

"How was your flight?" I ask her.

"Uneventful, which is the best kind, don't you think?" She laughs nervously. It can't be easy for her to walk into a room full of strangers.

"She was even a bit early," Raj chimes in. He turns to his mother. "I almost wasn't there to meet you!"

"But you were, *beta*." She smiles and reaches to squeeze his hand. "And even if you weren't, I'm certainly capable of taking a taxi."

Ron walks in with five glasses of wine on a tray.

"Oh, aren't you wonderful!" Varsha exclaims as though he has summoned our beverages out of thin air. We all take one, and Ron raises his glass to make a toast.

"To new friends."

"To new friends," we all repeat and take our first sips.

"Jen, Rajan tells me you teach exercise classes." Varsha looks directly at me.

"Well, it's part-time right now. I teach spin at a local gym."

"Ah. I've never tried that. The only exercise I get is a brisk walk in the park when the weather is good."

"Well, I'm teaching for the next two weeks, if you'd like to come to a class."

"That sounds wonderful!" she enthuses. She turns to Raj. "Would you come too?"

"Uh, sure." I think Raj is surprised his mother would even be open to something like that.

"You must be so happy to finally meet Maude."

Varsha's eyes light up. "Yes! She is so beautiful." She glances toward our shared granddaughter, who is hugging her mother's legs. "She's a little shy with me, but I'll win her over."

"Vivs, are you closed for the week?" I already know the answer, but my daughter's silence is bothering me, and I just want to hear her talk.

"Closed till New Year's Day," she confirms. "I'm really hoping business picks up after that."

"I'm sure it will, sweetie." As I say this, the front door opens, and Laura bursts into the foyer with an armful of presents, my parents right behind her, and what I'm guessing is my surprise right behind them. Standing there in a colorful Christmas cape is none other than Garth's mother, Yvette!

"Surprise!" my mom yells and gestures toward our unexpected guest. "Look who came for Christmas!"

"Yvette! What are you doing here?" I ask before I can stop myself. To make up for it, I give her a big hug.

"Your mother invited me when she found out I was going to be alone for the holidays," she says with a big dose of gratitude in her voice.

"Well, that's just . . . wonderful!" I hope I sound more enthused than I'm feeling. I really don't mind the surprise, but Yvette adds an element of crazy to the room that I have no control over. And I don't even have Garth to act as a buffer, because he and Nina have gone back to Mexico to finish the school they started building on their honeymoon. I was hoping to make a really good impression on Varsha, or at least have her think we're a relatively normal family. But God knows what Yvette and her spirit guides are going to bring to the conversation.

Introductions are made, and everyone settles in the living room, where I have set out cheese and crackers (the fancy kind!) for everyone to snack on. As per usual, my father is quiet, but my mom has brought the full Kay tonight, and she is in a very chatty mood.

"So, Varsha, you look very modern. Ray and I thought we'd be meeting Princess Jasmine!"

I cringe, but Varsha just laughs. "Oh, I only wear my harem pants when I take the magic carpet out."

Everyone laughs, thank goodness.

My mother has settled herself beside Raj and peppers him with questions about his work. Varsha is smiling at both of them.

Dinner is a big hit. Who doesn't love lasagna? And Varsha seems touched that I thought to make a vegetarian version for her, although she barely eats anything. I'm most worried about the conversation, but it never veers into dangerous territory, thank God.

When Vivs excuses herself to change Maude's diaper, I slip out after her.

"How's it going?" I ask her. "I mean, with Varsha?"

Vivs shrugs as she takes off her daughter's frilly diaper cover. "It's fine. She seems nice."

"That isn't exactly a ringing endorsement," I tell her.

"I know. It's weird—I mean, there's nothing wrong. She's been nice, and polite, and friendly . . ."

"What a bitch," I joke.

"I know, right? It's all good, but I just keep getting the feeling that the other shoe is about to drop."

"What shoe? Oh wow! Maudie, you little stinker!" I can't help reacting to the smell from my granddaughter's diaper. She just giggles.

Vivs frowns. "Don't make her feel bad!" She tickles her daughter. "*Tutti fanno cacca puzzolente, amore mio.*"

"So, what's the other shoe that's going to drop?" I get us back on track.

"I don't know. I just feel like something isn't being said." She shakes her head. "Maybe I'm imagining it."

"Well, she could be holding a bit of a grudge about the way you treated Raj. I know I would."

"Maybe Yvette's spirit guides can tell me." She winks.

Maude is all tidied up, so we head back downstairs to find everyone has moved to the kitchen and Laura is leading a massive cleanup. I have to say, ever since she started working in a kitchen, she has become impressively efficient at cleaning and even sanitizing all surfaces. Maybe I should send Max to work with her once a week.

Max, by the way, has been an angel all evening. He doesn't believe in Santa anymore, but he does know that things will go better for him on Christmas morning if he behaves himself on Christmas Eve. Varsha has been peppering him with questions about school and sports, and he's enjoying the attention. I'm touched that she's taking so much time to get to know my son. Just as I start to yawn, Vivs announces she needs to get Maude home to bed.

"Mummy and I will come with you," Raj says, and he and Varsha get up and head to the foyer. As I suggested previously, Varsha is staying with Vivs and Raj, and Laura is camping out with us.

"We should probably leave too, Ray," my mother shouts. "Yvette, you ready?"

"Just give me a minute." Yvette is sitting by the Christmas tree, looking up and to the right.

"Maybe the spirit guides are telling her what's under the tree," Ron mumbles to me as he hands out coats.

At the door, Varsha takes my hands. "Thank you for an enchanting evening, Jen. I felt so welcome."

"You *are* welcome," I assure her. "I'll see you this week."

As she floats down the walkway, I can't help but kick myself for being worried about such a lovely woman.

Yvette is the last to leave, and as she walks out the door, she leans in and gives me the worst Christmas gift I could have received.

"The guides tell me that woman is going to be big trouble."

11

To: The personal chefs of Mr. Green's Fifth-Grade Class
From: Jennifer Dixon
Re: Happy new year!
Date: January 8

Greetings, fellow food preparers,

Hope you all had a fine holiday season and are ready for the rigors of fifth grade, second semester.

A few notes as we sally forth into the rest of the year:

1) Sex education starts this month. Don't let the title panic you. It's basically personal hygiene and respecting other people's boundaries. Mrs. Seamen will be teaching the class (insert your own joke here), and she wants parents to be prepared to answer some new and interesting questions at the dinner table.

2) The big fifth-grade overnight trip to Topeka is definitely taking place May 18 to 19. I know it was up in the air after the boys in last year's class were caught streaking in the hotel hallway, but I have convinced Principal Jackowski that our kids are nothing like those hooligans. So please just remind your kids to keep their pants on.

This trip will be the perfect way to end the kids' yearlong study of slavery and the civil rights movement. I plan to chaperone, but I'll need two other parent volunteers. It's your chance to spend two glamorous nights at the Ramada Inn in lovely downtown Topeka. Full disclosure: I need both sexes represented, as we will be sharing rooms (Dad, whoever you are, you will be bunking with Mr. Green).

3) Our next class party will be for Valentine's Day. As always, if your children plan to give out cards or treats, please send enough for everyone. Hormones will be running high from sex education class, and we don't want any hurt feelings.

That's it for now. Just a reminder that the fundraising committee will be selling chocolate-covered sea salt caramels starting next week, so please order early and often for your special valentine. Your generosity will be judged.

Run along, I'm sure you have things to do.

Jen

My entire body hurts. I stretch back in my kitchen-counter-office chair and try for the umpteenth time to loosen up my joints. I was so excited to teach spin classes all through Christmas break, but I had no idea the toll it would take on me.

Not to mention the emotional toll of the three-ring circus that Varsha's visit has become. After Yvette's dire warning on Christmas Eve, I was on high alert for anything that would indicate Varsha was not who she appeared to be.

But she came to a spin class and told me she really enjoyed herself, and she cooked us a traditional Indian meal one night that I could tell she put a lot of effort into. Her chicken tikka masala was better than anything I've ever had at a restaurant. My parents bagged out on that dinner because according to my mom, Indian food gives my dad the trots. But everyone else loved it, including Maude.

Varsha spent a lot of time with her granddaughter and Raj, which is only right, and as far as I could tell, everyone was having a lovely time.

The first indication that something wasn't quite right came just before New Year's, when Vivs started complaining because she wasn't being included in any of their outings.

"They treat me like I'm the babysitter they can hand Maude off to when they're finished with her for the day," she griped while eating an acai bowl in my kitchen.

"Well, you *are* working, so they're really just taking Maude time away from me, and frankly, I was grateful for the help this week," I tell her.

"I just don't feel included in any fun things they do at home or when I'm working. All I do is bathe and feed her."

"Have you said something to Raj?"

"I told him I didn't like being excluded, and he was like, 'Oh really? You feel excluded? How the hell do you think I felt when I didn't know I had a daughter until three months after she was born?'"

"Well, you walked right into that one," I told her. "Has Varsha been unkind to you?"

"Noooo . . ." she says uncertainly. "She hasn't been anything. She kind of ignores me."

I frown. "What do you do?"

"I ignore her right back."

I'm so glad to see my mature way of handling conflict has rubbed off on my daughter.

This all went on while I was preoccupied with teaching my classes, making sure Max had friends to hang out with, and checking in on my parents, so I couldn't give Vivs's griping my full attention. But the hammer came down the first week of the new year, when, according to Vivs, Varsha sat her down and told her they wanted to take Maude back to India for a visit.

"I can't really take time off work right now" was her response. Varsha said she didn't expect her to come and wanted Maude to go for a few months. Vivs rejected the idea outright, and that's when things got heated. A few choice words were thrown out by my daughter, and then Varsha lashed out at the audacity of Vivs thinking she could keep Raj's daughter away from her. Then Vivs, who really is her mother's daughter, said there was no way they were taking Maude anywhere and reminded Varsha that Raj's name isn't even on Maude's birth certificate, so he has no legal claim to her.

"We've hired a lawyer to fix that," Varsha informed her. "And Maude needs to know her heritage and where she comes from."

"She comes from Kansas City. And she's two years old. It would very traumatic for her to be without me," Vivs shot back.

"Oh please," said Varsha. "You're never home. You work all the time. If it weren't for Rajan, you would put her in day care."

When Vivs told me this story later, I couldn't help but wish I'd been there—not as the voice of reason, mind you, but because I happen to be really good at giving dirty looks. I guess Raj wasn't present for that conversation, and he hasn't returned any of Vivs's calls or texts. None of us have ever known Raj to be so uncommunicative.

Since then, he and Varsha have moved to Raj's new apartment (the one none of us knew he'd found), and she's staying indefinitely. In the meantime, we have consulted a lawyer to see what rights Vivs has to keep Raj from taking her baby to another country.

✦ ✦ ✦

Ron saunters into the kitchen as I'm pouring myself another much-needed cup of coffee.

"What's on the agenda today?" he asks. I already know what's coming.

"Just another glamorous day in the life of Jen Dixon," I tell him. "Putting gas in the jet, buying diamonds, and getting ready for the cotillion."

"Any time for your man?" He moves behind me and starts rubbing my shoulders.

"Well, I do have a meeting with the stable boy, but I think I can squeeze you in before that." I turn to kiss him.

"I know exactly where I want to be squeezed," he whispers as he takes my hand.

This has become a bit of a routine for us. By the time we go to bed at night, neither of us has the energy to have sex. So, Ron has taken a liking to midmorning sexy time. If I'm home, and he's home, and Max and Maude are *not* home, I know it's going to be one of those mornings. It usually lands on a Thursday, so I don't make early plans that day, just in case. It's a nice time for us to just be together.

Afterwards, we shower, and Ron gives me a soapy back massage because he knows how sore I am. It feels amazing.

"When are you teaching again?" he asks. "I feel like you should be on the schedule by now."

"I know. But I don't mind having a little downtime. Those two-a-days really wiped me out."

My ten days of teaching at Fusion had some highs and lows. On the upside, my confidence as a teacher is definitely on the rise. I don't feel scared shitless when I get on the bike and face the class anymore, and I'm getting better at reading the room and knowing what the riders will want to hear. On the downside, people are still disappointed when they see their favorite teacher isn't there, and they have no problem telling me about it.

"You again?" was my favorite greeting of the week. That and "Don't play anymore yacht rock." I discovered this channel on satellite radio and fell in love all over again with the simple but satisfying musical stylings of Ambrosia, Boz Scaggs, and Steely Dan, to name a few. Little did I know that for most people, that kind of music just doesn't get their mojo going in a spin class. At all. Oh well, lesson learned.

"You need to do some yoga. We haven't done a class together in ages," says Ron.

"That's a great idea. Who's teaching tonight?"

"I think Yasmine is doing the six o'clock Ashtanga class at the old studio."

"I'll go if you go."

"Deal. What about Max?"

"Brinda's coming to tutor at five thirty, so we're good."

"Then it's a date." My husband smiles, and I silently thank the universe yet again for sending me someone I actually like as well as love.

✦ ✦ ✦

It's so damned cold today! I'm standing at school, waiting for Max with the pickup squad. We're all bundled up and huddled together against the subzero temperatures.

"I can't wait till middle school," Ravi announces. "No more standing outside for pickup."

"Is that true?" I ask.

"That's what I've heard. I heard you can just wait in your car for them."

"That's a game changer," Asami chimes in from beneath her neck gaiter.

I have updated my group on the Varsha/Raj/Vivs saga, and they are in complete agreement that this woman needs to be stopped. All except Ravi, that is. She just tries to balance the conversation, which can slip into "lock her up" territory pretty quickly.

"You need to put your feet in her shoes for a second," she has become fond of saying. "What if you just found out you had a granddaughter? Wouldn't you want to spend time with her?"

"Of course I would, but she didn't *just* find out—she's known for almost two years. And I'm all for her spending time with Maude, but she doesn't have to take her thousands of miles away to do it."

It goes on from there, back and forth and back and forth. I know Ravi is on my side in the long run, but she seems to understand Varsha's mind-set better than anyone, so I try to keep an open mind.

The bell finally rings, and the floodgates open. It's hard to identify any one kid unless you're familiar with their outerwear. Max used to be easy to spot when he was younger because he had a somewhat flamboyant way of dressing, but ever since third grade

(Ron likes to call it the "year of enlightenment") he runs with the pack, and his black down puffy jacket is anything but distinctive. Luckily, *he* recognizes *me*, so when he stomps by and yells, "Come *on*, Mom!" I know it's my own little darling and no one else.

Back at the minivan, I start the engine, then immediately unwrap the scarf around my mouth, so my son can get the full effect of my words.

"Max. In *no way* is it okay for you to speak to me like that," I say in my "I mean business" voice.

"Like what?" he scowls.

"Like I'm your servant. What's going on?"

"Nothing! Why do we have to talk?"

"We don't!" I snap back. "You can go straight to your room when we get home, and you won't have to talk to anyone."

"Fine! It's what I want anyway," he yells.

"Fine!" I yell back, and we drive home in a silence dripping with what's not being said.

Max was so great over the holidays. He was busy and happy and spent a lot of time with all of us. We kept him from the Varsha drama, and he seemed relaxed and ready to go back to school. This is the first time I've seen him in a bad mood in weeks.

When we get home, he rushes through the kitchen door and makes a meal out of running up the stairs and slamming his door with a window-shaking bang. My first instinct is to race right after him and give him shit for the door slam, but my cooler head prevails, and instead I grab a pamplemousse (that's French for "grapefruit"!) flavored LaCroix from the fridge and plunk myself down at the kitchen counter office. Yoga tonight can't come soon enough.

✦ ✦ ✦

"One final breath in as we thank the universe for the air in our lungs and this wonderful practice that has brought us to a peaceful place. Namaste."

"Namaste," we all repeat after Yasmine, and I finally open

my eyes. Ron is beside me, and I think we both feel ten pounds lighter.

"Well?" he asks as we exit the class to the sound of wind chimes and rushing water.

"I'm a new woman," I declare. "This was such a great idea."

"Free class whenever you want! I'm going to hit the john before we go."

As I'm packing my yoga mat into its carrying bag, the sound of a very familiar voice stops me short.

I poke my head around the corner and there, in the flesh, is the love of my life, the woman of my dreams and a vision in yoga pants—my former spin instructor.

"Carmen!" I shriek and immediately make myself the center of attention. "Sorry!" I'm embarrassed as I slink over to where she's standing by the front desk, and I take it down a notch. "I can't believe you're here!"

"Jen! What's up, girl? It's been ages." The cadence of her voice acts like a tonic on my soul.

"How's Peloton? We miss you so much at Fusion." I'm literally gushing, and I don't care who sees me.

"Aw, it wasn't for me." She shakes her long red locks. "I couldn't play all the music I wanted to, and they wouldn't let me call the riders my 'spin bitches.'"

"So, wait, are you teaching anywhere?"

"I'm actually hoping to teach here. Give my joints a break."

"Really? That's great." I look around for Ron, because I want him to hire her on the spot.

"I love this place. Do you come here a lot?" she asks.

"Not as often as I . . . Ron!" I spot him coming out of the men's room and motion him over.

"Carmen, this is my husband, Ron."

"Ron Dixon." He smiles and holds out his hand. "Wait, is this *the* Carmen?"

"I don't think I'm *the* Carmen—" she starts to answer.

"Yes! Yes, you are! This is her," I tell Ron. I really need to calm down and act a little cooler. I turn to her. "You're kind of famous in my house. I loved your classes so much, and I talked about them all the time."

"Literally, *all the time*." Ron emphasizes the point.

"Carmen wants to work here," I announce.

Ron's eyebrows go up, and he nods but doesn't say anything.

"Yes, so if you know anyone," Carmen jokes.

"I know us!" I tap her arm excitedly. "We own this place!"

Ron has put his hand on the small of my back and is now pinching it hard.

"Why are you pinching me?" I demand.

"Sorry, sweetie. I didn't realize I was." He smiles at Carmen. "So, I guess we should set up a time for you to meet the manager." He turns to the woman behind the desk. "Jayna, could you take Carmen's info so we can have someone call her?"

"Oh my gosh, thank you! This is crazy. You own Om Sweet Om? I had no idea! This place is amazing." Carmen seems a bit embarrassed by the whole thing.

"We'll see you soon, Carmen," Ron says politely and pushes me toward the door.

"I'm a spin instructor now!" I tell her as I'm being led away. "I've been filling in at Fusion!"

"Good for you," Carmen yells after me.

+ + +

"Do you want to tell me what that was all about?" I ask Ron.

He unlocks the car, and we both get in, out of the frigid air.

"Are you kidding me? You basically offered a stranger a job."

"She's not a stranger! I've known her for almost three years."

"Oh, really? What yoga does she practice? Where is she from? Where does she live?"

"Well, I don't know that stuff," I mumble. "But she's the best spin instructor I've ever had."

"Which totally qualifies her to teach yoga at our studio," Ron says sarcastically.

We drive in silence for a while, then Ron puts his hand on my knee. "So, that's Carmen, huh?"

"That's Carmen," I singsong.

He laughs. "You need a better poker face, my love."

"Will you hire her?"

"I'll consider her, like I do anyone who applies to work for me." He pauses. "And, Jen, you know how I run the business. Please don't put me in a situation like that again."

"Why would I?" I smile. "There's only one Carmen."

"Mmm-hmmm," was all I got in reply.

✦ ✦ ✦

"Are you ready to tell me what happened today?"

I'm up in Max's room, making sure his homework is done for the evening.

He sighs like he has the weight of the world on his shoulders. He's in his favorite Chiefs T-shirt and a pair of sweatpants.

"It's Zach E. He said something mean again, and I just got mad."

"What did he say to you?"

"He said I like boys."

Ho-ly *shit*. I did not see that coming. I take a deep breath. I feel like my whole life has led up to this moment, and I really don't want to screw it up.

"Why do you think he would say that?"

"He's been saying it since the summer." Max's eyes are watering. "At camp we were taking a pi—we were going to the bathroom together, and he told everyone I looked at his wiener."

I'm in so far over my head right now I need a thirty-foot oxygen line. I want to excuse myself and find out what Google has to say about this, but I don't dare. I ask my next question carefully.

"Did you?"

"No!" he says indignantly. And then he throws himself down on his pillow and starts to cry.

"Okay." I rub his back, and he lets out a few sobs. When he's calmed down, I continue.

"Are you upset because you think there's something wrong with being gay?"

"No. *I don't know!* Is that what liking boys means? That you're gay?"

I pull Max into my arms. "Yes. It's when boys like boys or girls like girls in a romantic way, and there is nothing wrong with that."

"Then why does it make me feel so bad when he calls me that?"

He takes a few deep breaths, then pulls away. "How do you know if you're gay?"

Do you like show tunes? I think but don't say.

"Well, I think if you'd rather kiss a boy than a girl, then there is a chance you might be gay."

Max looks completely confused. "But I don't want to kiss *any-one*. Well, except you. And Maude."

"I'm glad you still want to kiss me." I smile and plant a wet one on his cheek. "The next time Zach says you're gay, just tell him to stop using words he doesn't understand. And sweetie—" I pause to look him in the eyes. "If you ever think you're gay, you can tell me. It's nothing to be ashamed of."

"I will." He wipes the snot from his nose on his shirt sleeve. "But I don't think I am." He looks at me soulfully. "Maybe I'm nothing."

12

To: Jennifer Dixon
From: Shirleen Cobb
Re: Important question!
Date: February 5

Jennifer,

I don't want to alarm you, but we had an incident at the dinner table last night that I think you should know about.

Graydon asked us what is the difference between a boner and an erection? It was a conversation stopper, I can tell you that.

Have you had questions like this come up? It was my understanding that their sex education class would cover stuff like showering and wearing clean underwear.

I have half a mind to go to the principal, but I thought I'd ask you first.

Best,

Shirleen

To: Shirleen Cobb
From: Jennifer Dixon
Re: Important question!
Date: February 5

Hi, Shirleen,

I don't think there's any reason to be alarmed. I know the curriculum talks about changing bodies and feelings as well as hygiene. I think Graydon's question is probably something he's wondered about for a while. I'd encourage him to keep asking things. Better he asks you than someone he doesn't know or, even worse, a kid his own age.

By the way, how did you answer him?

Jen

To Jennifer Dixon
From: Shirleen Cobb
Re: Important question!
Date: February 5

I told him they were not the same. An erection is a tall building, and a boner is a stupid person.

Shirleen

Jeez, I really hope Graydon finds a good therapist when he's older.

I needed a laugh after the morning I've had. I got a call from Cathy Red Nails while I was driving Max to school. She's been spearheading the sale of chocolate-covered sea salt caramels for Valentine's Day. Apparently, she just heard from the supplier, and they've been shut down by the health department for code violations, whatever that means. So, more than two thousand dollars' worth of orders will not be filled by February 14. We either have to wait until they reopen or give everyone their money back. I was so frustrated I went down to the basement and hit the punching bag in Ron's Gym and Tan for the first time in ages. One of the many great things about wearing yoga pants all the time is you're always ready for a workout.

I gave that poor bag a good going-over, but it didn't do much to ease my frustration. What do I have to do to make money for this school?

It didn't help that when I was checking my email, I got one from PTA president Sylvie Pike.

To: Jennifer Dixon
From: Sylvie Pike
Re: Update please
Date: February 5

Hi, Jen,

One of the Cathy Reids just told me about the delay with the chocolate-covered sea salt caramels. I must say, I'm surprised you didn't vet the vendor more thoroughly. So . . . what's the plan? If I were you, I'd keep the cash and send an apology to everyone. At least we know the place will be spick-and-span when they start making our chocolates again.

Update me, please, and thank you. And there's no shame in asking for help if this task is too much for you. Lean on your team!

Regards,

Sylvie

So I was glad when I saw Shirleen's email. It was truly the laugh I needed. I'm still giggling as I craft a response to Sylvie Pike, letting her know I'm on top of things and we'll be just fine. But as I write it, I wonder if it's true. WeFUKCT seems to be operating under a dark cloud for some reason. It's February, and we aren't even halfway to our goal, nor do we have any real reason to believe we're going to get there.

I talk to Nina about it later in the day on our weekly call, and she suggests doing a raffle with two or three really great items—stuff people can get excited about.

"Like what?"

"I don't know. Maybe a designer bag, or sports tickets. You and Ron could put together a really nice workout package with spinning and yoga as one of the items."

"So, you think raffle over auction?"

"Definitely. Auctions are messy, and most people don't participate."

"You're right. I'll talk to Ron later. Hey, how's Yvette doing?"

"She's okay." Nina sighs. Yvette took a tumble down the front steps of her house just after the new year and broke her hip. She's been staying with Garth and Nina ever since, and I'm pretty sure she's driving Nina crazy. "She keeps talking about how much she loved spending time with your mom at Christmas."

"She and Kay seem to be soul sisters."

"Well, they're both a bit loopy. Maybe that's how they bond. By the way, Yvette's spirit guides have told her there's something in Kay's house that shouldn't be there."

"I'll tell you what shouldn't be in that house—Kay and Ray," I tell her.

"Ha-ha."

"I'm serious. I got a call from their doctor after my dad's check-up last week, and he was very concerned about Dad's weight loss and listlessness. He was also worried that my mother isn't being much help."

"She still has the blinders on, huh?"

"Yes, and it's so freakin' frustrating. The doctor said they could really benefit from an assisted living situation where they have independence but someone keeps an eye on them. He said it right to them, but my mother told him that when she wanted his opinion, she'd ask for it."

Nina laughs. "She's such a character. Why don't you bring it up?"

"Are you kidding? She'd kill me if she knew I talked to the doctor behind her back."

"Garth talks to all his mother's doctors all the time. It's kind of expected."

"Not in Kay's world." I sigh. "So, Ron and I decided to take a look at Riverview next week, just to see what's what. Laura thinks they'll like it."

"And she could low-key look after them. Maybe we can get a group rate, and I'll send Yvette up."

"Will she need a room for three?"

"Ha! Well, let me know how the tour goes."

"I will. Give my love to everyone."

✦ ✦ ✦

That night at dinner, I ask Max if he has any questions about his sex education class. He looks at me thoughtfully and says, "Well, I'm kind of wondering if it's funny that the teacher's name is Mrs. Seamen."

Ron smacks the table and lets out a barking laugh. "I'd say it's more ironic than funny." I give Ron a look that implores him to stop laughing. He doesn't. "I hope you guys don't make fun of her," he says through chuckles.

"We're not allowed to say much. And if you laugh at anything, you have to go stand in the hallway."

"What about asking questions?" I wonder.

Max nods. "Ya, she likes it when you ask questions, unless they're 'smarty-pants questions.'" He uses air quotes. "Then you have to go stand in the hallway. Yesterday there were five of us out there at one time."

"What's a 'smarty-pants question'?" Ron wants to know.

"It's hard to tell. I mean, I asked if you had to have a lot of sex to get twins or triplets, and she made me go outside. But I really wanted to know." He pauses. "Do you guys know?"

At this point I remember something I learned a long time ago with Laura and Vivs: answer the question that is asked and nothing more.

"No, you don't," I tell him. "It's the same amount. Some people just get lucky."

"I wish Maude was twins," is his reply. Max loves his little niece so much. He's always happy to sit and play with her whenever he can. I'm not sure if that's normal for a ten-year-old boy, but I'm glad he does it.

Later, when Max is in bed, I talk to Ron about Nina's idea of a high-end raffle for the fundraiser. He says we could do an Om Sweet Om package including a one-year membership plus a bunch of swag, and maybe even a private lesson with one of the instructors.

"I like it," I say.

Just then my cell phone rings, and I can see it's Fusion Fitness. "Hello?"

"Jen, it's Craig at Fusion. How are you doing?"

"I'm good, thanks." I take a peek at the clock and see it's nine forty-five. Kind of late to be calling, in my opinion, and then I remember I'm old. For Craig this is probably midday.

"Jodi wanted me to reach out and see if you'd be interested in teaching a regular class on Friday mornings at eight?"

"This Friday?"

"Actually, every Friday, if you want it."

I look over at Ron and mouth, *OMG*! Back on the phone, I try to act cool. "Yes, sure. That sounds great."

"We can pay you forty dollars a class, but if you fill the class, we'll double it."

"Okay." I'm a little less excited about that. Filling a class seems about as likely as finding diet donuts, but whatever.

"And now you'll be on the rotation to fill in for other instructors, so you can make extra money with that." Craig sounds like he's trying to convince me.

"It sounds great. Please thank Jodi for me."

"You can thank her yourself when you see her."

"You're right, I will. See you Friday."

"Well?" Ron looks at me expectantly.

"They offered me Friday mornings at eight on a regular basis." I grin.

"That's my girl! Way to go!" He moves over to hug me and starts rubbing my back. "How should we celebrate?"

Boy, this train is never late. Why do men always think that sex is the best way to commemorate everything? *We finished cleaning out the garage, let's have sex! Max got a perfect score on his math test, let's have sex! It's Thursday, let's have sex!*

So, I answer him the only way I know how.

"Let's have sex!"

13

To: WeFUKCT
From: Jennifer Dixon
Re: Mo' money!
Date: February 17

Hey team,

I know it's been a rough couple of weeks. Telling everyone their chocolate-covered sea salt caramels were delayed was tough on all of us. Did anyone besides Liana Jones get threatened with a lawsuit? Luckily, the Christmas candles arrived on February 4, so at least we had something to give out. With any luck the chocolates will be here by Saint Patrick's Day.

Going forward I want you to start thinking about items we could raffle off this spring. Do you know anyone who works for someone or knows someone who might be able to get us something good? Thinking caps on, please. We are in Hail Mary territory. Bring your ideas to the meeting this Thursday, in the cafeteria right after drop-off.

Let's keep the dream alive!

Jen

P.S. If anyone sees No-Tech Cathy, can you let her know about the meeting? Thanks.

"Are you about ready?" Ron asks as I send my email from the kitchen counter office.

"Yup. Did you change Maude?"

"Yes, I did," Ron says in his gruff baby voice and kisses his granddaughter on the cheek.

"I hate that we have to drop her with Raj and Varsha."

Ron shrugs. "It's their afternoon."

"I know. It's just so tense when we see her."

"Well, let's get it over with."

We haven't seen or spoken to Raj since Varsha dropped her bomb on New Year's Day. Any and all communication has been between our lawyers as they battle out some kind of custody-sharing plan that doesn't involve Maude getting on a plane to India. But we always see Varsha when it's our turn to hand off the baby. It's a tense, awkward thirty seconds during which I use all my inner strength not to say something that could hurt Vivs's chances in court. As it is, she is a wreck.

We pull into the apartment complex, and I'm stunned to see it's not Varsha but Raj standing there waiting for us. I jump out of the car, leaving Ron to get Maude out of her car seat.

"Raj! Where have you been? Why haven't we seen you?" I say as nicely as I can. It may or may not come out as a shriek.

"My mother isn't here today," he says, as though that's what I asked him.

"Raj." Ron walks up with Maude in his arms and shakes Raj's hand.

"Ron," Raj replies evenly and takes his daughter and her diaper bag.

I decide I might get better results with a softer touch. "Raj, sweetie. How did we get here? We miss you in our lives."

Raj's eyes won't meet mine.

"What can we do to make this right?"

He shakes his head. "I'm not supposed to talk to you guys."

"Have you considered how hard it is on Maude to be shuffled around like this?"

"Bye, Gee Gee!" Maude waves at me from her father's arms.

"Bye, Maudey-moo. I'll see you soon, okay?" I walk up to Raj and give her a kiss on her head. While I'm there I look him in the eye and say quietly, "You just need to know it doesn't have to be like this."

The look on his face is so conflicted. For a moment I think he's going to cry. I know I am. I truly love this young man. I've known him since his freshman year in college. He has spent so many holidays with us, even when he and Vivs weren't getting along, which was pretty much most of the time.

"Can't we work this out?" I plead.

He closes his eyes, and when he opens them again they are as cold as marble. "I have to go."

With that, he turns and takes Maude into his apartment building, and Ron and I silently return to the minivan.

✦ ✦ ✦

We ride for a few minutes, neither of us knowing what to say. Then Ron fills the space by asking yet again what time our appointment is.

"One o'clock."

Laura has set up a tour of Riverview so we can check it out for my parents. I haven't told them about it yet because I know having that conversation is going to be about as fun as passing a kidney stone. They're going to say they are fine, but the truth is they need help. Exactly how much help remains to be determined.

Riverview is so named because of its lovely setting near the Missouri River. The building looks a little like a southern plantation, with columns flanking the front door and a large wraparound porch with oversized planters that in the summer hold beautiful rhododendrons, or so I'm told.

We have to be buzzed in by the front desk, and as we enter the lobby, a petite, elderly woman with a pink sweater and a cane approaches us.

"Hello," she says, "are you here to see me?"

"I don't think so, Shirley," a young woman answers from behind the desk. "Hello. Who are you here to see?"

"Actually, we're here to see Shirley!" I say, and Ron gives me a nudge. No time for fun and games, I guess.

"We're here to see Laura Howard," Ron tells her.

"She's finishing up with lunch right now. Would you like to wait?"

"She's set up a tour for us with someone."

The girl consults a book in front of her and asks, "Are you the Dixons?"

"That's us," I say.

"So, you were supposed to be doing a tour with Gina, but as of this morning, she is no longer with us."

We look at each other. I for one am not sure if by that she means Gina quit or she's dead, so I don't know how to reply. Luckily, I don't have to.

"So, Mr. Price will be taking you around." She leans in. "He's the big boss. I'll just call him."

"The big boss!" I raise my eyebrows at Ron. "Nice."

While we wait, I look around the lobby area. There are about twenty residents sitting, either on sofas or in wheelchairs, reading or sleeping or staring off into the distance. A woman who I believe is also a resident is playing what I think is "Pennies from Heaven" on a shiny black baby grand piano. As she comes to a clanging finish, there is silence from her audience. I'm about to applaud her efforts when a gruff voice from one of the sofas yells, "Well, you don't think we're going to clap for that crap, do you?"

And without missing a beat, the woman starts playing "Pennies from Heaven" again.

"Hello. I'm David Price." A voice rises above the music.

I turn to see a tall man, probably in his midfifties, with a bald head that looks like it has just been spit shined. He's wearing black-framed glasses and looks impressively immaculate. I'm thinking he's ex-military.

"Hi." Ron shakes his hand and introduces both of us.

"So, Laura tells me you're thinking of finding a place here for your parents." He states it as a fact rather than a question.

"Yes, we think this might be a good next move for them, but we want to see what their quality of life would be." I can't help but glance at the array of people sitting in the lobby doing nothing.

"Please come into my office so I can tell you a little bit about us." Mr. Price gestures toward an office behind the front desk.

We settle into two armchairs in front of him, and he pushes a brochure across the desk to us.

"We offer different levels of care, from assisted living to full nursing. We don't offer any memory care, but Laura tells me her grandparents wouldn't need that."

I just smile, not sure if I should confirm that or not.

Mr. Price lists the facilities available—a game room, snack bar, salon, and post office, plus a full day of activities.

"For example, this afternoon we have Jack Cochran coming in. He has traveled the world extensively, and every week he brings slides from one of his exotic trips." He leans toward us with barely concealed excitement. "I believe we're going to the Amalfi Coast today!"

"That sounds fun," I say, even though it doesn't. I can't think of anything more boring than looking at a stranger's vacation photos.

"If you want to come with me," Mr. Price continues, "I can give you a little tour and then show you what suites we have available. Then we can come back here, and I'll answer any questions you might have."

"Sounds good." Ron immediately jumps up, and I can tell he's happy to get things moving.

After touring the lower level of Riverview, which houses a hair and nail salon and a party room, plus the aforementioned post office and snack bar, we walk up a circular staircase to the main floor and find ourselves in the middle of the lobby seating area, once again being serenaded with "Pennies from Heaven."

"Does she know any other songs?" I ask.

Mr. Price laughs. "No, I don't think so, but I'm sure she did at one time. Elaine used to play piano in an all-girl band that traveled the country during World War Two. I hear they were quite good."

We move along down the hallway, and I'm happy to see most people have their doors propped open and are wandering in and out. Mr. Price has a little word for everyone, and I can tell he really knows his residents. I peek in their rooms as we walk by and see most are furnished with what I'm sure are things from their original homes. By the reaction we're getting from the residents, our tour is the most exciting thing that's happened here all week.

We stop at Room 145. The door is closed, but Mr. Price has a card key, so he swipes us in.

The room is very small, especially for two people used to living in a house. It consists of two twin beds, a dresser, a small television, a gas fireplace, and a chair.

"This is too small," I tell him.

"I figured it would be, but I wanted you to see all your options. The next one is bigger, I promise."

We follow him out the door and down the hall to a talking elevator.

"Level one. The door is open," a robotic female voice helpfully informs us.

"Do you have a preference regarding what level you would like them to live on?"

"I'm not sure," I say as the elevator informs us that we have reached level three and the door is open. We follow Mr. Price down another hall, and I notice that people are coming to their doors. I'm not sure, but I think the sound of the talking elevator acts as a sort of Pavlov's bell for everyone to get up and see what's happening.

I smile and say hello as I walk by. When we turn to go down another hallway, who's there but Shirley and her cane! She's quick as a cat, she is.

"Hello. Are you here to see me?" she asks.

"Not today, Shirley," Mr. Price says kindly. Why don't you go get yourself a cup of tea?"

"Okay." She smiles but doesn't move. Mr. Price sighs and uses his key to open the door to Room 300.

We walk into a spacious living room with a sofa, two leather recliners, a large television, a gas fireplace, and a kitchenette with a small fridge and microwave. There's a full bathroom right by the door.

"You'll find another bathroom off the bedroom," Mr. Price informs us as we go through a set of French doors into a room with two full-sized beds, two dressers, and another television. This is definitely more in line with what I had been thinking for Kay and Ray.

"The rooms come furnished, but of course we can take anything out and replace it with something they would like to bring from home."

"I love this room, but I'm not crazy about the balcony." I'm realizing no matter how helpful the elevator is, my parents are not going to like having to get on and off it all day. "Do you have anything like this on the first floor?"

He looks down for a moment, thinking. "You know, let me just check something. You guys can stay here. I'll be right back."

"What do you think?" I ask Ron after he's left us.

He shrugs. "I mean, it's nice, but everyone here seems really old."

"What were you expecting? Spring breakers?"

Just then, Shirley comes wandering into the room.

"Hello," she says.

"Hi, Shirley. How's your day going?"

Shirley seems thrilled that someone has asked her a question.

"I had soup for lunch," she informs us.

"That sounds yummy." I glance at Ron, but he's opening up the glass door to the balcony.

Just then, an ear-piercing alarm starts blasting.

BEEP BEEP BEEP

Immediately, the door to our suite slams shut, effectively locking us in the room with Shirley.

"What did you do? What did you do?" she shrieks, obviously panicking at this turn of events.

"Did you set that thing off?" I yell at Ron. I'm in a low-grade panic myself.

"I don't think so." He's frozen in place by the glass door.

I run to the front door and it opens easily, thank goodness. While the alarm continues to blare, I notice other people coming out of their rooms or standing in their doorways.

BEEP BEEP BEEP

"It's his fault!" One woman with curlers in her hair points to her husband. "It's your fault, Perry. I told you not to touch anything."

BEEP BEEP BEEP

"Peggy, I didn't touch anything!" Perry yells back.

She looks at me. "I told him not to touch anything, but he never listens!"

"What? What did you say?" Perry yells.

Another couple in their doorway asks me what they should do. I get the feeling they think I work here, so I decide to pretend that I do.

"I think you should just stay put, and someone will let us know what's going on any minute now."

"What did she say?" yells a woman from down the hall.

BEEP BEEP BEEP

"She says to stay in your room, Ethel!"

Ron has calmed Shirley down, and they've both joined me in the hallway. We answer a multitude of questions from the residents as the alarm relentlessly blares at us.

"Will dinner be late?"

BEEP BEEP BEEP

"I didn't get my mail today. Can I go now?"

"I need to go to the bathroom!"

I tell everyone to stay put, and I go back down the hallway in search of the talking elevator and someone who can tell me what the hell's going on.

BEEP BEEP BEEP

I meet two guys from the cable company when I reach the elevator.

"Hi. Any idea what's going on?"

They shake their heads. "We were just hooking up some cable and the alarm went off."

"Do you think we can leave?" I ask this because the alarm incident has me wanting to get the hell out of this place.

BEEP BEEP BEEP

The elevator doors open.

"Third floor. The door is open."

Laura comes flying out. "There you are! Are you okay?" I'm so relieved to see her.

"Hi, sweetie." I give her a hug. I can't help but notice how adorable she looks in her chef uniform. "What's going on?"

BEEP BEEP BEEP

"They were burning garbage in the basement and it got a bit too smoky. Where's Ron?"

"He's waiting by Room 300." We start making our way back there, and I find myself checking in on people along the way.

"Are you okay, Ethel?" I ask as I'm passing the woman who had earlier wanted to know what to do.

BEEP BEEP BEEP

"I'm fine. Can I go to the beauty parlor now?"

"Why don't you wait just a bit longer, okay?"

We reach the couple that's still bickering about whose fault it was.

"Peggy, I don't think it was Perry's fault," I tell her. "My daughter says there was a small fire in the basement, but everything is fine now." Peggy doesn't look convinced, but Perry gives me a grateful smile.

"Jeez, Mom, do you, like, live here now? How do you know all these people?"

BEEP BEEP BEEP

"Just being my usual friendly self."

As we approach Room 300, we see Ron is standing with Shirley, holding her hand.

"Are you here to see me?" she asks Laura.

"Shirl, I'm always here to see you!" Laura replies.

When Mr. Price finally rejoins us, he's looking a little flustered.

"Mr. and Mrs. Dixon, I'm so embarrassed! This type of thing never—"

BEEP BEEP BEEP

"—happens. Why don't you come back down to the office with me? Laura, can you stay here and answer questions for a while?"

"Of course," Laura says, and I give her a proud smile. My little flibbertigibbet of a daughter is all grown up and taking care of people.

We say good-bye to our new friends, then follow Mr. Price down the stairs to the first floor. As we're walking, he turns excitedly.

"I went to see what the status is on Suite 100. It's the same room as 300, but it has a little fenced-in patio instead of a balcony."

BEEP BEEP BEEP

I look at Ron and roll my eyes. As we get near the front desk, I decide to let Mr. Price down easy.

"You know, I think we've seen a lot today. We're going to look at the brochure and talk about it."

"You should know"—he lowers his voice—"we think the gentleman in 100 could go at any time so the room could be yours in a matter of weeks."

We've arrived at the lobby, which is empty thanks to the alarm lockdown. No more "Pennies from Heaven" today.

"We'll definitely let you know." Ron shakes his hand, and then we're out the door faster than you can say **BEEP BEEP BEEP**!

14

To: WeFUKCT
From: Jennifer Dixon
Re: We're marching back!
Date: February 20

Hey gang,

Great meeting this week! I loved the ideas for high-end raffle items. We just have to keep our goals realistic. So next time we get together, please only bring to the table things you can definitely get—Delia, I think we'd all love to have dinner with America's Dad, Tom Hanks, but I'm not sure Tom would be up for it.

Just so we're all on the same page, below is a list of who's trying to procure what:

Alison Lody—Trying to get Prada to donate a handbag
Terry DiLorento—Trying to get decent tickets to Hamilton when it
   comes back to town
Liana Jones—Trying to get box seats to a KC Chiefs game plus swag
   bag
Delia Cramer—Trying to get dinner with Tom Hanks (or similar)

Jen Dixon—Om Sweet Om/Fusion workout package

Cathy Red Nails—Trying to get spa package from either Sunlight or Ultimate Escape

Cathy Funfair—Trying to get case of premium wines from Cellar Wine Rat

No-Tech Cathy—Trying to get 50" flat-screen TV from Costco

Please keep me posted on your progress. I'm feeling good about this effort. Also, we can look forward to the chocolate-covered sea salt caramels arriving the first week in March.

Stay classy, girls!

Jen

P.S. If anyone sees No-Tech, can you please read this to her?

Done. And off I go to Fusion for my 8:00 a.m. spin class.

Ron now takes Max to school on Fridays so I can be there for my small but growing cast of characters, the most loyal of whom is, you guessed it, Ron's ex-wife, Cindy. Her fellow cyclists include Bob, a forty-something chef who is looking to lose a few pounds; Donna, a woman in her sixties who always wanders in five or ten minutes late; a writer I have never heard of named Mary Willy; a guy (Jeff, I think) who always comes to class dressed as though he's doing the Tour de France; and a few others I have not had the pleasure of talking to yet, because they leave class before the stretch—one of my personal pet peeves.

What they all have in common is an indifference to the music I play. I don't get complaints or compliments, so I just play what I like. I get a kick out of slipping a random song in that I know they haven't heard in a while, just to see if I get a reaction. I played "Kodachrome," by Paul Simon, last week, and I think (I *think*) I saw Bob smile a bit.

When I walk into Fusion, the first person I see makes my heart skip a beat. Carmen is standing at the front desk in her workout clothes, talking to Jodi!

"Hi! What are you doing here?" I ask, while a small part of me hopes she isn't here to take over my one little class a week.

Carmen walks toward me and gives me a huge hug. "I came to take your class!"

"Oh my God, no." My insides turn to liquid.

"Oh my God, yes! Come on. I want to see you in action."

I can't. I'm truly not ready for this. And the people in my class are so lame! Ugh. This will be too humiliating.

"I also just wanted to thank you so much for helping me get the job at Om."

"You got hired? That's amazing! Congratulations!" I'm wondering why Ron hasn't told me.

I glance at Jodi, who seems less than thrilled by this entire conversation.

"It's after eight, Jen," she informs me, which makes me rush to the spin room, with Carmen hot on my heels.

"Would you want to teach?" I ask Carmen as we enter the spin room.

"Hell no! I'm here to learn." She laughs—at the ridiculousness of her statement, I'm guessing—as she finds a bike in the front row.

My regulars are all on their bikes, waiting. Defeatedly, I climb onto the instructor bike, say good morning, and start the class.

"Okay, eight a.m., let's see what you've got!"

"It's eight-oh-three," Bob says helpfully. I can see Carmen roll her eyes.

The playlist is a bit of a mixed bag today—some eighties rock, some nineties pop, and just for shits and giggles I threw in a little Captain & Tennille. Had I known Carmen would be here, I'd have put a little more razzle-dazzle into it, but whatever.

A glance around the room tells me I have two new riders, but it still looks empty with only eleven people. Any other day I would have been thrilled with this number, but today, I just feel lame.

Donna comes sashaying in right on time, ten minutes late, but I'm grateful for the extra body. I'm doing my best to get this group motivated but getting the usual nothing in return—except from

Carmen, who is smiling her encouragement and giving the odd "Woo-hoo!"

After the third song, I'm really warm, so I take off my hoodie and throw it behind me. I'm not sure why I hadn't noticed that the 7:00 a.m. teacher left her mood candles burning . . . I'm guessing I was too preoccupied with Carmen. So, it isn't until the middle of the fourth song that I notice the burning smell, just about the time everyone else does.

"Keep going," I encourage as I get off the bike and try to find where it's coming from.

"Behind you!" Carmen yells from her bike.

I look and see a nice-sized hole burning into the arm of my hoodie. I take it off the candle and stomp on it until it isn't smoking anymore. I blow out the other three fire hazards behind the instructor bike before I get back on and pretend like nothing happened.

"This girl is on fire!" Carmen yells in her most effective teacher voice, and you'll never believe what happens next: the whole room erupts in whoops and hollers and whistles and cheers.

Seriously? I sweat my boobs off trying to motivate my classes to no avail, but Carmen comes in and says *one* thing, and everyone is all over it.

The last four songs fly by, and the class's energy is off the charts, especially for the final song, "Livin' la Vida Loca," by Ricky Martin. For the first time ever, everyone stays for the stretch, and I get a record number of smiles and thank-yous. Carmen hangs back to talk to me.

"Great playlist," she enthuses, but I'm not having any of it.

"How did you do it?" I demand.

"Do what?" She wipes her face with a towel.

"You made this room come alive. I was dying up here until I almost burned us down. Then you say one thing, and *bang*, everyone goes crazy."

She shrugs. "Sometimes all you need is one person to break the dam. People are self-conscious by nature and don't want to seem different. But if one person lets their freak flag fly, maybe the rest will follow along. I didn't say anything groundbreaking, I just said the right thing at the right time."

I follow her out of the spin room, and we pause by the water fountain.

"You're a good teacher, Jen, you just need to loosen up. You should have been the first person to yell something after you put out the fire. Make fun of yourself! Have a good time, even if no one else is. If they keep coming back, it's because they like what you do, and it'll only be a matter of time before they join in."

"Thanks for saying that."

"I mean it. And thank you for helping me get the job at Om. You have no idea how happy I am about it."

"Will you come do another of my classes?" I ask.

"Of course. This one made me realize I need to keep up with my cardio. You kicked my ass!"

I don't even care if she's telling the truth. I definitely learned something today, and it's no surprise Carmen ended up being the one to teach it to me.

✦ ✦ ✦

I'm on quite the high after class. I race home, shower up, and belt out "Girl on Fire," by Alicia Keys, as I'm getting dressed. I choose the super-comfy flared yoga pants for the mom uniform today, because I need all the good juju I can get.

Vivs arrives on time and immediately announces that she will be driving. We're going to see her new lawyer about this whole Raj-taking-Maude-to-India business, and I think she needs to feel in control of something, so I don't argue.

The law offices of Drake and Crenshaw are decidedly understated—located in a strip mall along with a Bed Bath & Beyond, a Dollar Tree, and a Pilates studio—but the lawyers come highly recommended by Peetsa. She used them for her divorce from Buddy and pretty much got everything she wanted.

We sit and wait until the receptionist tells us Mr. Crenshaw is ready.

I do admire that these guys haven't spent all their money on furniture and artwork to impress clients, but I expected more than the folding chair that is offered me.

"Hello, Vivs. Nice to meet you face-to-face," says a man of medium height and build with the beginnings of male pattern baldness on his medium-sized head. He is so completely unremarkable that I'm positive I will forget what he looks like as soon as we leave. I'm starting to doubt Peetsa's judgment.

"Hi, Mark. Nice to finally meet you too." She pauses, and they both look at me like I'm some kind of outlier.

"Hi. I'm Jennifer Dixon. I'm Maude's grandmother and part-time caregiver."

I'm expecting the usual *Wow, you don't look like a grandmother* response, but Mark Crenshaw just nods at me to sit down in my folding chair. He opens a folder that's front and center on his desk and consults it. "Are you aware that Mr. Basak has obtained a paternity test?" he asks us.

Vivs frowns. "But we aren't contesting his paternity. Maude looks just like him."

"Yes, well, he needed it in order to petition the court to have his name put on the birth certificate as her father."

"So, what changes when his name is on it?" she asks.

"Now he has the legal right to petition for custody or shared custody."

Vivs takes a big breath in and reaches for my hand.

"Can he take Maude away from her?" I ask.

"Not unless he can prove she's an unfit mother."

"Well, he can't. She's a wonderful mother," I tell him as only a mother could.

"There seems to be an issue of how much you work." Crenshaw consults another piece of paper.

I'm thinking this has Varsha written all over it. "Three of the days she works, I take care of Maude," I inform him.

"I realize that. But they're claiming Mr. Basak has had to cover for *you* when you're supposed to be looking after Maude so you could"—he looks for something on the page—"go exercise. And he claims he has even had to look after your child as well."

"What? That was one time! And he stayed for dinner." I'm fuming now.

"Calm down, Mom," Vivs orders. "They're just trying to make us look bad." She turns to Mr. Crenshaw. "Is it working?"

"Not if I have anything to say about it." He consults his papers again.

"Has Mr. Basak ever hurt Maude or put her in any danger?"

"What? No. I mean, I don't think so. He loves her." Vivs shrugs.

"That doesn't mean he hasn't been careless," Mr. Crenshaw replies. "If you can think of any instance where his inattention could have harmed her, it would be very helpful."

"I mean, I can think about it . . ." Vivs seems reticent.

"Good. Thank you. So, tell me what a typical week in Maude's life looks like."

While Vivs goes through the details with him, I silently plot some kind of evil revenge on Varsha. I know I should be putting part of the blame on Raj as well, but none of this was an issue until his mother came to town. I think his only crime is he told her too many details that are now being twisted to work against us. Not to mention he's being a total wuss. I could tell by the look in his eyes that day when we handed off Maude that he's hurting too. I wish he would man up and tell his mother where to go.

"I think you should know that none of us saw this coming," Vivs informs Crenshaw, her voice strong and steady. "Ever since I told Raj he was the father, we've had a very friendly relationship. I've never tried to keep Maude from him, and I welcomed the idea of his moving back to Kansas City." She shifts forward in her seat to emphasize her next point. "But there is no way in hell I'm letting his mother take my child to India. Maude's only two, and she's just met the woman. I think it would traumatize her. We can share custody and do whatever else he wants, but I will not agree to international travel without me, until she's at least ten."

With that, she sits back in her chair and bursts into tears.

"Oh, sweetie." I put my arm around her.

"I'm fine!" she insists and shrugs off my embrace. "I'm just tired of this. It's all just so unnecessary."

Mr. Crenshaw has been listening, in all his mediumness, but suddenly clears his throat. "Okay. My turn to talk."

We both look up, surprised.

"I'm not going to let anything happen to your daughter. From what you've told me, she is a very well-cared-for child, a happy child, and most certainly a loved child."

We nod.

"You aren't asking for anything unreasonable, and any judge should be able to see that. If you're saying you agree to shared custody, then I can almost guarantee we'll be able to keep international travel off the table—maybe not for eight years, but certainly for the next five."

"So, what's next?" Vivs asks.

"I'm going to meet with their lawyer this week and see if we can come to some kind of understanding without going to court. Have you thought about a financial agreement at all? Will you be asking for child support?"

"We split everything now. Could we just keep doing that?" Vivs asks.

"I think it would be better to have something on paper that is legally binding. Is there a chance he would ask *you* for child support?"

Vivs barks out a laugh. "I doubt it."

Mr. Crenshaw's eyebrows shoot up. "It isn't unheard of."

"Raj makes more money than I do."

Crenshaw nods and stands up. "Okay. Leave this with me. I'll be in touch." As we're walking out of his office, he stops us. "And please, no more contact with them about this case."

"I never talk to them," Vivs assures him.

"It's not you I'm talking to."

Vivs looks at me, stunned. "What did you do?" she demands.

"Nothing!" I feel my face getting hot. "It's just, when we

handed Maude off to Raj the other day, I asked him what we could do to make this all go away."

"Mom!"

"Nobody told me not to talk to him! And he seemed so sad. I really don't think this is coming from him." I direct the last part to Mr. Crenshaw.

"Be that as it may, please don't talk about this case to them."

"I won't." I look at Vivs, who gives me the mother of all dirty looks. I really hope I haven't ruined it for her.

✦ ✦ ✦

By the time I get home, I'm exhausted. I know life is a juggling act, but I have way too many balls in the air right now. Between Vivs's custody drama, concern for my parents, Max being bullied, the fundraiser, and my budding career as a spin instructor, I have more gum than I can chew. Trying to prioritize is like trying to pick a favorite child (Max). Plus, I've twice missed my weekly therapeutic phone call with Nina. So, after Max goes to bed, I try her to see if she's free.

"What's wrong?" She's whispering.

"Were you sleeping?" I immediately feel bad that I didn't check the time before I called her.

"No. But Garth is." I can hear rustling as she moves to another room. "Okay, so what's wrong?"

"How do you know something's wrong?"

"Because it's ten thirty, and on any given night you'd be asleep by now."

I sigh. "I don't like to go to sleep anymore. I keep having these really weird dreams."

"What about?" I can hear Nina stifle a yawn.

"It's all different things. The other night I dreamed I was in the hospital and my roommate was Kanye West."

She laughs. "That's random."

"I know! I literally never think of that guy."

"Did you play his music in your class?"

"No."

"Maybe your subconscious is telling you to."

I doubt that, but I don't say it. "I guess I just have more anxiety than usual."

"Talk me through it," Nina offers, and so I do.

When I wrap things up with a recap of today's meeting with Vivs and the lawyer, there's silence at the other end of the line, and then: "Damn, girl. No wonder you aren't sleeping."

I laugh. "So, what do I do?"

"You're asking me?"

"Yes, I'm asking my brilliant, multitasking best friend what to do."

"I'm guessing that dropping a couple of these projects isn't an option."

"Correct."

"I hate to say it, but I think this is one of those times when you just have to put your head down and drive through it. Take it one thing at a time. Make lists and check things off. And try to use your spin class as stress therapy for yourself."

"Did I tell you Carmen came to my class?" I'm finally surfacing from the "poor me" plunge dive I'd been taking.

"*The* Carmen?"

"Yes, *the* Carmen. She was great. Gave me some solid teaching advice."

"And what was that?"

"To be myself. Sounds simple, but it never occurred to me."

"Maybe you should take that and apply it to everything in your life right now. You're a world-beater, girlfriend. It's time you remember that."

"God, I miss you. You're the best."

"I know, right? Now go get some sleep."

15

To: Jennifer Dixon
From: Scott Green
Re: Overnight Field Trip
Date: March 1

Hi, Jen,

    I'd love for you to stop by the classroom before pickup today. We need to start discussing the details of our Topeka trip.
    Thanks,

Scott Green

Normally a surprise meeting at pickup would have me shaking in my boots, but since this clearly isn't about Max, I breathe easy. However, I'm already spread too thin today, so I need to get going if I'm going to get it all done.

"Want to go for a ride in the car, Maude?" I ask my granddaughter, who's playing on her activity mat.

She nods and comes running to me. "Go! Go!" I probably

shouldn't have said anything until I was actually ready to leave. I pick her up, and we head upstairs to change our clothes—me from my sweats and Maude from her jammies. It's a chilly March morning, so I bundle us both up and head to the minivan.

After hitting the gas station, the post office, Party City (Max's eleventh birthday is coming up!), and the dry cleaner, we stop by the deli to pick up sandwiches for my parents.

I haven't approached Kay and Ray with the idea of moving into assisted living yet. After our event-filled tour of Riverview, I was having second thoughts, but Ron convinced me to go back and look again, so I did. No fire alarm this time, and I bumped into some of my friends, including Shirley and Ethel. This time I observed that the people who live there are in various stages of retirement. There are people who are still completely with it—they function on their own for the most part and enjoy each other's company. And then there's an older crowd who sit around much of the day and don't interact a whole lot. After that visit I could definitely see Kay and Ray interacting with the cool kids—well, Kay, anyway. So now I'm back to wondering when and how I should throw this at them.

"We're here!" I yell as I carry Maude across the threshold. I'm glad to see the house continues to look and smell good. My parents are in their assigned seats in the kitchen as usual—my dad reading the paper and my mom looking through a Target flyer. What's odd is they're both in their pajamas.

"Maude, you little gingersnap, come here and give Nana a hug!"

Maude walks slowly over to my mother with a coy smile and crawls into her lap.

"Jennifer, I'm so glad you're here. I'm hungry."

"Didn't you have breakfast?"

"We just got up twenty minutes ago."

"You didn't get up until eleven? That's not like you."

My mother lets out a huge sigh. "Well, there's no reason to get up early these days. We like to relax in bed for as long as we want."

I start unpacking the sandwiches. "Dad, how are you feeling?" He seems to look smaller every time I see him.

He shrugs and smiles. "Oh, about the same, I guess."

"Are you hungry?"

"Not really."

"Are you losing weight?"

"Jennifer, please stop asking questions. He's fine." Kay sounds exhausted.

I frown at her as I put their lunches in front of them and take Maude into my own lap.

"After lunch, do you want to go do a bit of grocery shopping?"

"Amelia brings groceries every Wednesday," my mother informs me with a mouth full of egg salad.

"Well, why don't we just go out for a drive, maybe stop and get ice cream somewhere?"

Maude has been busy eating the turkey out of my sandwich, but at the mention of ice cream her eyes light up.

"Scream! Scream!" she says excitedly, and I curse myself for not spelling it out. Clearly now I'm committed.

"Oh, I don't know. I have a headache, and it takes forever to get your father ready to go out."

"I can help with that." I am *not* taking no for an answer.

My mother rubs her temples. "Whatever you want, Jennifer. I'm in no mood to argue."

"Good. Neither am I." We finish lunch in silence except for the odd reminder from Maude that she was promised "scream." When we're done, my father has barely eaten half his sandwich.

✦ ✦ ✦

After the drama of getting my parents dressed in something other than pajamas and finding my father's shoes (the people in the basement think it's funny to hide them, according to my mother), we pile in the minivan and drive around Overland Park for half an hour, then stop at Twisters Frozen Custard. Along the way I update my parents on the trials and tribulations of WeFUKCT and where we're heading.

"That's a very unfortunate name you have for your committee," my mother observes. "It sounds dirty."

"Well, it really isn't supposed to be said out loud. It's an acronym that works best in emails. It's kind of an inside joke," I explain.

"For a name that isn't supposed to be said out loud, you certainly say it enough," she sniffs.

My parents enjoy the outing but don't seem to want to prolong it, so I take them home. I feel sad and a bit helpless as I watch them shuffle into the house, and once again I consider the idea of assisted living.

As I'm driving home, Maude falls asleep in her car seat, so I end up driving around instead of trying to do the transfer. It was much easier when she was a baby.

My phone rings, and I see PTA president Sylvie Pike is calling me. I entertain the thought of not picking up but realize she'll just track me down.

"Hi, Sylvie. You're on speaker, and Maude is taking a nap in the back of the car," I say quietly as I glance in the rearview mirror at my sleeping beauty.

"Oh, okay," she whispers. "I'll make this quick."

I should use this excuse every time.

"So, where are we with the fundraiser?"

"We've decided to do a raffle of high-end items."

"Great. What have you got so far?"

Nothing, I want to say, but I don't dare. "Umm . . . my husband and I have put together a yoga/spinning package with private lessons and free classes at Om Sweet Om for a year."

"Uh-huh" is all I get for that. "What else?"

Now I'm getting annoyed, mainly because I have nothing else to tell her.

"Wouldn't you rather be surprised?" I ask.

"No. I need to know what you have, what the timeline is for the raffle, when you plan to get tickets printed, and how you plan to sell them." She's kind of whisper-shouting at this point.

"All good questions, and if I had my notes in front of me, I could answer them." It's just a small lie.

"Get back to me as soon as you can. I don't need to remind you that it's March already."

March! "Yes, I know. The sea salt caramels should be in any day." I figure I should give her something from the win column.

"Finally," is all she says.

"Okay, well, I'll have that information for you after WeFUKCT meets tomorrow."

"Sounds good. Thanks." She hangs up before I can say goodbye. She was definitely more curt than usual on this call, and I wonder whether she's getting tired of her job.

By the time Maude wakes up, it's time to meet Mr. Green. I pull into the school parking lot, then I crawl into the back seat of the minivan and change her soaking diaper.

"Okay, baby. You're going to be a good girl while Gee Gee has her meeting, right?"

"Gu grl," she agrees with that killer smile.

I stand outside the open door of Room 252 and eavesdrop on the tail end of Mr. Green's English lesson.

"'I won't describe what I look like. Whatever you're thinking, it's probably worse.'" He finishes reading to the class. "That's what Auggie says in chapter one. Your homework for tonight is to read chapter two and, based on what you've read so far, draw a picture of what you think Auggie looks like."

He looks up and sees me skulking in the doorway, Maude on my hip, with her thumb in her mouth.

"Actually, if you want to get started on the reading, you can do it now. I'll be right outside the door, and if I hear anything other than pages turning, I'll be giving out demerits."

"Hi, Jen," he greets me. "And is this the famous Maude?" he says in a typical adult-talking-to-a-toddler voice.

"This is Maude. Did I come too soon? I didn't want to interrupt your lesson."

"No, no, you're right on time. I just wanted a quick face-to-face about the things we'll need to start doing now to get ready for the trip."

"Sure." I'm secretly wondering if I should be taking notes, and how that would be possible with a child in my arms.

He must see my concern, because he offers for me to come in and sit at his desk. As expected, when we walk in, there is a chorus of "awww"s from the class. Maude is playing shy, burying her face in my shoulder and peeking out, until she spots a familiar face.

"Max!" she yells and tries to wiggle out of my arms.

"Let her go. It's okay." Mr. Green laughs, and Maude runs to Max's desk in the second row. He puts her on his lap and enjoys the attention everyone is giving her.

"Jen, why don't you write a few things down." He hands me a piece of paper and a pen. Immediately I feel ashamed that I didn't think to bring these things on my own.

"Oh, I usually just take notes on my phone," I lie.

He proceeds to go through the things he needs me to champion for this trip—permission forms, health forms, special requests from parents (he's dreaming if he thinks I'm inviting that can of worms to be opened), and roommate suggestions.

"Got it," I say as I type an email to myself. Suddenly the crowd of kids around Maude erupts into laughter. I glance over and see my son with a look on his face that says he's trying not to smile but he's losing the battle. Maude is clapping, clearly thrilled by all the attention.

"What's so funny?" I ask the kids, which prompts another burst of laughter.

"Are you being a silly girl, Maudey?" I ask my granddaughter, to which she replies, in a crystal-clear voice, "Gee Gee, WeFUKCT!"

This elicits yet another burst of cackles from Max and his friends while I slowly die inside.

"It's not what you think," I tell a bewildered Mr. Green. "It's the name of my fundraising committee," I explain. "And it's only supposed to be used in emails." I'm having to raise my voice to be heard over the laughter.

Thank goodness the bell rings, and the kids start packing up their things. Max brings Maude over to me and shakes his head.

"Vivs is going to be so mad at you."

"Only if she finds out," I tell him. I can see that negotiations for his silence are going to be held in the car on the way home.

I apologize to Mr. Green on our way out, but he waves me off. "Maude can come back any time." He smiles.

On our way to the minivan I'm approached by a number of mothers, asking for various pieces of information that I luckily have crammed into my head. The last is No-Tech Cathy, who wants to know if the meeting is on for tomorrow morning.

"Yup. Have you got something for us?"

"I might. I'll let you know tomorrow."

"That's the first good news I've had all day," I tell her.

After we're all belted into the minivan, I turn to Max.

"Okay. What's it going to take?"

He can't help but smirk. He knows he has the upper hand right now. My potty mouth has gotten me into some sticky situations, but today's slipup is next level.

"Can I uninvite Zach E. to my party?" he asks hopefully.

"You really can't, sweetie. Your whole class is coming. You can't leave just him out."

"I didn't think you'd say yes," he grumbles.

I take a deep breath, knowing I may regret what I'm about to say. "How about you have a small sleepover after your birthday party? Maybe like three friends?"

The look of shock on his face doesn't surprise me. After the now-infamous birthday sleepover fiasco of last year, I declared in no uncertain terms that Max would never, *ever* have a group sleepover again.

Let me set the stage for you. It was 12:30 a.m., and Ron and I were relaxing in bed after the hell of settling down six fourth-grade boys who were sleeping over for Max's ninth birthday. Just as we were drifting off to sleep, there were three loud bangs on the front door. We both sat up, and Ron said, "Stay here." Since I don't like being told what to do, I followed him down the stairs. He grabbed a baseball bat from the front-hall closet and opened the front door to find two of Overland Park's finest standing on our porch. One was on the younger side, but he had the body of a linebacker. His partner seemed to be the veteran of the two, with graying hair and a bit of a belly.

"There was a nine-one-one call from this house. Is everything all right?" the older policeman asked while the linebacker eyed Ron's bat.

"Everything is fine," Ron assured them. "No one called."

"Do you mind if we come in, sir?"

"Can I see your badges?" Ron asked.

They showed them, and Ron stepped aside to let the officers in.

"Sir, can you please put the bat down?" The older officer talked to Ron like he was negotiating with a crazy person.

"Is there anyone else in the house?" the linebacker asked.

"Yes." I stepped forward. "We have six little boys in the basement." As I said it, I heard how it sounded, and understood the looks I got from the police.

"Can we see them?"

"Oh, they're all asleep," I assured them.

"Ma'am, we need to see the boys. Where is your basement?"

They both had booming baritone voices, so no matter what they said it came out as a command.

Ron and I walked them to the kitchen, and as we turned the corner, I saw two pairs of eyes peeking through the basement door.

"Max!" Ron said sternly. "Get over here right now."

Max and Zach T. came shuffling over, their eyes big as saucers.

"Sir, please let me talk to the boys," Gray Hair commanded.

"What are your names?" he asked them.

"Max Dixon."

"Zach Tucci."

"Did you call nine-one-one tonight?"

The silence was deafening.

"Boys!" the linebacker boomed. "Did you call nine-one-one tonight?"

Max stepped forward and into my arms. He was shaking.

"Well, *we* didn't, but one of our friends did," Zach T. offered up.

"Do you live here, son?" the older one asked Max.

"Yes."

"And are these your parents?"

"Yes."

"Who's downstairs?"

"My friends. It's my birthday." At this Max broke and buried his head in my chest.

The older officer walked down to the basement, and I heard him asking if anyone was hurt or being held here against their will. I couldn't hear the answers.

"You boys should know that calling nine-one-one as a joke is against the law," Linebacker said.

"Yes, sir." Zach T. had his head down. Max wouldn't show his face.

"Mr. Dixon, is anyone holding you here against your will?"

"No, sir," Ron assured them. "You can look around if you want."

The gray-haired officer came up from the basement, followed by four ashen-faced boys. I was pretty sure that in the retelling of this story, the boys would portray themselves as total badasses, but right then they all looked like they needed their mommies.

"Everything checks out," he said to Ron and me, and we all headed to the door.

"I'm really sorry for the trouble, officers," I offered.

"Maybe next time you can keep a better eye on them, ma'am," Gray Hair suggested. *Ouch.*

When the police finally left, I was seething and couldn't wait to speak my mind to these juvenile delinquents. But Ron insisted I go back to bed, and he ended up talking to the boys for more than half an hour. Apparently, they had been making prank phone calls, and then Graydon Cobb—Shirleen's son—decided to call 911. You know the rest.

"Really? You'd let me?" Max asks now. He is truly shocked.

"I'll have to talk to Dad, but I think it'll be okay. It goes without saying that there will be no access to phones."

"I won't invite Graydon," he says sincerely.

16

To: The fun-killers of Mr. Green's Fifth-Grade Class

From: Jennifer Dixon

Re: Field trip to Topeka

Date: March 2

Greetings, party people,

And what a party it's going to be when the William Taft Elementary School's fifth grade tears up the town of Topeka in May!

Thanks to Ali Burgess for stepping up to chaperone. I'm still looking for a dad to room with Mr. Green, and I really don't want it to be my husband, so gentlemen, please don't be shy.

I know the trip is two months away, but I need to get a head start on the paperwork. Attached you will find a trip permission form, a medical release form, and a brief questionnaire about any special needs your child may have. I'd like these filled out and sent back to school in a timely manner. As always, lollygaggers will be humiliated in the parking lot at pickup time.

Also, there's a rumor that we will be getting the chocolate-covered sea salt caramels in sometime next week, so if you ordered any, you've got that to look forward to!

Gotta go! See you when I see you.

Jen

I'm in the school's parking lot, typing this email on my phone and killing time until my meeting with WeFUKCT.

A knock on the passenger-side window startles me, but I'm happy when I see Ravi's smiling face. *Get in!* I motion to her.

She does. "Whew! Thanks. It's cold out there."

"What's up? I haven't seen you in ages," I tell her.

"I know. I had the flu for two weeks."

"Are you okay?" I unconsciously lean away from her.

"I'm finally better, but it took a while. I lost five pounds!"

"Why don't I ever get the flu?" I joke, but Ravi looks horrified. "Ravi, I'm kidding!"

She gives a gratuitous chuckle and then changes her tone.

"How are you doing?" she asks me earnestly. I've been talking to her on and off about Vivs's custody situation, and she's been very insightful in her comments about Varsha's possible state of mind.

"We're fine." I smile at her. "Vivs is very strong."

"What's the latest?"

"Not much is new. I told you about the meeting with our lawyer, right?"

"Yes, you did."

"So, we're waiting for him to update us on what the other camp wants."

"And you still don't want Maude to go to India, right?"

"Right. I mean, can you blame us?"

Ravi takes a minute before she answers. "Nooo, I can't blame you. But you know why she's asking for that, right?"

"To take control of Maude's life and ruin ours?"

"No! If you look at it through her eyes, she's not the bad guy here. When did Raj's father die?"

"Umm, ten years ago? I'm not a hundred percent sure."

"So, once she lost her husband, she probably realized she needed her son to help take care of her, financially and emotionally. Indian mothers are especially close to their sons, so it couldn't have been easy for her to have him halfway across the world, having babies with a woman he didn't marry."

"I know he sends her money every month, so she's hardly neglected," I tell her.

"The money is one thing, but I think she also wants the emotional connection and knowledge that she's still in his heart. I would bet anything that's why she came on so strong. She might be hoping that Raj will move back to India, and she knows he would never go without Maude."

"If they take her to India"—the words feel like sandpaper in my mouth—"is there a chance they won't bring her back?"

"I doubt it. Unless Raj gets Vivs's permission, that would be kidnapping."

"Shit." I sit back in the driver's seat and bang my head against the headrest.

"Listen, I have to run, but keep me posted. I'm sorry you're going through this." She gets out of the car and wraps her scarf around her head to keep the cold away.

"Thanks, Ravi." I try to put myself in Varsha's shoes, now that I have a bit more insight into what she may be thinking. Would I do the same thing if Vivs and Raj were in India? It's a question that must remain unanswered for now, because I have my WeFUKCT meeting.

I walk into the cafeteria, and even though I'm two minutes late, I'm the first to arrive, which pisses me off.

To kill time, I make a list of things I'm going to need for Max's birthday party. I'm happy to announce that gone are the days of the theme party. While he used to want ninjas and cowboys and Pokémon parties, now he just wants junk food and games. So, next Saturday, we have his whole class going to Dave and Buster's for the afternoon, then Zach T., Zach B., and Alison Lody's son, Draper, will sleep over.

I check my email and find one from Mary-Jo Baton.

To: Jennifer Dixon
From: Mary-Jo Baton
Re: Field trip to Topeka
Date: March 2

Hi, Jen,

If you're still looking for a father to chaperone the trip, Luc said he would do it. We have held off because Nick doesn't want either of us to go.
Let me know!
Thanks,

Mary-Jo

Forty-eight hours with the hottest dad in the grade? Yes, please! Luc and Mary-Jo have always fascinated me. I used to think they were such a mismatched couple because he is male-model gorgeous, and she . . . well, she looks like the rest of us. Shame on me for being such a shallow thinker. Over the years I have seen that these two have a great marriage—they are always holding hands and seem to have the same sense of humor.

Finally, WeFUKCT starts trickling in, and once we're assembled, I ask each of them for an update.

"Alison, how are you doing on getting the Prada bag?" Alison Lody is so interesting. She's a petite and preppy woman whose diminutive stature masks a fireball of a personality.

"I've put in a call to an old friend who works in their PR department. I'm going to need a letter on school stationery formally stating that this request is for our annual fundraiser. When I get that, I'm feeling good about our chances."

"Fantastic. I'll talk to Sylvie Pike about getting a letter like that for all of you. Terry?"

"Still waiting for *Hamilton* to announce new dates. They're definitely coming back, but until they set a date, the box office won't guarantee me tickets. Sorry."

"Not your fault. Are any other shows coming that would be a slam dunk?"

She looks at her notes and makes a face. "Would anyone want to see *The Phantom of the Opera*?"

We all groan. It comes around more often than any other show. "Let's keep hoping for *Hamilton*," I suggest. "Who's next? Liana?"

"I scored tickets to sit in the owner's box for a Chiefs game."

We all clap and whoop. "That's terrific! How did you get that?"

"My husband plays golf with one of the Hunts' cousins." She's blushing. "I'm working on a swag bag."

"Well done. Delia, has Tom Hanks called you back?"

Delia rolls her eyes. "I have calls and emails in to his people, but no one has gotten back to me. It's very frustrating, because I feel like if Tom knew we wanted him to do this, he'd say yes. I've heard he's super nice."

It takes me a moment to realize she's serious. "Why don't we shoot for someone a bit lower on the celebrity food chain?" I suggest. "Does anyone have any ideas?

"Ryan Reynolds?" Delia says without a trace of sarcasm.

"Lower," I say to her.

"How about the weatherman on Channel 2?" Cathy Red Nails lobs out there. "He's hilarious."

As I'm saying, "Great idea," Delia gives a resounding "*No*. I'm going to get someone good," she promises.

"Well, you have about two weeks before we need to get tickets printed," I tell her. "We're going to start selling right after spring break."

No-Tech Cathy jumps in. "I got Costco to give me a TV!" she announces jubilantly. We all applaud again, and she beams. "Seventy-inch flat screen, and they threw in a sound bar. Oh, but I'll need one of those letters too."

I nod and give her the thumbs-up. The irony is not lost on me that No-Tech just got us the big tech item.

"Cathy Funfair, what have you got?" I'm feeling very chirpy now that we are on a roll.

She looks up from her phone. "What was I supposed to be getting?" she asks.

Seriously?

"Some premium wine from Cellar Wine Rat," Alison Lody answers.

"Oh." She shrugs. "Ya, I can get that. Just let me know when."

"When is now," I tell her, barely containing my frustration. "I need to know how many bottles, what the wines are, and how much it's all worth. We're hoping for at least five hundred dollars' worth of wine."

She looks at me as though this is news to her. "Really? I thought I'd just ask them for, like, three bottles of rosé or something."

"Well, do what you can do, but these are high-end raffle items. We want people to feel good about spending twenty-five dollars a ticket," I tell her.

"This isn't how we do it at the funfair," she replies dismissively.

A slew of snappy clapbacks rush to my mind, but I choose to simply gift her with a silent glare before I move on. "Red Nails, how is the spa package looking?"

She looks up and crosses her beautifully manicured fingers. "I'm hearing back from them tomorrow. I know they'll give us something. I requested the Pure Bliss package, which is like seven hours long."

"What the heck do they do to you for seven hours?" Delia asks.

"Mani, pedi, facial, massage, body scrub, and infrared sauna."

"I'd buy that!" Alison says enthusiastically.

"So, how is this all going to work?" Cathy Funfair asks.

"My plan is to have people buy tickets only for the items they want. We'll sell tickets before and after school every day for a month, and there will be separate jars for each raffle item. You buy a ticket and put it in the jar of your choice."

There's silence in the room.

"What? Is that a bad idea? I'm open to suggestions."

"Why doesn't it all go into one big jar?" Terry asks.

"Because if you win the wine lot but you don't drink wine, it's going to be very disappointing for you."

Alison raises her hand. "I think we need to widen our selling circle. Maybe ask parents to sell tickets at their work or take some to their church."

"That's a great point. Do you want to coordinate asking parents to help us out?"

"Do I *want* to? No. Will I?" She sighs. "You bet." She gives me a wink.

"Okay, so what we have as of now is the spinning/yoga package, the TV, the Chiefs owner's box tickets, probably a Prada bag, maybe some wine, hoping the spa package comes through, and Delia is waiting on word from Tom Hanks. Did I miss anything?" They all shake their heads. "Great. We'll meet again next week. Terry, could you work on descriptions for the items that are definite?"

"Sure I will!" God bless her, she actually sounds happy to be asked.

✦ ✦ ✦

The next morning I'm up like a rocket and busting to get to my spin class. Ever since Carmen's pep talk, I've approached my class with much more personality. I play the songs I want (Rick Astley!), I say all the things that I observe (hey, Mary Willy, nice haircut!), and I talk about my life struggles. Talking it out with my class has become the best therapy I've ever had.

"Good morning, eight o'clock! Let's get things going. I have a busy day," I tell them.

"It's eight-oh-two."

"Thanks, Bob."

While we're warming up—to "Boogie Wonderland" by Earth, Wind and Fire—I let them know that I'm going to tell my parents about the retirement home next week. There are oohs and ahhs from the class, and one person yells, "Good luck, Jen!" I've been sharing bits of the saga with them over the past few weeks, and many have approached me afterwards with words of encouragement and stories of their own.

After the stretch, during which only one person leaves, Crazy Cindy approaches the instructor bike with purpose.

"I'm sure Ron has mentioned that my fifty-fifth birthday is coming up . . ."

"No, he didn't." *Why would he?* "That's great. Any big plans?"

"Well, I was wondering if you would teach a birthday ride for me."

"Oh" is all I say, so she continues.

"Fusion says it will let me rent out the studio, and I'm going to invite all my friends to come for a spin-class party."

"That sounds like fun," I tell her.

"So, will you do it? Will you teach the class? Of course, I'll pay you for your time."

Wow, she really wants me. I can't help but be flattered.

"If the date works out, I'd be happy to teach for you." I smile at her, and for the first time, my defenses are down and I embrace the new Cindy.

Shame on me.

17

I'm cleaning up the last of the pancake mess made by Max and his three sleepover friends. Miraculously, we got through the birthday party and overnight without one appearance by the police.

Dave and Buster's was a hit. The kids ran around playing games and getting tickets so they could buy something at the "store." I tried not to hover, but I kept my eye on Max's interaction with Zach E. To the naked eye, it did indeed seem as though Max was actively avoiding him and even leaving him out of things, which I really didn't like to see. But if Zach is still attacking him with gay slurs, I can't blame him.

We surprised Max with a phone for his birthday. We were one of the last holdouts in the grade—most kids got them for their tenth birthday—and as a reward for our abundance of caution, we had to suffer a year of stories about all the things he was missing out on via Snapchat and TikTok. Needless to say, he was thrilled and then horrified when he got the phone and then realized he wasn't allowed to use it during the sleepover. But hey, a deal is a deal, and he may as well learn that now. To make him feel better I took his friends' phones too. So, you can imagine how popular I was last night—ergo the pancakes this morning.

But now I want these boys to go home, because today is the

day I talk to my parents about moving into assisted living. Peetsa is the last mom to pick up, so I invite her to stay for coffee so we can catch up.

"How's work?" I ask her.

"Oh my God, we had such a drama last week. Some guy bought an Elantra and had it custom painted this really ugly chartreuse color, and when he saw it, he refused to pay for it. There was a huge scene in the showroom." She shakes her head. "I thought someone was going to get punched."

"Why would anyone want a car that color in the first place?"

"I think it was supposed to match a company logo or something, but it just looked *so* bad."

We chat about school and the boys for a minute, then I tentatively ask about her dating life.

"It's been pretty dry," she confesses. "I did take your advice and went on one of the over-fifty sites."

"Did you lie about your age?" P is only forty-six.

"I did."

"So . . . good new crop of men?"

"Define 'good.'"

"Oh, come on."

"Well, I did learn that men don't stop being idiots after fifty. They're just more gentlemanly about it."

"Like how?" I ask.

"Like, I went out with this guy, Barry. He's in his early sixties and not bad looking. Widower."

"Okay."

"So, we have dinner, it's very pleasant, and at the end I was thinking I might even consider going out with him again."

"That's great."

"*And then,*" she says loudly, "he leans in for what I'm thinking is going to be a good-night kiss, and instead *he licks my nose!*"

"*What?*"

"Yup!"

"Who thinks that's okay to do on a first date?" I exclaim.

"On *any* date!" Peetsa counters. "It was disgusting. I haven't even told you about the other 'mature'"—she uses air quotes—"man I went out with. He was so old that he couldn't hear anything I was saying in the restaurant, and afterwards, he insisted on walking me to my car, which was a few blocks away."

"Well, that was nice of him."

"Yes, but he had two bad knees and could barely walk. It took me more time to walk to the car with him than it did to drive home." She looks at me, then bursts out laughing. "This cannot be what's left for me in the dating pool."

"It isn't," I say, but really, how the hell do I know? I try to think if I know of any eligible men, and randomly, Jeff, the Tour de France rider in my spin class, comes to mind. I wonder if he's single. At the very least he has two good knees.

✦ ✦ ✦

Once Peetsa and Zach T. leave, Ron and I head over to my parents' house. Our plan is lunch, then intervention. I've got the girls coming, without Maude, and I've gone back and forth on whether Max should be included but decided he doesn't need to be there.

It's a beautiful Saturday afternoon in late March. There's a chill in the air, but because the sun is shining, there's a feeling of hope that winter is finally gone. You know how you can smell the wet mud that's on the ground after the snow melts? I love this time of year.

On the way to my parents' I casually lob out the fact that Cindy's fifty-fifth birthday is coming up.

"It is?" Ron frowns. "How do you know?"

"Because she wants to have a spin birthday party, and she's asked me to teach it for her."

"I hope you said no."

"Actually, I said yes. I'm telling you, Ron, she's a different person. She seems happy with her life. She has a boyfriend . . ." I trail off.

"Whatever. Just don't be surprised when the shit hits the fan."

I see Vivs's car in the driveway, so we go right in without

knocking. Big surprise, everyone is in the kitchen, and Laura is making grilled cheese sandwiches and tomato soup for lunch.

"Hi." We hug everyone before settling at the kitchen table.

"How are you feeling today, Mom?" I ask Kay.

"Okay." She rubs her temples.

"Just okay?"

"Yes, Jennifer. Just okay. What do you want me to say?" my mother snaps at me uncharacteristically.

"How about you, Dad?"

"Oh, well, about the same, I guess. Kind of tired. We had to get up early because you guys were coming."

"Early? Poppy, you said you got up at ten," Vivs points out.

"It seemed early." He shrugs and goes back to his newspaper.

Once Laura has served our food and we're all settled in and eating, I decide to jump in with both feet.

"Mom and Dad, I want to talk to you about something."

Everyone stops eating and looks at me. I look at Ron for support, and he gives an encouraging nod.

"We all think it might be time for you to move into a smaller place—maybe even an assisted living facility."

Silence. Ron picks up the ball.

"We think it would be helpful for you to have someone to cook your meals and help with your medications."

"Amelia does that," my mother informs him.

"Also, you'd have people around, right outside your door. Plus, there are lots of activities every day," Laura adds.

I'm not sure what the look on Kay's face is telegraphing, but her answer floors me.

"You do know those living places are just a sex den for old people, don't you? I hear klamafia runs rampant in them."

Klamafia?

"Nana, that is not true! I work at one of those places, and it's very clean and disease free."

"My friend Gert Cohen told me it's like Sodom and Gomorrah where her sister lives!"

"Mom!" I say, because I can't think of anything else.

"Nana, I'd really like for you to come and see where I work. I think you and Poppy would be really happy there, and you'd get to see me every day!"

My mother looks at her suspiciously. "We would?" It seems this is a selling point, so Laura jumps on it.

"Yes! It would be so fun. Maybe you could even help me in the kitchen."

I'm about to laugh, but Kay beats me to it.

"Uh, no thank you!" she sputters. "I don't know." She looks tired. "Ray, what do you think?"

"Oh, well, I guess I'll do whatever you want to do."

Kay sighs deeply, and I can tell she just wants us to leave.

"I'll think about a visit," she tells Laura. She hasn't made eye contact with me in a while, so I know she's not happy with me, but that's okay. I'll take that bullet if it means getting them some good care.

✦ ✦ ✦

When we get home, we find Max in the kitchen, on FaceTime with Asami's daughter, Suni.

"We're doing a history project together," he explains.

I poke my head in front of his. "Hi, Suni!"

"Mom! Don't!" Max seems embarrassed by me. It isn't the first time, and sadly, it won't be the last.

"What's your project about?" Ron asks.

"The assassination of Abraham Lincoln," Max says.

"And the Emancipation Proclamation," Suni adds. I can tell they feel very important using these big words.

"That's heavy stuff," Ron says.

"Mom, don't you wish Martin Luther King could have met Abraham Lincoln?"

"I'm sure they would have really liked each other," I agree.

"Jennifer, is that you?" Asami's voice comes blaring through Max's phone.

"Hi, Asami." I stick my face in front of the camera again.

"I have questions about this trip to Topeka."

"Okay. Why don't you call me on my cell so the kids can get back to work?"

She nods and walks out of frame. My phone rings almost immediately. Jeez, does she have me on speed dial?

"What's up?" I say as I settle onto the living room sofa.

"I'm unsure about this trip."

I roll my eyes. "What are you unsure about?"

"Well, to start with, a bunch of eleven-year-olds all together in a hotel is just a recipe for trouble."

"Asami, from what I hear, they keep the kids really busy all day touring around. And when they finally go to the hotel they're exhausted. Plus, girls and boys are on different floors."

"Oh, like that's going to stop them."

"Stop them from what?"

"From fraternizing, Jennifer!"

"I think the point of the trip is for them to bond, Asami, so fraternizing is encouraged."

"I want you to promise me to keep an eye on Suni. I don't want any boys getting her into trouble."

"I promise I'm going to be vigilant with all the kids."

"But especially Suni," she insists.

"Sure." Asami clearly needs this assurance.

"Good. And I want her to share a room with Lulu Burgess. I know Lulu's mother is going to be there, so that way Suni will get extra attention."

"I'll do what I can," I promise her.

"Good."

We hang up, and I try to think of what she could possibly be worried about.

✦ ✦ ✦

On Monday morning we have an emergency meeting of WeFUKCT to finalize the raffle items. Things have been flip-flopping so much that I feel we need to sit down one last time before we go to print with the raffle tickets.

"I won't keep you guys," I say as we assemble around a table in the cafeteria. "Just one last go-around. Alison, what's up with Prada?"

"She promised me a bag but just came back and told me she can only get a wallet." I can tell Alison sees this as a failure.

"Well, how much is it worth?"

"Five hundred dollars." She shrugs.

"That's great!" I tell her, and everyone murmurs their approval. "Good job. When will you have it in your hot little hands?"

"I can pick it up tomorrow."

"Great. Liana, owner's box seats all set?"

"Got the tickets in my desk drawer at home. I had to hide them from my husband."

We all laugh.

"Red Nails, what was the final final with the spa?"

"We got the Pure Bliss for sure!" She smiles, and we all cheer.

"No Tech—TV delivered?"

She nods. "Sitting in my garage."

"Delia, did you get a final answer from Tom Hanks?"

Delia looks chagrined. "I did finally talk to his manager's second assistant, but apparently he's unavailable for the foreseeable future. But they were really nice about it—wanted to know what we were raising money for and wished us luck."

"Well, you tried. Any other thoughts on celebrities, anyone?"

"I read somewhere that Steven Seagal is willing to do dinners with fans, but you have to pay him," Alison said.

"Well, that's not going to happen. Moving on, has anyone heard from Cathy Funfair?"

Everyone shakes their heads.

"Any idea if she ever got the wine?" I ask while I text her that very question.

Cathy, what's the status on the wine for the auction?

"I think she's really busy with her church's funfair right now," Delia attempts to explain.

"Uh-huh." I'm looking over my list. We have some good items, but—

They said no. Sorry.

I wish I was shocked, but I'm not. "The wine is a no-go," I tell the group. They groan.

"I feel like we should have one more thing," Alison muses.

Everybody looks around, hoping someone has an idea.

"What's one thing everybody wants?" No-Tech Cathy wonders.

"A vacation?" Red Nails suggests.

"A car?" Terry adds.

"Cash," Liana says definitively.

"Grrrrr." I let out a frustrated groan. "There has to be something."

My team starts to collect their things. I guess this meeting is over. "Okay, well, I'll send the final five to the printer, and we'll start selling right after spring break. Thanks, everyone. Have a good vacation."

Feeling deflated, I head to the minivan and just hope we've got enough fancy raffle items to get people excited.

18

To: The daily companions of Mr. Green's Fifth-Grade Class

From: Jennifer Dixon

Re: Don't delete this! It's important to me.

Date: March 23

Greetings,

Before we all head off to places unknown for spring break, I want to leave you with a few thoughts.

First, a reminder that we will begin selling raffle tickets for some amazing high-end items right after break. Please consider volunteering to sell some at your places of work or worship.

Second, there are still twelve parents who have not yet turned in their permission and medical forms for the trip to Topeka. I don't want to be the buzz saw in your head, so please just get them done. I'm happy to report that even world-champion procrastinator Jackie Westman has already turned hers in. This should put the rest of you in a shame spiral.

And finally, Mr. Green asks that you guys be more vigilant in sending fresh gym clothes for your kids. I won't name names, but I'm told there are a couple of real stinkers out there.

And on that nifty note, I bid you adieu and a safe vacation week.

Jen

I smile at my last official class duty for a week. Tomorrow we're heading out to see Garth and Nina and Chyna in Memphis for a few days. We've only ever visited once, and I'm feeling a strong need to see my friend. It's a seven-hour drive—almost all of it highways—so it should be a fun trip.

I feel badly leaving Vivs and Maude. I offered to take Maude with us, but my daughter assured me Raj and Varsha would have kittens if we did. She and Laura are going to check in on my parents, so I'm feeling very responsibility-free. Or I will after I teach my spin class.

When I get to Fusion, I see the parking lot is relatively empty, which doesn't surprise me. A lot of families leave on either Thursday night or Friday morning to beat the traffic or the airport rush. But I'm surprised and happy to find the spin room almost half full. My regulars are all there, including Mr. Tour de France.

"Hey, Jeff! Looking sharp today." And he does, having traded his usual Tour de France garb for a simple tank top and cycling shorts. His hair is dark and straight, with just a hint of gray at the temples, but I know after class it will be curly, which makes him even cuter.

"Thanks, Jen." He seems open to conversation, so I press on with the subtle grace that I'm known for.

"Hey, are you single by any chance?"

He looks down and smiles. "I thought you were married."

Oh God.

"I am! I'm very married." I have no idea what that even means. "I was just asking for a friend."

"Ah, the old 'friend,' huh?" He laughs.

The class is now all saddled up and listening to our conversation.

"No, really, I have a friend."

"Well, I'm married"—he pauses for effect—"but I do have a brother who's recently divorced."

"How old is he?" I ask, a bit too eagerly.

"He just turned fifty."

"Let's talk after class," I suggest, with a quick glance around the room. "Okay, eight o'clock, let's get to it!"

"It's eight-oh-five," Bob yells as I turn on the music.

"Thanks, Bob!" I say into my mic, hoping he catches the sarcasm in my voice.

✦ ✦ ✦

After class, Crazy Cindy stops by to tell me her party is May 11 and asks if I'm free that day.

"As far as I know, I am," I tell her and she promises to get back to me with details about her theme.

When she leaves, I see Jeff has been waiting to talk to me.

"Tell me about your friend. Is she hot?"

Why is that always the first question?

"Well, I'm no expert, but I think she's beautiful." Peetsa is a classic beauty not unlike the actress Sophia Loren: dark hair, dark hazel eyes, and a figure that doesn't even suggest she's had three kids. "How about your brother—is *he* hot?"

"He looks like me, but older." That little tidbit lingers in the air for a moment before I continue.

"Would he be open to a blind date?"

"I don't know, but I'll ask him. Do you have a picture of her?"

"No! Take my word for it, she's gorgeous."

"Okay. I'll tell you what he says next week."

✦ ✦ ✦

"How was the drive?" Garth asks warmly as we groan our way out of the minivan. After seven hours and two stops, Max is the only one with energy.

"Just fine," I tell him as he gives me a big hug. I really adore Garth—and I have since he was my trainer in Kansas City. The fact that he married my best friend is just icing on the cake.

Nina comes running out with her arms open.

"Yay yay yay!! I'm so glad you're here!" She hugs my son first. "What are they feeding you, Max?" She stands side by side with him, and I'm not surprised to see he's taller than her.

"Just the usual stuff," Max assures her.

Nina grabs my arm and pulls me in the house as the men unload the minivan.

"Yvette is here." She whispers what I guess is a warning that Garth's mother is still staying with them. It's not a surprise. I knew she was still convalescing.

"Great! Oh, hi, Yvette!" I say as we enter the living room and I see her sitting on the sofa in a colorful caftan.

"Hello there! I can't get up because of my hip," she says with a smile. "How is your mother doing?"

"She's good! Thank you for asking. She told me to send you her best."

"I know." She nods. "I already got the message from the guides."

Everyone else joins us after dropping the bags in our rooms.

"Where's Chyna?" I ask.

"Lacrosse practice."

"Over spring break?" That seems a bit unfair to me.

"Her spring break was last week," Nina explains. "She'll be home later."

We spend an hour catching up with them and letting Max show off the apps on his new phone, and then Nina and I head to the kitchen to start dinner.

"It's pretty much ready. We just need to heat a few things up," Nina tells me. "Want some wine?"

"Oh, hell yes."

After she pours us each a glass, I start heating up the turkey chili she's made, and Nina puts together a salad.

"How's work?" I ask.

"Great! I got two new commissions—one's a dental office downtown, and the other is a woman who wants to sell her custom-painted plates online."

"You always have something on the go," I tell her admiringly.

"Ya, I guess I'm lucky that way."

There is a disruption by the kitchen door, and then Yvette shuffles in using her walker.

"Mind if we join you?" she asks. By "we" I'm guessing she means her guides.

"Of course." I get up to help her into a kitchen chair. "How is it going here?"

"Garth and Nina have been so wonderful to let me stay with them. But as soon as I can walk without this damned thing"—she points to the walker—"I'm going to be out of their hair."

"You've been no trouble at all." Nina smiles.

Yvette turns to me. "Pizza."

Oh God, here we go again. "What about it?"

"The guides are still insisting I tell you it's the answer. Did you ever try to do anything with pizza?"

"I did try, Yvette," I say patiently. "I went to a couple of big pizza restaurants, but it didn't seem like something they could help—" I stop and stare at her, and for the first time I actually hear what she's saying. Not "Pizza is the answer." *Peetsa* is the answer! My friend is the answer! And like dominoes, the pieces fall together. God, why am I so dense?

I hug Yvette and tell her she's a genius, then run out to the backyard to call P. She answers on the third ring.

"He wore a puffy shirt" is her greeting.

"Who did?"

"The guy I went out with last night."

"Like from *Seinfeld*? That kind of puffy shirt?"

"Yup. I thought that's why you called."

"Honestly, I forgot you had another date. How was he otherwise?"

"*He wore a puffy shirt, Jen!*" Peetsa yells into my ear. While I'm laughing, she says, "So, what's up?"

"Okay, I have a weird question for you: Remember the ugly green car you told me about?"

"How can I forget it? I see it on the back lot every day. Why?"

"Do you think your boss would be interested in donating it to our school raffle?"

"I doubt it. But who would want a car that color anyway?"

"If it's a free car, whoever wins can spend the money to have it painted, don't you think?"

"I guess. But Hyundai can also have it painted any color and re-sell it so why would they donate it?" She has a good point.

"Can you just ask your boss?"

"I can, but don't get your hopes up. In the two years I've been there, I've never seen them donate a car to anyone."

"I *do* have my hopes up. I know he's going to say yes."

"Why are you so sure?"

I can't believe I'm saying this. "Because Yvette's guides said so."

There's silence, and then Peetsa says, "No, really, why?"

"I told you why."

"Are you drunk?"

"No! And I know how it sounds, but please, please, *please* just ask."

She sighs. "I'll try."

"You're the best," I tell her.

"Don't thank me yet. Let's see what Big Lou has to say. It may take a few days. He's gone to Las Vegas with his wife for a long weekend."

We hang up, and I walk into the kitchen beaming with what I think is the first genuine smile I've worn in months. Yvette looks up at me.

"So, is pizza the answer?" she asks knowingly.

"I do believe she is," I tell her. "Please thank your guides for me."

"They don't need thanks," she assures me. "But I wouldn't mind a scarf or something."

✦ ✦ ✦

Four days in Memphis flew by, helped along by trips to Beale Street, the Peabody Hotel, and Charlie Vergos's Rendezvous, where I had the best barbecue of my life.

The highlight for me and pretty much no one else was our trip to Graceland. I'm not a huge Elvis fan, but his home is an American institution, and I wasn't going to miss it again. Last time we were here I got so much pushback from Ron that I finally gave up asking. But this time I informed him I would be happy to go alone, which in our marriage is code for "Come with me, or there's going to be trouble." So we all went, including Max, who at least kept an open mind.

It was everything I could have wanted and more. Between the grounds, the costume museum, an insane house tour (*the Jungle Room*!!), and a guide who choked up when she referenced "the tragic death of the King," it was kitsch at its finest. And we got to try a deep-fried peanut butter and banana sandwich (Elvis's favorite!), which I expect I'll be dreaming about for the rest of my life.

Peetsa finally called while we were driving home after a tearful good-bye with Nina and Garth.

"Hello?" I sniffled.

"What's wrong?" she asked.

"Just sad to say good-bye to Nina."

"Aww. Well, this should cheer you up: Big Lou said yes."

My eyes popped open.

"He did? That's great! Oh my God! We're going to raffle a car!" And to myself I thought, *Oh, crap, I'm going to have to print new tickets.*

Ron looked at me from the driver's seat and raised his eyebrows. I gave him an excited nod and a thumbs-up.

"You need to come into the dealership and bring some kind of official paperwork confirming it's a donation for a legitimate cause."

"Yes, yes. Of course. I'll come in on Friday with everything. P, thank you so much! I totally owe you."

"Ya, well, just find me a great guy and we'll call it even."

"I'm on it," I promise her.

✦ ✦ ✦

Back in KC, Max still has the rest of the week off, so I recruit him to help me with Maude. I promise to pay him ten dollars if he plays with her all afternoon so I can get my housework done. He proves to be a very responsible babysitter, and I realize, not for the first time, that this has been a real year of growth for him.

He hasn't been grumpy for a couple of months, and he never mentions Zach E. anymore, so I'm hoping this means they have reached the stage of bygones.

My phone rings while I'm vacuuming. It's Laura, so I pick up immediately.

"Hi, sweetie."

"How was Memphis?"

"So great! I finally got to Graceland!"

"Oh wow! What was it like?"

"Very retro. I think you'd like it."

"I doubt it. I don't really get the whole Elvis thing."

"Well, you kind of get sucked into it when you're there. So, what's up?"

"Okay, so I wanted to tell you I have arranged for Nana and Poppy to take a tour of Riverview, *and* they're going to let them sleep over for the night."

"Seriously? That's incredible."

"I told Mr. Price they'll be a shoo-in if they have a good experience."

"Well, I wouldn't have gone that far, but it will be great for them to really spend some quality time there. I just don't want Mr. Price hovering with contracts the second they get in the door."

"He won't," she assures me.

"So, when is this happening?"

"He said any time the first week of May, so I thought the third?"

"That sounds good, and it'll give me time to find an appraiser to look at their house."

"Oh my God, it never occurred to me that their moving means they have to sell the house!"

"How else would they be able to afford to live there?" I ask her. Does she not realize that living in Suite 100 at Riverview is easily going to cost them five thousand dollars a month?

"I don't know. I just never thought about it. I love that house so much. It's where we grew up."

"I know, sweetie." I try to comfort her.

"Could you and Ron buy it?" she asks hopefully.

"I don't think that's in the plans, my love." Laura's never been very fiscally in touch with reality. "Listen, you should tell Nana. She'll be more excited about it if she hears it from you." My mother has barely had two words for me since I ambushed her (her word, not mine) with the idea of moving. It makes my daily visits a bit awkward, but I still insist on stopping by. I feel like they're standing still in life right now, and I want them to move forward.

"Okay. I'll call her now."

"Let me know how it goes." I cross my fingers that Kay hasn't changed her mind.

19

To: WeFUKCT
From: Jennifer Dixon
Re: Raffle update
Date: April 20

Hi,

Just wanted to give you an update on raffle ticket sales. We are kicking ass and taking no prisoners!

Thanks to all of you and your efforts, we have sold almost two hundred tickets. Add that to the proceeds from the candles and chocolate and we're pretty close to our goal of ten thousand dollars.

Well done, all of you!!

Thank you, Alison Lody, for taking on the role of treasurer and making sure all the money we're raising gets put into the PTA reservoir.

We still have a few weeks left before the big raffle party just before Memorial Day weekend (kudos to Delia Cramer for that idea and for the name she came up with: Raffle Mania!), so let's keep pushing and see how far past our goal we can get. After the year we've had, it's nice to be putting one in the win column.

See you at the meeting next week.

A very happy Jenny D.

P.S. If anyone sees No-Tech, can you tell her about this?

I've never been so happy to send an email. Scoring the car as part of the raffle has been a game changer for our little team. It is by far the most popular item despite the color, although people seem to be excited about the Chiefs tickets too. I've actually bought two tickets—one for the spa day, and one for the flat-screen TV. Sadly, the Om Sweet Om fitness package is the least popular at this point, but I'm hoping for an eleventh-hour surge.

I went to meet Peetsa's boss, Big Lou, a few days after we got back from Memphis, and I was a bit nervous. While I was getting ready, Ron asked the always annoying question, "Is that what you're wearing?" I looked down at my dressy yoga pants and T-shirt and gave him a thumbs-up.

"You might want to switch it up. This is a business meeting, right?"

"I guess." I shrugged.

"Maybe dress up a bit. Show the guy you're meeting that you're taking him seriously and he should do the same."

"But these are the *dressy ones*," I argued.

"Jen, I love you, but I feel like you don't even care what you wear anymore. You wear yoga pants every day. Not that you don't look great in them, but I wouldn't mind seeing you in something other than the 'I give up' pants."

It was obvious that Ron had been thinking about this for a while.

"They aren't 'I give up' pants! They're comfortable. Every woman I know wears them."

"Does Peetsa wear them to work?"

"Probably," I said without much conviction. "Women wear yoga pants at *your* work." It was a ridiculous thing to say, and I knew it, but my ego had been bruised.

"At the yoga studio, yes, they do," Ron said condescendingly. "Look, it was just a suggestion." He sidled up to give me a kiss, but I wasn't ready to make up, so I gave him my cheek.

"I'll take your suggestion under advisement," I said stiffly.

Half an hour later I went down to the Hyundai dealership decked out in a pencil skirt and blazer, equipped with all my WeFUKCT paperwork, ready to take on Peetsa's boss.

Let me just say, if Central Casting is ever looking for a mob boss, they should hire Big Lou. He's a gruff, tough-talking guy with a big heart and a big stomach. I'm serious about the stomach. He looks like he could give birth any day.

His office was right in the middle of the showroom floor, with glass walls so he can see everything, and he's known to jump into any sale that might be going on to give the customer an extra something, to make them feel like they're getting special treatment.

"Usually it's a protective coating for the leather interior," Peetsa told me. "We do it anyway, but Big Lou likes to make it seem like it's an add-on."

"Come in, sweetheart," was how Big Lou greeted me. He had on a pinstriped suit, a burgundy shirt, and a black tie. His salt-and-pepper hair was slicked back.

"So, you want the shit-green car, huh?"

"Umm, well, if you want to give it to me then I definitely want it."

"Have you seen it yet?"

"Yes, Peetsa showed it to me on my way in." And boy, it did not disappoint. I tried to imagine the most offensive shade of green I've ever seen, but when I saw the Elantra in person, it took my breath away. Calling it lime green would be an insult to colors everywhere. It actually hurt my eyes to look at it. It's as if Kermit the Frog and the Grinch had a baby, then soaked it in neon. But if you looked past the color, the car was really nice, and I told Big Lou as much.

"So, who am I donating it to?" He asked this question as if he didn't have a clue, but I didn't doubt for a second he knew exactly where it was going.

"It's our primary school in Overland Park. We're holding a raffle to make money to buy tablets for the fourth and fifth grades," I explained.

"Overland Park, huh?" He looked at Peetsa. "Those rich assholes never buy my cars." He glanced at me. "No offense."

Ouch. I wasn't sure how to react to this, but Peetsa knew exactly what to say.

"I know, right? They're a bunch of snobs."

Big Lou looked at me. "What do you drive, sweetheart?"

"A minivan."

"Oh ya? Ours?"

"No, but I'm actually looking for a new car. Maybe an SUV." It wasn't a total lie. Ron and I had been talking about it for months.

"Maybe we can put you in a Palisade." Big Lou was obviously always selling. But I suddenly wondered if this was going to be a quid pro quo situation. Did I have to buy an SUV for him to give us the car? Explaining the merits of that transaction to Ron would be interesting.

"Lou, she isn't here to buy a car." Peetsa jumped in to save me.

"No harm in looking." Big Lou shrugged.

I slid the official request for donations across his desk. He barely looked at it before he signed it and slid it back.

"Okay. Done." He looked up and smiled at me. "You look like my sister."

"Really? That's cool. Do you have a picture of her?" I'm always curious to see what people think I look like.

Lou pulled out his phone and scrolled till he found one. "Check out the ice on her finger," he said proudly.

I looked and saw a woman with frizzy brown hair and a *huge* diamond on her finger. "Wow," was all I could think of to say. This woman looked nothing like me. Or, she didn't look the way I like to think of myself as looking.

Big Lou showed it to Peetsa. "Dead ringer, am I right?" he asked her.

"Totally," Peetsa agreed, and I made a mental note to egg her car later.

"All right, ladies, I gotta get back to work. Peetsa says she's gonna do all the paperwork so you can get that thing out of here tomorrow."

We both stood up, and I thanked Big Lou again for his generosity.

"You're very welcome. Go test-drive the Palisade on your way out. Peetsa, grab the keys from Shelly."

And that, my friends, is the story of how I bought my first SUV. And Big Lou threw in the protective coating for free.

✦ ✦ ✦

So, now a brand-new black Palisade sits in my driveway, and a very green Elantra rests in the front yard of the school, parked on the lawn like a chartreuse beacon, reminding people that the raffle tickets are on sale. Every night, No Longer Homeless Mitch covers it up, much like Ron does for Bruce Willis, and in the morning, he unveils it again.

I'm still a bit hung over from my birthday dinner, but I have to get to Fusion for my 8:00 a.m. class. Ron surprised me two nights ago with an amazing yoga party at Om. He had all our friends show up for a class (taught by Carmen!) and had wine and beer and pizza brought in afterwards. It was a blast, but unfortunately, I had a little too much fun, and I honestly don't remember going home. All in all, a perfect way to turn fifty-four.

I'm hurrying to get to my spin class a bit early this morning because I'm dying to talk to Tour de France Jeff about his brother, who, from what Jeff has said, sounds like a great guy. He's divorced with two kids in high school, works as a pharmacist at Walgreens, loves to ski, and belongs to the Kansas City Running Club. We have been colluding to get him and Peetsa together for a blind date, but Brian (Jeff's brother) keeps getting cold feet. I don't want to even bring it up to P until Brian says it's a go. But Brian doesn't want to pull the trigger until he sees a picture of Peetsa, which I refuse to provide. My word that she's beautiful should be enough.

When I walk into Fusion at 7:50 I see Jodi, the manager.

"Hey, Jen, can I talk to you for a minute?"

"Sure." Why do I feel like I'm being called into the principal's office?

"So, are you okay to teach Cindy Dixon's birthday class in May?"

I will never get used to that name. "Yup. I already told her I would."

"Is she a relative of yours?"

"No, she's my husband's ex-wife."

"Wow, that's very progressive of you." Jodi's impressed.

"It wasn't always cool between us, but you know, time heals all wounds." I shrug.

"Or wounds all heels," she counters, and I smile. Am I the heel in this scenario?

"Anyway, just wanted to check in with you about that and tell you what a great job you're doing. We're looking for another slot on the schedule for you to teach."

I practically burst from this news, and I don't even bother to hide my excitement. "Seriously? That's so great! Thank you!"

"Well, you've earned it. Now get to class."

Shit! I just spent all my early time with Jodi, so now I won't be able to talk to Jeff until after class.

✦ ✦ ✦

As we're dripping and stretching to "Bridge over Troubled Water," by Simon and Garfunkel, I update the class on my parents.

"And they're going to be able to stay overnight, so they'll get a real feel for what it's like to live there."

"What if they don't like it?" Mary Willy asks.

"I haven't thought that far ahead," I tell her. "Okay, one last breath in. Fill your heart with love and release it out into the world. Good job."

Tour de France Jeff comes straight to my bike with a big smile on his face. "Brian said yes."

"Really? What changed?"

"I told him you showed me a picture of her, and I thought she was pretty. You said she has dark hair, right?"

"I did. Well, this is exciting! What's the next step?"

He shrugs. "Should I give Brian her phone number?"

"Let me talk to her first. I'm sure she'll be up for it."

✦ ✦ ✦

"No freaking way." Peetsa is adamant when I tell her about it over lunch the next day.

"Oh, come on! He sounds like such a nice guy."

"I can't believe you would even do this!" she exclaims.

"You asked me to!"

"When did I ever ask you to set me up?"

"After you told me Big Lou said yes! I told you I totally owed you, and you said, 'Find me a great guy and we'll call it even.'"

"And so you find some random guy's brother and think it's the perfect fit?"

"He isn't some random guy," I mumble. I hadn't mentally prepared for this scenario.

"I would rather light myself on fire than go on a date with a guy I don't know and have never seen, recommended by someone who has never met him either."

I'm starting to see her logic, but I give it one last shot. "Seriously, what do you have to lose?"

"Are you kidding? Have I not been telling you my stories?"

"P, I just have a feeling about this. I can't tell you why, but it's in my gut."

"You've been hanging around with Yvette too much," she grouses, but I can tell she's thawing.

"How about coffee on a Saturday afternoon?"

"What kind of coffee?" She smirks.

"Whatever kind you want. Please?"

She shakes her head. "I'm not sure why you're so invested in this, but okay. I'll meet the pharmacist for coffee."

"Great! Yay. I'll set it up. I'm so excited!"

"I'm glad one of us is."

✦ ✦ ✦

After my lunch with Peetsa, I meet Vivs at the law offices of Drake and Crenshaw. I didn't know lawyers worked on Saturday, but Mark is right there, sitting in his humble office in what I'm guessing is his casual weekend lawyer attire of a golf shirt and khakis.

"The meeting has been set for May tenth," he tells us. "The goal is to facilitate a mutually agreeable resolution of the issues through arbitration."

"What is arbitration?" I ask. It's one of those words I hear and kind of know but, gun to my head, I wouldn't be able to actually define it.

"A mediator will listen to both sides and decide on the best course of action for Maude. You should know that it's binding."

"Meaning?" Vivs says.

"Meaning you have to abide by whatever the mediator says."

"Do you know who it's going to be?" Vivs asks.

"I do. Her name is Chinda Grover, and she's tough, but she's fair. It's hard to say which way she'll go on this. Most people side with the mother, but she's been known to take the road less traveled when it suits her. Plus, she's—you know—she's . . ." He trails off.

Vivs and I look at each other.

"What?" she says.

"Well, she's Indian." He scratches his chin.

"And you think that gives Raj and Varsha an edge?"

"I honestly don't know. She's a mediator—being fair is in her job description—but I can't guess."

"Should we ask for someone else?" Vivs asks.

"Definitely not. The optics of that would be terrible."

We nod our agreement and decide to put our fate and our faith in the fairness of a woman we have never met.

"God, this is awful," Vivs groans. She sounds defeated.

"I don't want you to worry. We've got a strong case. And you can bet I'll be bringing my A game."

That should go without saying, I think to myself.

Mark stands to indicate we're done, so we head out to the lobby. Vivs walks straight out to the parking lot, but I linger to ask Mark one final question.

"Would you like to buy a raffle ticket to win a car or other wonderful prizes? The money goes to buy tablets for our fourth and fifth graders at William Taft."

When I join Vivs outside, twenty-five dollars in my pocket, she turns to me. "Could you go pick up Maude from them? If I see Raj or Varsha right now I won't be responsible for what I do."

And I will? Have you met your mother? "Of course. What time?"

"Now, if you can. They've had her since Thursday."

"I can't even imagine how hard that is on you." My eyes start to water, and I can see Vivs is holding back tears too. I give her a hug and run to my car. Losing my shit right now would help no one.

✦ ✦ ✦

"Gee Gee!" Maude leaps into my arms, and I feel myself start to well up again at the sight of her. But I quickly pull it together when I see Varsha watching me.

"Hello, my love! Are you ready to see your mama?" I take the diaper bag and her new Princess Jasmine rolling suitcase and nod to her other grandmother as I walk away.

"Jen, do you have a minute to talk?" Varsha reaches for my arm.

"I'm not supposed to discuss anything with you," I tell her.

"I know. We've been told the same thing. But surely you can see how happy the baby is here with us."

"Just as she is at home with her mother," I counter.

"Yes, of course. But we would never hurt Maude or put her in any danger."

"Neither would we." I decide I don't want to know where she's going with this, so I turn quickly and start singing Maude's favorite song to her as I dash to my car.

20

To: *Those who are spiritually responsible for the kids in Mr. Green's Fifth-Grade Class*
From: *Jennifer Dixon*
Re: *Taking our show on the road!*
Date: *May 2*

Hello, and happy May!

It's a little more than two weeks until the big fifth-grade trip to Topeka! Kudos to all of you for getting the permission slips and medical slips in on time. It's nice to know that selling my soul to the devil was worth it.

As for the room requests, we will do our best to make everyone happy, but don't get your hopes up. This is harder to figure out than the seating chart at my wedding.

I've attached a suggested packing list that has been handed down from years gone by. It looks like it was written a very long time ago, so ignore suggested items like clean handkerchiefs and the advice to leave your beeper at home.

See you on the other side!

Jen

I look at my watch. I'm waiting for a call from Peetsa telling me how her coffee date with Brian went. They were supposed to meet at Grab A Java at 1:30. It's only 2:30, so I need to cool my jets.

It's a glorious Sunday afternoon, so Max and Ron have gone to meet the other fathers and sons for a pickup soccer game, and I'm in the basement doing laundry. What's wrong with this picture?

I've contacted a real estate agent and a house inspector to meet me at my parents' house tomorrow, after they leave for their sleep-away at Riverview. Amelia, their cleaning lady, is going to go in the morning and make the place look good, then the others will show up at one.

This couldn't come at a better time. My parents have been getting so confused that I'm worried whenever they're in the house alone. My dad has taken to sitting in the kitchen in his pajamas, watching TV for hours on end. My mother has no energy, and any she does have is put into labeling everything in the house so the people in the basement know what's theirs and what isn't.

I check my watch again just as my phone rings. It's Peetsa.

"How did it go?"

"Did you know he's five foot eight?"

Shit! Peetsa is five feet eleven inches tall.

"No. Oh my God, I didn't even think to ask."

"Ya, well, it's one of the first things in my dating profile for a reason."

"Oh, P. I'm so sorry." I curse myself for not thinking of it.

"But besides that, it wasn't horrible."

I brighten a bit. "Really?"

"He's a nice guy. Really good looking in kind of a nerdy way, very smart, and oh my God is he funny. He told me the craziest story about the first time he ever got a massage, and I was dying." She's laughing at the memory of it, so I decide to laugh right along.

"He was already there when I showed up, and when he stood to greet me and basically came up to my nose, we both cracked up. It was actually a good ice-breaker."

Relief is washing over me. "So, what did you guys talk about?"

"Our jobs and our kids mostly. A little bit about our exes, but it didn't seem like the right time to get too into it."

"How long did you stay?"

"Two hours. The time flew."

"So . . . do you think you'll see him again?" I ask tentatively.

"I'm seeing him tonight," she says casually as if a second date on the same day is an everyday occurrence.

"You are? Oh my gosh, I can't believe it."

"We're going to see a movie. Can you believe neither of us has seen one in over a year?"

"What movie?"

"The new Matt Damon. Brian pointed out that he's short too."

I laugh. "He *is* funny. And I'm so glad you got past the height thing."

"Well, I always think the guy is going to have a problem with my height, but Brian doesn't seem to mind at all."

"So, am I out of the doghouse for setting it up?"

"We'll see."

I can hear Ron and Max stomping around in the kitchen, so I wish Peetsa good luck tonight and head upstairs with my basket of folded towels.

"How was it?" I asked my two obviously worn out and sweaty men.

"Great," Ron says. "Max played goalie, and he didn't let one ball get by him."

"Wow! Good for you." I give my son a thumbs-up, and he smiles.

"Who was there?" It's my casual way of asking for the gossip of the day.

Ron takes a swig of water before he answers. "Uh, the usual suspects—Buddy was there with his child bride and their newborn."

I consider telling him about Peetsa's date but decide to hold off until I hear how tonight goes. As Max wanders upstairs, I ask if Zach Elder was there.

"He was there, and so was Dean. He just got back from an eight-month tour in Qatar. He looks exhausted."

"How were Zach and Max with each other?" I wonder.

"They didn't even interact." Ron shrugs.

"I just can't figure out what the real story is. Max says he's being bullied, but all I see is him ignoring Zach, which is bullying in another form."

"The truth is probably somewhere in between. Don't sweat it. Today was a good day." He comes and gives me a sweaty hug, and I don't mind at all.

✦ ✦ ✦

I'm up and at 'em at the crack of dawn. It's a full day, and I need to be present for all of it.

Fusion found another time slot for me on the schedule, on Mondays at 8:00 a.m., so once again, my little family has to disrupt its morning routine for me.

This is only my second Monday teaching, so it's still a mystery as to who is going to be in my class. When I get there, I'm thrilled to see Tour de France Jeff adjusting his second-row bike.

"What did Brian say?" I figure, why beat around the bush?

"He said she's tall." Jeff laughs.

"Funny how we never talked about that."

"I know," he agrees. "It never even occurred to me to ask. I mean, how many six-foot-tall women are even out there?"

"Five-eleven," I mumble.

"What did Peetsa say?" he asks, and I'm wondering how much I should share. She called me late last night and said the movie was great and cocktails after the movie was even better.

"She said Brian's really funny." I cherry-pick one of the many nice things she said about him.

"Sounds like we did good." He offers me a fist bump.

"Too early to say, but it looks promising." I turn and get on my bike.

"Good morning, eight o'clock! Let's see what you've got!"

"It's eight-oh-four!" a familiar voice yells from the back.

"Thanks, Bob!" I smile at him as "You Ain't Seen Nothing Yet," by Bachman-Turner Overdrive, kicks in. I look out and only see two or three familiar faces in the half-full class, but I'm heartened when Donna, my always-late rider, ambles in at ten past eight.

"Good morning, Donna!" I say cheerfully. She waves and rushes to her seat.

By the time we're stretching to "It's Quiet Uptown" from the *Hamilton* soundtrack, I'm feeling energized and ready to start my day. I thank everyone for coming and, just for the hell of it, I tell them that I'll see them on Friday. Nothing wrong with the power of suggestion!

I race home to take a quick shower, and while I'm squeezing myself into jeans to prove to Ron that, indeed, I have *not* given up, I call Vivs. She has taken her first-ever sick day in order to look after Maude, because I have to deal with my parents' house.

"Hello?" a little voice answers the phone.

"Is that my Maudey?" I'm immediately reduced to mush.

"Hi Gee Gee! Mama! It's Gee Gee!"

Hold up. Was that a full sentence? I ask Vivs when she gets on the phone.

"Ya, she's been much more verbal lately. I'm still getting used to it."

"Any updates from Crenshaw?" I ask.

"Mom! No. I'll tell you if I hear anything. We're still set for a week from today."

"Okay." I sigh. "I'm heading over to Nana and Poppy's to see them off."

"Better hurry," she advises.

"Are you guys ready?" I ask my parents when I get to the house. It's a rhetorical question, because they're both still in their pajamas, even though it's nine thirty and I'm supposed to drive them over at ten.

"Obviously not, Jennifer," my mother snaps at me. "Can we just have a minute to finish our coffee before you haul us off to be locked up with the rest of the old people?"

"Mom, stop. It's one night. Let's go up and get you dressed."

"I can dress myself, thank you very much. Come on, Ray."

My father looks up, surprised to hear his name. He looks at me and smiles. "Hello, you."

"Hi, Dad. Let's get you dressed, okay?"

He amiably follows my mother upstairs, and half an hour later they come ambling down again.

"Where's your luggage?"

"Why would we need luggage?" my mother demands.

"Mom, we talked about this. You're going to stay the night at Riverview."

"I realize that, Jennifer, but I don't plan to take my clothes off at any time with all the disease that's there. We'll sleep like this and leave first thing in the morning." Well, that explains the velour tracksuits they're wearing.

"What about toiletries?"

"I have our toothbrushes and our medications in my purse."

I give up. They've agreed to stay the night, and that's the most I can expect from them. I drive them over in my mother's car because they have a very hard time getting into my new SUV. As we pull up to Riverview, we're met by Laura and Mr. Price.

"Welcome to Riverview!" he says warmly, and my mother just nods to him, but she gives Laura a very warm hug.

"Are you here to see me?" Shirley comes wandering over to the entrance.

"Hi, Shirley! Would you like to meet my mom and dad?"

"No, thank you," she says and strolls toward the snack table outside the dining room.

"Okay, I'm going to leave you guys in Laura's capable hands. I have some things to take care of."

"Oh, of course. Off you go, Jennifer. Go live your busy life.

We'll just fend for ourselves here." My mother rubs her eyes and grimaces.

"Are you okay?" I lean in close and put my arm around her.

"I'll be fine," she says, tight-lipped, but she gives me a half hug.

As I turn to go, I can hear her say, "What's that awful piano racket?"

✦ ✦ ✦

Back at my parents' house, Amelia has made their bed, cleaned their bathroom, and tidied the kitchen. They really only use the three rooms. I make my way down to the basement to make sure no one's there, and to clear a path to the furnace for the inspector.

I pop a Lean Cuisine into the microwave and pour myself some water. It feels very strange to be here without them, and part of me feels guilty that they don't know what I'm doing. While I eat, I look around the kitchen that is such a reflection of my parents' life. The calendar of kittens that hangs beside the fridge and is usually chock-full of their upcoming activities hangs with the month of March still showing—a tabby licking her paw. The fridge is covered with old pictures of the girls and new ones of Max and Maude. February's church bulletin is hung with a thumbtack on a little corkboard over the counter, which I'm guessing indicates the last time they went to church. That's kind of alarming, now that I think about it. Church is the biggest part of their social life. It's like time has stood still in this kitchen for the last couple of months.

Is this inevitable? Are we all headed in this direction, no matter how well we care for ourselves? I'm suddenly saddened by the ines-capability of aging and start to sob my heart out over my half-eaten Lean Cuisine.

Things change all through our lives, and for the most part, you roll with it and even embrace it. But when you start seeing your parents round the corner to the last stretch of their lives, it puts your own mortality into razor-sharp focus. I'm not sure if I'm crying for my parents or myself, but either way it feels really good.

At one o'clock sharp, the doorbell rings. I quickly splash cold water on my face, but I don't think anything but time will erase the effects of the ugly cry I just had.

Georgia DeBarge shakes my hand while she takes in my parents' foyer.

"What a lovely house!" she tells me. "It looks a bit dated, but nothing that some furniture and a fresh coat of paint can't fix. At least it doesn't smell like old people live here." I see her frankness as a realtor has not been oversold.

I start to follow as she walks through the house, but a knock takes me back to the front door to greet Steve Grimes from Inspector House. After pleasantries, he tells me he needs to check the roof first, and then he'll look in every room for water damage, mold, cracks, and so on. So I leave him to it and go in search of Georgia. I find her upstairs, in my parents' room, with a tape measure.

"Do you know if your parents have a layout of the house?"

"A layout?"

"Yes, something that shows what the upstairs and downstairs look like on a map."

"Like blueprints?"

"That's a start." She smiles and forges ahead to my old room.

"Great closets!" she enthuses. "Of course, you'll have to clean them out before we can show the house. Messy closets make people feel dirty."

This woman is never coming to *my* house.

Georgia talks me through the good, the bad, and the ugly of my parents' house. Seen through her eyes, it's a bit more of a fixer-upper than I would have thought, but she's very good at her job and assures me that everything she's talking about is cosmetic, so I'm feeling pretty good.

Then Steve Grimes comes up from the basement and says something that completely rocks my world.

"Did you know there are people living down there?" he asks.

I'm actually kidding. He didn't say that, but compared to what he really did say, it would have been a relief.

"You know you have a carbon monoxide leak, right?"

"Uh, no."

"It's coming from the water heater. It's small, but it's there." He holds up a contraption to show me that I'm guessing proves what he's saying.

"Carbon monoxide?" Georgia races into the kitchen from the pantry, still holding her tape measure. "How bad?" she asks Steve.

"It's fixable. It looks like someone tried to seal it with duct tape, but it came off."

I'm having a stop-the-bus moment. I need everyone to slow down so I can absorb what's being said. I've heard of carbon monoxide, but I'm not sure what it means that it's leaking. I ask them to fill me in.

"It's called the silent killer, because the gas is invisible and odorless. But it can really fuck—excuse me, ladies—mess with your health," Steve explains.

"How?" I ask, my heart racing like a thoroughbred's.

"Well, it can kill you if it's really bad. You don't have that kind of leak," he assures me.

"But it can give you headaches or stomachaches. You can lose your appetite, lose your energy, and sometimes even hallucinate," Georgia confirms.

I'm gobsmacked. My mind races through the past few months and my parents' slow and steady decline. Headaches for my mother. Loss of energy for both, but mostly my dad. Hallucinations? Hello, people in the basement! I immediately call Laura and explain the situation to her.

"Can you have the nurse over there check them out?" I'm trying to relay a sense of urgency without completely freaking out.

"I think they're taking a nap now. Should I wake them?" she asks with a frightened voice.

"Go talk to the nurse right now, tell her the situation, and see what she recommends. I'll be there soon." I hope I don't sound as panicked as I'm feeling.

Steve and Georgia are watching me for any clue as to what they should do next.

"Steve, can you recommend someone to come and fix the leak?"

"My brother-in-law does stuff like that. Let me call him." He picks up his cell and walks into the living room.

I look at Georgia. "I think we should put any thoughts of selling on hold for now. I need to see what's going on with my parents." I feel an unfamiliar weight on my chest, and I take some deep breaths.

"I get it. We can talk next week. I hope your mom and dad are okay."

"Thank you."

"My brother-in-law can stop by tomorrow morning," Steve informs me. "Will anyone be here?"

"I'll make sure someone is here," I tell him as we all head for the front door.

Driving to Riverview, I call Ron and, in what I'm sure sounds like an unhinged rant, tell him what I have learned in the past hour.

"You should pull over."

"No! I have to get to them. They were being poisoned for months! This could have killed them."

"Jen! Pull over. You need to calm down."

I do as he says and realize for the first time that I'm crying so hard I'm gasping just to get a bit of breath. The guilt is literally suffocating me.

"Easy, sweetie. Just let it out." Ron's calm voice makes me cry even harder. But soon I have myself under control enough to talk to him.

"Okay. I'm okay."

"Just take another minute. Do you have any water?"

I grab the bottle in my cupholder and down the whole thing. I can feel my body respond almost immediately.

"Can you pick up Max from school?" I sniffle.

"Of course I can. Don't worry about us. Just take care of your parents. Now, are you okay to drive?"

I take a breath and tell him I am. "I'll call you later. I love you."

"I love you too."

✦ ✦ ✦

"Jennifer, I'm glad you came back. These people are trying to put me in the hospital. I knew no good would come from being here."

My mother is in the small infirmary at Riverview, along with my father, a doctor, a nurse, and Laura, who comes running to hug me when I walk in the door.

"It's okay, Mom. They want to check you're getting enough oxygen," I tell Kay.

"Well, why wouldn't I be?" she asks through the oxygen mask she is wearing.

"Mom, you have a gas leak in the house. That's why you and Dad haven't been feeling well."

"I know that, Jennifer. They've already told me. But frankly, it's hard to believe."

My father has a mask on as well, but he seems completely unfazed by everything.

"How are you feeling, Dad?"

"Oh, well, pretty good, I'd say."

I turn to the doctor. "How are they?"

"They're doing well." The doctor puts her hand out and smiles. "I'm Dr. Singh. We're waiting for the blood tests, which will take twenty-four hours. Do you know how big the leak is?"

"The inspector said it was small."

"So, their exposure was a little bit over a long period of time." She nods. "And when did you start seeing symptoms?"

"I didn't know I was seeing symptoms. I just noticed they were tired all the time and getting confused. Then my mother started talking about people living in the basement."

"They're still there!" my mother assures us.

I motion for the doctor to follow me into the hallway.

"We thought it was just old age catching up to them." My eyes start to water, but I refuse to cry three times in one day. "So, what should we do?" I ask Dr. Singh.

"If it's possible, I'd like to keep an eye on them for a couple of days. Can they stay here?"

"I'll have to ask Mr. Price. They were only supposed to be here for a night, but I don't want to take them home until I get that leak fixed."

"I'll have a word with him if you like."

"I'd really appreciate that. Thank you, Doctor, so, *so* much."

I go back into the infirmary to find Laura gone and Kay regaling the nurse with the story of how she beat breast cancer. The oxygen is clearly kicking in.

"Jennifer, I was just telling Bianca here about our first Race for the Cure."

I nod to the nurse. "It was pretty great," I tell her.

"We're going to keep your folks on oxygen for the rest of the day, but they can walk around with these." She shows me two slim canisters on wheels. "You can take them back to their room if you like," Bianca tells me. "I'll be around in case they don't feel well."

"Sounds good. Thank you, Bianca."

"See you later, Mr. and Mrs. Howard!" She raises her voice to talk to them, and my mother rolls her eyes. "I'm not deaf!" she lets Bianca know.

"Are you guys ready to go back?" I ask my parents and their rolling oxygen tanks.

"What I'd like is to see the downstairs. They toured us through here this morning like they were late for lunch, so I didn't get to see everything," Kay tells me.

"Are you up for it, Dad?"

"Sure."

I can tell the pure air they are breathing is doing wonders for their energy. We walk through the lobby and take the talking elevator down to start our tour in the basement.

"Basement level. The door is open," the elevator chirps to us.

"Well, isn't that helpful!" my mother murmurs, and I'm glad to hear the sarcasm in her voice.

We walk the length of the basement slowly and see many

residents using the facilities, including the gym, the pool table, and the snack bar.

"Lots going on," I muse.

My mother doesn't say anything, but I can tell she's taking everything in. When we stop by the activity room, we see a group of women playing cards.

"What are you playing?" she asks them.

Three of them answer "Bridge," and one says, "I don't know."

"Boy, do they need a fourth," she informs me.

As we're passing the post office, we all hear Kay's name being called by an elderly gentleman dressed in khakis and a sweater, carrying his mail. When she sees who it is, she rips the cannula out of her nose with the speed of a ninja.

"Sam? Oh, my goodness, what are you doing here?"

"I live here. How about you?"

"We're just visiting," she says coyly. "This is my daughter, Jennifer. Jennifer, this is Sammy Leighton. We went to high school together."

"Nice to meet you!" I shake his hand. He has a solid grip for an old guy.

"Kay Crosby! I can't believe I'm running into you after all these years." His smile is addictive.

"Oh, I'm Kay Howard now—been so for more than fifty years. This is my husband, Ray." *Is she blushing?*

"Nice to meet you, Ray."

My dad smiles, shakes hands with Sam, and says, "Same here."

"I moved in a few months ago . . . after my wife died and my kids didn't know what to do with me." He laughs, but it has a hint of bitterness in it.

"Do you know anyone here who has klamafia?" Kay surprises us all by asking. "I hear it runs rampant in these places."

Sam looks confused, so I explain that she means chlamydia.

"Oh, I know what she meant," he says jovially. "I just haven't heard that particular rumor. Although I have to say"—he leans in toward all of us—"I've had my fair share of ladies offer to walk me home after supper!"

My mother thinks this is hilarious for some reason and lets out a long and loud laugh.

"Are you feeling all right?" Sam asks, gesturing toward the oxygen tanks.

"We just found out we may have carbon monoxide poisoning! We have a leak in our house."

"That can be serious!" Sam is alarmed.

"I think we're fine," Kay assures him.

"I'm glad." He reaches out and touches her arm, and I'm thinking, *Okay, just slow your roll, Mr. Handsy.*

"I'm on my way to get a cup of tea. Would you all like to join me?"

He asks all of us, but he's looking at Kay, so I let her decide.

"We can't right now, but maybe we'll see you at dinner," she offers.

"Ah, so you're staying for dinner. Wonderful! I hope to see you later." Sam ambles off toward the stairs.

"Wow, Mom, is he an old boyfriend?" I tease her.

"Hardly. But he always was a big flirt. You saw him, didn't you, Ray? Making eyes at me?"

"I sure did," my dad agrees.

"Do you guys want to go back up to your room? There are some things I need to go over with you."

They agree, so we take the talking elevator to level one and then walk down the hall to Suite 100.

"How do you like it?" I ask as we all settle into the living room.

"The furniture isn't much." Kay scrunches up her nose. "But I like that there are two bathrooms."

"The doctor wants you to stay a couple of nights so she can keep an eye on you, and I think it's a good idea."

Kay eyes me suspiciously.

"Is this some elaborate plan you've concocted to move us in

here without telling us? If it is, I'm on to you, and we can go home right now."

"No, Mom, I don't have time to concoct elaborate plans just to trick you. It's just two nights instead of one."

"Well, I guess that would be all right. Is it okay with you, Ray?"

"Oh sure. Whatever you want to do."

"But someone will have to bring us some clothes." I forgot that my parents only brought toothbrushes.

"I'll text Vivs to go get you some things."

My mother nods, then furrows her brow. "So, how did you figure out we had a gas leak?" she wants to know.

I was hoping this wouldn't come up. I really don't want to lie to them, so I tell a half truth. "I had a house inspector come today to make sure the house is still sound and safe, and he found the leak."

"Without telling me?" She stares me down.

"It wasn't a big deal."

"You brought someone into our house, for an inspection we didn't ask for, without telling us," Kay repeats the facts. Coming out of her mouth, it does sound like I've committed a federal offense.

"Mom, I'm sorry . . ."

"Well, what do you think of that, Ray?" This is her constant default. She consults my father, who she knows will agree with everything she says. But today my father surprises both of us.

"Well, I think I'm glad she did it." He smiles at me, and I give him a grateful nod. My mother is not pleased.

"Please don't surprise me with anything else. I may be old, but I'm still in charge of my life, thank you very much."

We hear a chime, and then a voice over the loudspeaker says, "Dinner is served." I look at my phone and see it's five o'clock.

Jeez, why do they make old people eat so early? It reminds me of having small kids.

"That's us!" my father says and walks to the door, his oxygen canister in tow. My mother and I follow, and I'm thrilled to see my father excited about a meal for a change.

I walk them to the dining room, then peel off to find Mr. Price's office.

He's sitting at his desk, on the phone, but he waves me in. "How are your parents?" he asks kindly.

"They're fine. Did Dr. Singh talk to you about them?"

"Yes, and if you want them to stay an extra night, it's fine. We're just going to need their medical insurance information to pay for the oxygen."

"No such thing as free air, huh?"

"Not in this place."

21

"Whatever happens, stay calm," Ron whispers to me as we walk into the mediation room for Maude's custody hearing.

"I'm not going to say anything," I whisper back, and I'm rewarded with a look from my husband that perfectly captures the sentiment. *Ya, right.*

Varsha, Raj, and their lawyer are sitting on one side of the table, so our team sits down on the opposite side. Vivs and Crenshaw sit together. Ron and I are just here for moral support, so we sit off to the side. There are strained pleasantries and then silence as we wait for the mediator. Crenshaw has told us he's only there to answer legal questions, otherwise, he will not be talking. I can't help but wonder how much we're paying for him to grace us with his presence.

"My apologies," Chinda Grover says when she finally shows up. "I got into a fender bender at the gas station."

She's dressed in a skirt and blazer, both navy and a little too small for her, and has her hair pulled back in a tight knot. She is all business.

"My name is Chinda Grover," she says matter-of-factly. "And I am here to mediate a custody dispute between"—she checks her notes—"Rajan Basak and Vivs Howard. The child in question is Maude Howard."

"We will be petitioning to have her name legally changed," Varsha tells her.

Chinda nods and continues. "This arbitration is binding, so I want a verbal confirmation that both sides have agreed to this."

Vivs and Raj both say yes.

"Okay, I'll hear from the mother first. Ms. Howard? Please tell me what the dispute is."

I could not be prouder of the way Vivs presents herself during the next ten minutes. She is eloquent, succinct, and passionate in her explanation of why she doesn't want Raj and Varsha to take Maude to India. She says she is willing to discuss coparenting with Raj and promises there will not be a hostile environment for him in her house. "I just don't want my two-year-old daughter to be taken to another country—especially a country where her father doesn't even live. She's too young."

"Thank you, Ms. Howard." Chinda asks if anyone needs a bathroom break, but everyone declines. "Mr. Basak, I'll hear from you now."

Raj has prepared remarks in front of him. He talks about how he didn't know he was a father until Maude was three months old, and how he uprooted his life in Brooklyn and moved back to Kansas City to be with his daughter. He describes his time with her in detail, including what he feeds her and what books they read together. He wraps things up with a powerful statement. "I feel that I have been unfairly treated by Ms. Howard. I would like to take my daughter home to India with my mother so she can have the same luxury of time to get to know her granddaughter that Mrs. Dixon has enjoyed."

At the sound of my name I look up at him, but he avoids eye contact with me.

Chinda nods at Raj's last comment and calls a recess. We all file out to grab some fresh air.

"You did great," Mr. Crenshaw tells Vivs. "You weren't adversarial, and you didn't paint him in a bad light. Well done."

"What about the mediator—do you think she's on our side?" I ask.

"I have no idea. She didn't seem pleased that you kept the pregnancy from him, but so far, you've presented your point very well."

"What happens next?" Vivs asks him.

"Ms. Grover is going to ask each of you a bunch of questions, and those answers will help her decide."

I shudder, and Ron puts his arm around me.

Back in the room, the mediator starts her cross-examination of Raj and Vivs, asking them what their work schedules are and what backup they each have in case they can't take care of Maude. Vivs explains that she has her mother, stepfather, and sister as backup and adds that we would be available for Raj too, since he doesn't have family in KC. There are a few questions about Maude herself, her schedule and her temperament. It's all very civil until Chinda asks Vivs if she feels Raj has ever put Maude in a dangerous situation.

"Absolutely not. As I've said, I think Raj is a wonderful father and I have no problem sharing custody with him at all."

I'm not sure, but I think I see Raj give a grateful smile.

"Mr. Basak, do you have any concerns that Ms. Howard has ever put Maude in a dangerous situation?"

And that's when the shit hits the fan.

Raj starts to answer, but Varsha interrupts with a resounding "Yes, we do."

"What?" I say, much too loudly, and Ron grabs my leg and squeezes it hard.

"Mrs. Basak, may I remind you that you are here simply as support? But I will let you speak on this one important issue."

I put my hand over my mouth to stop any words from coming out.

"Thank you, Your Honor. I apologize for my outburst, but I think you should know that Maude was left in the custody of her mentally questionable great-grandparents, who didn't tell anyone where they were taking her."

Vivs looks at Raj. "You must be joking." He doesn't say anything.

"Ms. Howard, please don't direct any comments to Mr. Basak. Mrs. Basak, please explain," Chinda says.

"Ms. Howard was on a shopping trip with her mother, sister, and grandparents. At one point they couldn't find Maude or Mr. and Mrs. Howard, and it was several minutes before they reappeared."

"Was anyone hurt?" Chinda asks.

"Thank goodness, not this time," Varsha says, suggesting that there will be other times when we won't be so lucky. I'm writhing in my seat, but I know I can't say anything. This is my version of hell.

"Ms. Howard, can you tell me what happened?"

Vivs explains the details of that day and how her grandparents had taken Maude back into the store to buy her a drum without telling anyone. "But they were all fine," she concludes. Then she looks across at Raj and says, "I can't believe you. I tell you things, and you use them against me? My grandmother adores you, and this is what you think of her?"

"Ms. Howard, I've asked you before—"

"They had no business being entrusted with the baby," Varsha interrupts Ms. Grover.

"They weren't!" I shout as I shake off Ron's restraining hand. "They were pushing her in the shopping cart. That's all."

"Mrs. Dixon!" the mediator reprimands me.

"Anything could have—" Varsha begins, but Raj cuts her off.

"No, Mummy, stop." He puts his hand on her arm.

"Rajan, don't," she pleads.

"There's nothing to win, Mummy. They're good people." He looks at us across the table. "They're like family." He shrugs.

"*I* am your family. They don't want you and they don't love you."

"That is *not* true! Vivs is the only one who doesn't love him."

That sounded so much better in my head than out loud. "I mean, she *likes* him . . ." I trail off.

"Everyone, please!" Chinda Grover is exasperated. "I've seen and heard enough." She takes a deep breath and straightens the papers in front of her. She asks Vivs and Raj to write down their custodial and financial requests, and after they hand them to her, she says she will make a decision within a week.

✦ ✦ ✦

At dinner that night, we rehash the highlights of the day with Laura and Max and my parents—yes! my parents, who are back home and doing well.

They ended up staying three nights at Riverview, and when their blood tests came back they confirmed that they both had mild to moderate carbon monoxide poisoning. But after a few tanks of oxygen and three square meals a day, they seemed like new people. It was such a relief to see my dad walking around the grounds outside Riverview, checking out the lawn and talking to the caretaker about what type of fertilizer he uses for the perennials. My mother inserted herself into the bridge game we had come across when we were touring that first day, and she would have gone on the shopping excursion to Oak Park Mall with her new friends, but it was set for the day they left.

"Well, I'm glad Raj came to his senses," my mother said after we finished our story. "Sweet boy."

"If he'd really come to his senses, he would have dropped this whole thing," Laura grumbles.

"He's not going to completely abandon his mother," I tell her. "But the fact that he wouldn't let her use that incident with Nana and Poppy as a strike against us was huge."

"Incident!" my mother sniffs. "That child was never safer."

I guess we can agree to disagree on that one.

✦ ✦ ✦

"What are you working on?" Ron asks as he slides into bed beside me.

"My playlist for Cindy's birthday spin tomorrow."

He rolls his eyes. "Can I make a few suggestions?"

"Sure."

"How about 'Crazy,' by Patsy Cline?"

"Helpful, thanks," I say dryly.

"'Crazy on You,' by Heart? 'Psycho Therapy,' by the Ramones?"

"You know, you're being very unkind," I tell him.

"I'm sorry." He pats his pillows, lies down, and closes his eyes. I think he's gone to sleep, but after a minute he starts to hum the Ava Max song "Sweet But Psycho." I reward him with a pillow in the face.

✦ ✦ ✦

"Ron, help!" I yell from the driveway. I'm leaving to teach Cindy's birthday spin but find a flat tire waiting for me on the brand-new Palisade.

"What's up?" He walks out the back door of the house chewing on a sandwich. I gesture toward the flat tire. He looks surprised.

"How does this happen on a new car?" I ask no one in particular.

"You probably caught a nail or something. Where's the spare?"

"I don't have time for that. I have to be at Fusion in ten minutes. Can I take Bruce Willis?"

"No, I need him. But I can drive you. Just give me a minute."

He dashes inside and is back out in a minute with his keys and a bottle of water.

"I thought of more songs for your playlist," he teases.

"No, thanks, got it covered."

"'Maneater,' by Hall and Oates? 'The Bitch Is Back,' by Elton John?"

"Enough!" I can't hold back a laugh. "It's her birthday. Can you just be nice?"

"Not as nice as you're being."

"How am I going to get home?" I ask as we pull into the parking lot at Fusion.

"You might have to take a—oh shit!"

"What?"

But Ron doesn't need to answer, because Cindy is suddenly

knocking on the driver-side door, all decked out in her birthday spin outfit, which includes rainbow pants, a low-cut pink top, and a plastic princess crown on her head.

"Hey, you two!" she yells through the window.

Ron reluctantly rolls it down.

"Hey, Cindy. Long time no see." I've never seen my husband so uncomfortable.

"Happy birthday!" I chirp from the passenger seat, hoping to make this less awkward than it is.

"Thanks! Ron, you aren't coming to my birthday spin, are you?" She seems concerned.

"Uh, no. I don't spin. But happy birthday."

"Do you remember my thirty-fifth birthday?" She leans into the car, her boobs on full display, and Ron physically recoils. To me she says, "He took me for a couples massage."

"I remember you thought the massage girl was touching me too much, and we got in a big fight."

Cindy stares at him. "Really? I don't remember that at all." She looks at me and giggles. "Men, am I right?"

"I'll find a ride home," I tell Ron and get out of the car before we go any further down memory lane.

"Thanks for coming to wish me happy birthday!" Cindy says to Ron as he rolls up the window and pulls away. I try not to think about how mad he probably is.

"I'm so excited!" She hooks her arm through mine as we walk into Fusion and down to the spin room.

"Oh my gosh!" I'm shocked when an almost-full spin room bursts into applause as we walk in and I see gold balloons and a banner saying:

55 CINDY HITS DOUBLE NICKELS!! 55

Cindy claps her hands and waves to everyone. I don't recognize any of the riders—she has clearly filled the room with her own people. There are whistles and cheers as she walks with me up to the instructor bike.

"Thanks for coming, everyone! I'm so glad you could all join me for the moment I've been waiting for for God knows how many years." She takes a deep breath and looks at me and—*Oh my God*—I see it. I see the crazy eyes that have always been her tell. I suddenly realize that whatever comes next is not going to be good.

"And this"—she puts her arm around me—"is the famous Jen I've told you all about. And she's here to teach my birthday class. For those of you who bet against me on this: pay up!"

Everyone laughs, so I join in, although I'm not sure what I'm laughing at. "What were they betting against?" I ask her.

"Well, Jen," she says loudly so everyone can hear, "I told my friends six months ago that I was going to get the woman who broke up my marriage to basically be my bitch for an hour while she teaches my birthday spin." The room laughs again, but this time I don't join in.

"Most of my friends said I wouldn't be able to do it, but here you are! My ex-husband's wife is working for me on my birthday. Best gift ever!"

I'm so confused at this moment. Either this is a hilarious joke and I'm just not getting the punch line, or Cindy has gone to insane lengths just to embarrass me in front of her friends. I'm guessing it's the latter. I say the first thing that comes to my head.

"So . . . you're still crazy."

There are boos from the riders, but Cindy yells over them. "Oh, you thought I just loved your classes so much I would just forget that you stole Ron right out from under me? You're such an egomaniac."

I want to tell her that I didn't meet Ron until they were divorced, but I decide it would fall on deaf ears, just as it has for over a decade. Instead, I decide to play it straight.

"So, just to be clear, you *don't* want me to teach your class?"

"Wow! Look who just woke up. No thank you. You've served your purpose. You can go."

And with that she plugs her phone into the sound system, and

Kelly Clarkson's "Since U Been Gone" starts blaring. I'm in a bit of a daze as I walk to the door of the spin room, but I do have the presence of mind to turn and give Cindy the finger as I walk out. There are so many thoughts and emotions going through my mind, but the worst one is that I'm going to have to live through yet another episode of Ron Dixon's favorite show: *I Told You So.*

22

To: Luc Baton, Ali Burgess
From: Jennifer Dixon
Re: Chaperone rules
Date: May 15

Hello, fellow chaperones,

Are you thinking what I'm thinking? Rules? There are going to be rules? Sadly, yes, there are. Mr. Green sent these little beauties to me last night, and I'm just going to say it: they suck. Hopefully we will be able to find a little wiggle room along the way. I mean, no alcohol for the grownups? In the name of Cuervo, why not?

The bus leaves Monday morning at 10:00 a.m. sharp, so please don't be late. I have it on good authority that the bus driver, Mrs. King, will leave your ass on the sidewalk if you're even one minute late. I'm not sure how she has the authority to do this, but I'm not going to be the one to test her power.

See below for the aforementioned rules, and I'll see you Monday!
Thanks,

Jen

Chaperone Rules for Overnight Trip to Topeka

1. You must do a head count every half hour while we are outside the hotel.
2. You must do a hall check every hour between 11:00 p.m. and 4:00 a.m.
3. Absolutely NO ALCOHOL—even after the students are in bed.
4. No wandering away to shop or do personal business.
5. Stay off your phone as much as possible, but have it handy in case of an emergency.
6. Report any bad behavior to Mr. Green immediately.

I'm trying to do the math on the hallway checks in the middle of the night. Do we take turns? Do we have to set an alarm and wake ourselves up? I'm going to be useless on day two if that's the case.

I'm still in my spin clothes, having just returned from my Friday class. I have come to love my regulars for the quirky little group of misfits and weirdos they are. When I walked in earlier today, I was greeted with concerned questions about my parents and my granddaughter, and in turn I asked about ailments and family dramas that they've mentioned to me.

One noticeably empty bike was Crazy Cindy's. No surprise there. After the tongue-lashing I took at her birthday party/ambush, Jodi, the manager, reached out to give me crap for leaving a class unattended and letting a student take over. When I explained to her what had happened, she seemed endlessly entertained by my public shaming. So, it was an unexpected surprise when she called later to inform me they had revoked Cindy's gym membership.

"That woman has quite a mouth on her," Jodi told me. "It's pretty hard to offend me, but when she called me a C-U-Next-Tuesday, I drew the line."

"You got off easy," I informed her.

I run upstairs for a quick shower and a change of clothes. I'm having a lunch meeting with WeFUKCT to finalize the plans for Raffle Mania. They don't know it yet, but I've planned a really special lunch to thank them for all their hard work. The party is a week away, but as luck would have it, I'll be in Topeka the first part of next week, so this is really our last chance to have a full meeting.

On my way to YaYas Euro Bistro, I voice-dial Vivs. "Any word yet?"

"God, Mom, don't you think I'd tell you?" she barks at me. We haven't heard anything from Chinda Grover yet, and tensions are high on all sides.

"I'm sorry, sweetie. I know it's hard."

"I've got to go." She hangs up, and I choose to believe it's because she's busy at work and not because she's mad at me.

When I walk into YaYas I see the majority of WeFUKCT is already seated at our table by the window. The only one missing is No-Tech Cathy, and I have a horrible moment wondering if anyone told her about this.

"Where's No-Tech?" I ask the group.

"She said she might be a bit late," Delia offers. "I think she has a doctor's appointment."

"We've asked for menus three times, and no one has brought them," Cathy Funfair informs me.

"I know. It's okay. We have a special menu today." As if on cue, waiters start bringing out flatbread appetizers and asking for our drink orders.

Alison Lody is looking at me like the cat who swallowed the canary, so I ask her what's up.

"I was going to wait for No-Tech to get here, but I can't!" Her smile is infectious. "As of this morning's ticket sales, we have raised"—she pauses for effect—"seventeen thousand two hundred and fifty dollars!"

The group gives a collective "*What?!*" and then we all start clapping and laughing.

"That's insane!" Cathy Red Nails exclaims.

"That's amazing!" Terry DiLorento cheers.

"That's impossible!" Cathy Funfair yells. We all look at her.

"Why is it impossible?" Alison scowls. "I think I know how to do basic math."

"It's just—" Funfair realizes she has nowhere to go from here, so she backpedals. "It's just, I've never seen any one group raise this much money without a clear plan." I'm guessing that was directed at me, and who can blame her? Not everyone likes to fly by the seat of their pants. And let's face it, I got really lucky with the car.

"Well, what we lacked in leadership we made up for in pure determination and a never-say-die attitude," I say to everyone. "You guys have been a pleasure to work with." I raise my water glass and toast my team. "To WeFUKCT!" We all clink glasses and drink to our success.

No-Tech comes rushing in half an hour late, as we're enjoying a variety of YaYas's amazing salads.

"Sorry I'm late." She plops down beside Delia. "What did I miss?"

"Only the greatest success story in the history of fundraising," proclaims Liana Jones. Did I mention we had ordered a bottle of champagne? Everyone is feeling festive.

"Grab a glass, No-Tech!"

"Uh, no thanks. I'm good with water."

"Why?" asks Delia. "We're celebrating!"

"So am I, but in a different way." She gives us a smile. "I'm pregnant!"

We all whoop and holler much too loudly for a lunchtime crowd, but who cares? Our little ragtag group has pulled off the Miracle on Ice of fundraisers, *and* one of our own is having a baby! I wouldn't want it to be me, even if they threw in free delivery and a million dollars, but I'm thrilled for her.

Thank goodness we talked through the details of Raffle Mania before we got too giddy, so I'm feeling very accomplished as I head to my car.

I check my phone when I get into the Palisade and am surprised to see I've missed three calls from Vivs. I call her back immediately.

"We lost." She's sobbing. "V-V-Varsha can take M-M-Maude to India." The sound of her anguish makes me physically ache.

"I'm on my way," I tell her and head to where she works.

✦ ✦ ✦

When I get to the Jenny Craig that Vivs manages, the girl out front tells me she's in her office. She's sitting at her desk, eerily still, when I walk in. She's stopped crying, but her eyes are swollen and red. I walk right over and wrap my arms around her from behind. She leans her head back against me and takes a deep, shuddering breath.

"Tell me what happened," I say into her hair.

"Crenshaw called." She takes a gulp of air. "He said the mediator is recommending joint custody, and that means Raj can take Maude wherever he wants when it's his time with her." She starts hyperventilating.

I have so many questions, but I don't think Vivs is in any shape to answer them, so I tell her I'm going to call Crenshaw. On a normal day, my bossy firstborn would tell me to stay out of it, but the fact that she doesn't object tells me she's in a bad place.

"How did this happen?" I ask when I get him on the phone.

"It's a reasonable settlement," he tells me. "In fact, Vivs gets Maude more than fifty percent of the time. But when Mr. Basak has her, he is not restricted on what he can do with her. But as I tried to explain to Vivs before she hung up on me, he can't take Maude outside the country without written consent from her."

"So, she can just refuse to give her permission," I reiterate.

"Yes. However, Mr. Basak can choose to challenge her in court every time she refuses him, and that would become very costly for both of them."

"Goddamnit!!" I yell. "How did someone else get to be in charge of what happens to my granddaughter?"

"I know it's frustrating. But as I told Vivs, this isn't a bad settlement. I'll be in touch when I know more."

"Thank you," I say vaguely and hang up.

"Where is Maude now?" I ask Vivs.

"She's with Varsha. I'm supposed to pick her up at five."

"Let me get her. She shouldn't see you like this."

"Okay."

"Can you take the rest of the day off?"

"No, I'm better here, keeping busy."

"Okay. Why don't I take Maude to my place, and you can meet us there and stay for dinner?"

Vivs nods and looks completely defeated.

"It's going to be okay," I tell her.

"How, Mom? How is it going to be okay?"

"I don't know, sweetie. I just know it will be." It occurs to me that I might just be putting my faith in something bigger than myself. My mother would be so happy.

✦ ✦ ✦

Varsha is all smiles when I pick up Maude. "I'm not trying to take Maude away from you, you know. I just want my fair share of time with my granddaughter."

"Varsha—" I take a deep breath and try to keep my voice even. "I've tried to put myself in your shoes many times, so I understand where you're coming from. But I could *never* wrap my head around taking a child away from her mother." At this, I reach out for my granddaughter. "Hi, Maudey-Moo! Say bye-bye to Grandma Varsha."

"Bye, Daadi Maa!!" Maude blows her a kiss. It heartens me to see she never cries when she's leaving either camp. It lets me know she is a loved and happy girl no matter who she's with. But no one will ever convince me she wouldn't be traumatized by being taken away from Vivs for any extended period of time.

On our way home, I call my parents and Laura and invite them for dinner as well. I hope my instincts are right and Vivs will appreciate being surrounded by the love of her family tonight.

✦ ✦ ✦

"This was delicious, Jennifer." My mom is wiping her mouth after devouring the Moroccan chicken dish I threw together. It's one of those one-pan recipes that's so easy to make and just happens to be very yummy.

"Thanks, Mom." I look around the table, and everyone has cleaned their plates except Vivs. She's holding Maude on her lap and kissing her head every ten seconds. We haven't said anything about the arbitrator's decision during dinner, but I know we need to talk about it, so I ask Max to take Maude up to his room to play a game.

"I think we all need to realize that this is not the end of the world," Ron says after the kids have left the room.

"Well, not *your* world," Vivs snaps. It's uncalled for, and she knows it, but Ron takes it in stride.

"We can certainly make it very hard for them to take Maude outside the country," I say.

"Yes, but how much is that going to cost us?" Vivs asks.

"Well, it's going to cost him too—maybe that will keep him from doing it," Laura offers.

We're discussing next steps going forward—what Maude's schedule will look like and who will be taking her to her activities—when Vivs suddenly stands up and says, "I need to see Raj." She yells for Max to bring Maude down, which he does reluctantly.

"We were playing Chutes and Ladders," he gripes.

"Sorry, buddy." She smiles at Max and reaches her hand out to her daughter. "Let's go, sweetie."

As she grabs her car keys and opens the kitchen door with Maude in tow, we're all surprised to see Raj standing there.

"Daddy!" Maude screeches and gives her father a leg hug.

"Hi, baby!" He picks her up and kisses her cheek.

"What are you doing here?" Vivs asks in a light tone that belies her foul mood.

"I came to talk to you," he says simply. "I went to your apartment first and then I came here."

"Come in, Raj." I stand and gesture for him to enter. There are hellos all around and then an awkward silence that is broken only when Kay says, "Boy, Raj, you really stepped in it."

Raj chuckles. "Indeed I have, Kay." He looks around at all of us sitting at the kitchen table and gives a heavy sigh.

I know it's taking everything Vivs has not to let loose on Raj in front of their daughter, so when she says, "How can we help you?" it has a little more of an edge than it should.

"I want you to know I would never take Maude to India unless you came with us. Or at the very least you agreed that I could take her."

It's so quiet that I can hear the dryer humming downstairs. I want to say something, but I know it isn't my place. Luckily, my mother isn't burdened with that kind of thinking.

"Well, it took you long enough to come to your senses," she informs him. "Now come sit beside me. Are you hungry?"

"Wait." Vivs blocks Raj's path to my mother. "Why are you here? Where is this coming from? Where is your mother?"

"Vivs!" I look from her to Maude and give her a *shut the hell up* look, but she presses on.

Raj, who really understands Vivs better than any of us, smiles and simply answers her questions.

"I'm here to tell you I'm sorry, this is coming from a need for us to be at peace, and my mother"—he sighs—"is very angry with me right now."

"Vivs, move out of his way," Kay demands, and she does. Raj takes a seat next to my mother, and she puts her arm around his shoulder.

"Tell us what happened," she encourages.

Raj looks at Maude and then back at Vivs, who asks Max to take her upstairs again.

"But I just brought her down!"

"Max. Be helpful, please," I say, and he acquiesces.

"The first thing I want to say is that this whole thing got way out of control."

"Ya think?" Vivs snaps, and we all shush her.

"You have to understand that my mother is the most important person in my life—or she was, until Maude." He smiles. "So, when she came here and wanted my daughter to know her heritage, it sounded reasonable to me. I had no idea it would take such a dark turn." He turns to Vivs. "I'm very sorry," he says sincerely, then looks around the table. "To all of you. I meant what I said at the arbitration. You're like my family. You've been so kind to me, and I wouldn't intentionally do anything to hurt you."

"We know that," Kay assures him.

"Vivs, in all my talks with my mother about taking Maude to India, I never once considered doing it without you. If you don't go, Maude doesn't go. I finally told Mummy that."

"And?" Vivs looks at him expectantly.

"She isn't happy." He shrugs.

"Is she going to stay and live with you?" I ask.

"She's still deciding. I want her to stay. She should be in Maude's life. Things are just very emotional right now."

"You'll make it right with her." Kay pats his hand.

"I know. It's just . . . I'm really all she has. I don't have any siblings . . ."

"You're a good son. We've all seen that," Ron says.

"That's why I promised that if she does go back to India, I will go to see her at least once a year. And I'll bring her here as often as I can." He turns to Vivs. "But I will never take Maude until you say it's okay. I'm saying this as a promise in front of your family." He pauses. "But I hope you'll consider taking a trip to India together sooner rather than later."

"Thank you," Vivs whispers. She has tears in her eyes as she goes to him, and he stands to hug her. "I promise I will."

In this moment, I can't help but wish these two would find their way back to each other. But if that can't happen, I'm glad they're now showing a united front.

"You two should get married," my father declares out of nowhere. The man says nothing nine days out of ten, and when he does speak, it isn't usually something this pointed. Everyone laughs, because it's awkward, and there isn't much else to do.

23

"*Roxanne, Roxanne, all she wanna do is party all night!*"

Max and his friends are singing at the top of their lungs on the bus to Topeka. Since we have the no-cell-phone rule, the kids are being forced to find ways to entertain themselves that don't include TikTok or selfies. So far singing has been the activity of choice.

The fifth grade is split up onto two Greyhound buses, so the chaperones are split between the buses as well. I get to sit with Ali Burgess, whom I've barely seen this year. When I first met her, six years ago, she was sharing custody with her baby daddy, Don, who just happened to be the boy I had the biggest crush on in high school. I nicknamed him "Suchafox," because that's how people described him back then. They are now happily married, and their daughter, Lulu, is a great kid.

"How is Don doing?" I ask her as we bump along the highway.

"He's good. Loving his new job."

"He has a new job?" As far as I know, Don still works at the city's recycling center.

"They put him in charge of a big new project. It's something like 3-D printing from recycled plastic. I'm not a hundred percent sure exactly what he's doing, but he's really pumped."

As the kids sing a Jonas Brothers song, Mr. Green makes his way to the back of the bus where we're sitting.

"Jen, do you have a copy of the room assignments with you?"

No one is more shocked than me that I actually do. I pull a hard copy out of my backpack and hand it to him.

"Any last-minute changes?" I ask.

"We won't know until we get there and tell the kids who they're rooming with." He scans the list. "There's always one or two who freak out and cry until they're moved." He goes back to his seat.

"Is Lulu okay rooming with Suni?" I ask Ali. "It was a special request from Asami."

"It's fine, although Lulu thinks Suni is boy crazy."

"She said that?"

Ali nods. "But they're still friends."

"What does 'boy crazy' even mean at their age?" I wonder aloud.

"I think she just talks about them, like, all the time—especially Max. You know that, right?"

"I've heard. But Max is clueless. He's all about his buddies."

"Sometimes I think boys are much easier than girls."

"Not in the early years, but getting to this age and beyond I can tell you they're *much* easier. My daughter Vivs is the reason I drink."

Ali laughs because she thinks I'm kidding.

✦ ✦ ✦

"Topeka in ten!" the bus driver, Mrs. King, informs us over the loudspeaker. I pull a trash bag out of my backpack and start walking up the aisle, collecting trash from the snacks we had the kids eat on the way. Will the glamor of this job never end?

✦ ✦ ✦

Our first day is jam-packed. We have opted for the Rediscover Freedom's Pathway tour, which is a five-hour experience that includes tours of the Kansas State Capitol, the Historic Ritchie House, and the *Brown v. Board of Education* National Historic Site. All of this covers over one hundred years of history involving the struggle for Black civil rights. It really is a great way to cement the things the kids have learned in American history this year.

I do a head count as the kids get off the bus. Thirty-two, plus thirty-three from the other bus, and the magic number is sixty-five. The teachers have assigned each kid a number so we can do a count-off after every tour. I personally feel they're kidding themselves if they think everyone is going to remember their number, but we can always hope.

"What are your numbers, boys?" I ask my son and his friends as they cruise by me on their way into the capitol building.

"Thirty," Zach T. says.

"Seventeen!" Draper Lody yells unnecessarily.

"Mom, stop," Max grumbles. I can see I won't be getting much companionship from him on this trip.

"Number, Max," I demand.

"Twelve. Jeez!"

"Don't forget them!" I call after the boys.

The state capitol building is truly stunning. They finished a multimillion-dollar renovation in 2014, and it looks so much better than it did when I came here as a sixth grader. The murals by John Curry are stunning. Funny how you don't appreciate any of it when you're a kid, but as an adult I'm completely captivated.

The highlight for the kids is the walk up to the dome. Two hundred and ninety-six steps gets you to the top, where you can enjoy the artistry of the dome itself and get a great view of the surrounding area. Ali and I are near the front of the group, but sadly we fall behind as a bunch of eleven-year-olds decide to jog past us. When we get to the top, I can't help but wonder what all that spin cardio is actually doing for me. I'm light-headed and have an overwhelming desire to throw up. We do a head count at the top, and everyone is accounted for. The walk down is much easier, but I'm still dizzy.

After an endless stop at the water fountain, we walk to Ritchie

House, which is known as one of the historic stops on the Underground Railroad and the oldest house in Topeka.

The kids are surprisingly subdued during the visit and actually spend time reading and viewing the exhibits. I mention this to Mr. Green, and he tells me they're getting tired. It's all part of the master plan to exhaust them so much that they won't fight their room assignments.

After Ritchie House, it's another head count and on to the *Brown v. Board of Education* National Historic Site. We actually start across the street, where a colorful mural exudes the power of equality and inclusivity. It's very moving. Then we tour Monroe Elementary School—the school at the center of the desegregation push of 1954. It feels like it's been frozen in time. I wonder if Max and his friends can truly appreciate the struggle this place represents. I like to think this generation will be the first to finally overcome systemic racism. It has to start somewhere.

As we all congregate in front of the school after our tour, we do another head count, getting the kids to yell out their numbers in order. We're running smoothly until Hunter Alexander yells, "Forty-two," and then . . . silence.

"Forty-three! Who's forty-three?" Mr. Green yells.

"It's Graydon," Hunter tells him.

"Graydon Cobb, are you here?"

No answer.

"I'll go back inside and see if he's there," I say. "I'll call you if I find him."

This feels like déjà vu for me. On the very first field trip we took in kindergarten, to the Kansas City recycling plant, we lost Graydon while everyone was watching a video on how to turn plastic bottles into jeans. Six-year-old Graydon had wandered off in search of a "clean" bathroom. I sprouted six gray hairs looking for him, and when he finally showed up I almost cried. This time, the bathroom is the first place I check, and that's exactly where he is.

"Graydon, if you go to the bathroom you have to let someone know."

"Sorry. I needed to wash my hands."

"I know you did, sweetie." Graydon has inherited Shirleen's germ phobia.

When we join everyone outside, they're already on the buses. Our next stop is dinner. We've rented out the back half of an Olive Garden. There's a little drama as everyone decides whom to sit with. This can be a minefield of social anxiety for the kids, and I feel badly when Michael Parker, from Ms. Stone's class, is left with nowhere to sit except the adult table.

"How was everyone's day?" Mr. Green enthusiastically asks our table of eight grown-ups and one eleven-year-old.

"I'm exhausted," Ali announces. "You do this every year?"

Mr. Green nods. "For the last five anyway. It's a lot."

Luc Baton somehow looks like he's ready for a *GQ* photo shoot. He raises his arms over his head in a stretch, and I'm almost relieved to see pit stains under the arms of his red polo shirt. He *is* human!

"Everyone at work thought I was lucky getting two days off, but man, I'd rather be in my office. It's so much easier." He laughs. He has the slightest French accent that I find very appealing.

"Any chance of getting some wine to go with our pasta?" I ask, because I just know it's what everyone else is thinking.

"You read my rules, right?" Mr. Green asks.

"Yes, and I committed them to memory. But can we really call wine alcohol?"

They all look at me like I'm asking if the sky is blue.

"White wine?"

No one backs me up on this.

After I've had my fill of pasta, salad, and breadsticks, I cruise the kids' tables under the guise of checking to make sure everyone is behaving themselves, but I'm really just spying on Max, who has basically ignored me all day. He's at a table with Zach T., Draper, and a new kid named Josh, plus four girls—Suni, Lulu, Alex, and Josie—and they seem to be discussing something very serious. I know this because there is a lot of shushing when I draw near.

"'Sup, Mom?" Max asks, so casually that it's hard for me to keep from bursting out laughing.

"How was dinner?" I ask the table.

"Good," they answer in unison.

"We're going to do a head count soon, so if you have to go to the bathroom, do it now."

"'Kay," is all I get. I debate standing there and really killing any fun they had been planning to have, but I decide to leave them alone. But not before I give Max the *I'm watching you* sign with my fingers. He just rolls his eyes.

◆ ◆ ◆

I flop on my bed in my hotel room and sigh.

"That check-in wasn't as bad as I thought it would be," I say to Ali Burgess.

"Really? How many kids have to cry for *you* to call it bad?"

"Seven."

She smirks and starts to go through her overnight bag. We're on the fourth floor and have twenty-two girls in our charge. The rest of the girls are one floor down, and Mr. Green and all of the boys are two floors up.

"All I want is a shower and bed."

I yawn. "You and me both, but I think we have to stay up until after lights-out for the kids."

"How serious are they about patrolling the hallways all night?" she asks as she holds up the master key we were given for the twelve rooms we have dominion over on our floor.

I make a sour face. "These kids are exhausted. I say one of us does a lap at eleven o'clock and we call it a night."

"Works for me. I'll leave this here." She puts the key on the dresser by the bathroom. "Mind if I shower first?"

"Go for it."

I pull pajamas out of my suitcase, along with my toiletries kit, then lie down on the bed and turn on the TV. I'm surprised to see it's only nine thirty. How the hell am I going to stay awake for an hour and a half?

As it turns out, I don't. I wake up at 11:37, still fully clothed and confused as hell. Ali is fast asleep in the next bed. I want to wake her up to ask why the hell she didn't wake *me* up so I could put myself to bed properly. I quietly get into my PJs and brush my teeth. I lie back down, only to realize I'm wide awake after my two-hour nap, so I decide to do a lap of the hallway.

As I expected, all is calm on our floor. I take a minute to enjoy the peaceful hum of the ice machine down the hall and try to appreciate this moment in my life when things seem to finally be calming down. And then I hear it—a squeal, followed by a bunch of shushing. The noise is close, but I'm not sure which room it came from, so I slowly walk down the hall, hoping to hear it again. My vigilance is rewarded on my third lap as I hear another squeal followed by an even louder "SHHHH!" I run back to my room and grab the master key from the dresser, then sprint back to the room where the noise came from. I pause for half a second, wondering if I want to be the killjoy who makes these girls quiet down, then I think, *Hell yes! It's pretty much what I'm here for*.

I slip the card key into the slot quietly and open the door. The room is dark except for a light coming from the floor. I reach for the light switch by the door and turn it on. The room is immediately filled with light and a bunch of audible gasps.

A group of kids are sitting in a circle on the floor between the two beds, and there is a cell phone in the middle. It takes me a minute to realize there are boys and girls together, and they seem to be playing some kind of a game.

"Mom, no!" I hear Max say.

"What's going on here?" I demand.

"We're just playing a game," he answers me.

"What game?" My voice is getting louder.

Silence. Then Suni Chang says meekly, "Spin the Bottle."

I freeze as I process her answer.

"But we only hug," her roommate, Lulu, adds.

I don't know what to address first: the obvious cell phone contraband that is providing the bottle part of Spin the Bottle (who knew there was an app?), or the fact that there are boys on an all-girl floor, or that they are all in violation of curfew, or that my son is among this pack of truants playing Spin the Bottle? It's a veritable potpourri of offenses.

"Boys, get back to your rooms immediately and quietly." I take note of who, besides Max, is marching past me. Zach T. (of course), Draper, and, most surprisingly, Zach E., my son's alleged bully.

Lulu and Suni have climbed onto their beds by now. I pick up the cell phone from the floor.

"Whose is this?"

"Mine," Suni says without looking at me. I hold on to it.

"Did you invite the boys to your room?" I look directly at her. She nods, then bursts into tears.

"Please, Mrs. Dixon, don't tell my mother."

This whole situation is way above my pay grade, so I tell the girls to go to sleep and we'll talk in the morning.

Back in my room, the thought that there were four boys and two girls keeps running through my head. Suni Chang sure knows how to stack the odds in her favor.

+ + +

I tell a shocked Ali Burgess about my midnight adventure early the next morning as we're packing up, ending the story with Lulu's assurance that "We were just hugging."

"Are you going to tell Mr. Green?" She asks the question I've been pondering since I woke up.

"Should I? I mean, no one was hurt. And it would mean both our kids getting in trouble."

"I kind of think we have to. I mean, something could have happened. If I were one of the parents, I'd want to know," Ali says. "As it is, I'm going to have a *long* talk with Lulu about following rules."

"Can you hold off until we get home? I think she's been scared straight."

"Well, maybe the talk should be about thinking for herself instead of following the crowd."

I let that simmer on the back burner while I finish packing, and then we start knocking on doors to make sure everyone is up and at 'em.

After the included continental breakfast off the hotel lobby, I take Max aside.

"Spill it," I say. Normally he would start by asking me what I was talking about, but since I caught him red-handed, he knows his only choice is to come clean.

"It was Suni's idea." He immediately throws her under the bus. "But I helped get the guys to her room."

"You did it knowing you were breaking like, five rules, right?"

He nods.

"I really didn't think I was going to have to worry about you behaving yourself. I'm very disappointed."

He nods again.

"I was surprised to see Zach E. there."

Max looks straight at me. "I wanted him to see me kiss a girl."

I'm deflated. "Max, you have nothing to prove to him!"

"I just wanted to show him I like girls."

I don't even know what to say to this, and then something occurs to me. "I thought you said you guys were just hugging?"

"That was Lulu's rule. Everyone else kissed."

"So . . . you kissed Suni?"

He lowers his face to hide a smile. I want to ask him more, but the group is assembling in the lobby, and we have to get going.

"To be continued," I warn him.

"Did you tell Mr. Green?"

"Not yet. You guys better not step one inch out of line today."

Max runs to his group of friends, and I join the chaperones as we count luggage and heads. Today looks to be a lot of fun for the kids. We're spending half the day at the Kansas Children's Discovery Center and the other half driving home. Apparently, the discovery center has a couple of great hands-on activities, including something called the Forensic Techniques Science Lab and another exhibit called Introduction to Robots.

"Hey, good mornin', Jen. How did you sleep?" Mr. Green approaches me as I'm getting on the bus.

"Really well, thanks. How about you?"

"Like a baby! I cried and wet the bed." He laughs at his own joke. "Seriously, though, anything to report?"

It's now or never. Either I fess up and the kids suffer the consequences of their deviant ways, or I keep my mouth shut and they get away with it.

"Nothing at all." I smile. It might be the wrong decision, but it's the one I can live with. I just really hope Asami never finds out.

24

To: WeFUKCT
From: Jennifer Dixon
Re: Are we ready?
Date: May 20

Hello, fellow WeFUKCTers!

I can't believe we're in the final stretch of this death march. And it looks like we'll have perfect weather for our outdoor Raffle Mania—good call, Red Nails!

The actual draw will take place at six thirty sharp—that will give people about an hour to buy last-minute tickets.

The food and drinks are in good hands thanks to Delia Cramer sweet-talking Grimaldi's into donating pizza, sodas, and water, and kudos to Funfair for getting Cellar Rat to give us some wine. We've also got a keg of beer coming from Alma Mader Brewing, so everyone should be happy happy happy.

In conclusion, I'll leave you with a quote from Les Misérables:
"One more dawn, one more day, one day more!"
See you tomorrow,

Jen Dixon, proud team leader

I really don't know what I was thinking, only giving myself one day between Max's overnight trip and Raffle Mania. Chances are I wasn't thinking at all, which is something I really need to work on.

For some reason I was bone tired from two days on the road. We got home yesterday in the late afternoon, and I don't think I even said hello to Ron. I walked straight upstairs to my bedroom and passed out. I woke up around five this morning completely naked and tucked in under the covers. I'll always be thankful I married a man who knows how to put an unconscious woman to bed.

It's still early, and Ron and Max are sleeping, so I call the one person I know will be awake at six thirty.

"How was the trip?" Peetsa asks in a hushed voice.

"Exhausting. And I caught our boys playing Spin the Bottle in Suni and Lulu's room."

"Seriously?" she whispers.

"Yup. Why are you being so quiet?"

"Hang on." I hear muffled movements, then she's back. "Sorry. I was in the bedroom."

"I thought Buddy had the kids—he picked Zach up from the bus last night."

"He does," is all she gives me.

"Do you have company?"

"I do."

"*What??* Who? Wait, is it Brian?" I'm bursting inside.

P is laughing when she answers, "Yes, it's Brian."

"Oh my God! This is so great. Tell me everything."

"I can't right now, but I will, I promise."

"Just tell me if it was any good."

"Jen!"

"Come on!" I beg.

"Yes, it was good. Really, really good."

"All right, you don't have to brag."

"Yes, I do! I haven't had sex in so freaking long."

"Okay, call me later when you can talk. I'm so happy for you!"

"It's all thanks to you, my friend."

"Whatever. Talk to you later."

"Bye."

I wake Max at seven, but I wish I could let him sleep. I know he's as tired as I am.

"Come on, buddy. Two more days of school, then you have a nice long weekend."

Over breakfast we tell Ron all about the trip, but we leave out the most significant detail. I'll fill him in on that later.

As Ron is leaving to take Max to school, Vivs shows up with the love of my life, who's looking sporty in little Adidas track pants and a white polo shirt that I know for a fact won't be white for very long.

"How was the trip?" she asks me.

"Well, it was a lot more interesting than I remember it being when I was a kid, that's for sure."

"It's because you're old," Vivs assures me.

"Yes, thank you, dear heart, for continuing to remind me. Any special instructions for today?"

"Nope. Just the usual." She looks at her daughter with pure adoration. I haven't seen Vivs this relaxed in months.

"How is Raj doing now that Varsha is gone?"

"He's fine. I think he misses her, but we'll see her soon enough."

" 'We'?"

Vivs lets out a sigh. "Yup. I've agreed to go to India with him for Christmas."

"This is new."

"Well, he's paying for it, and I've come to realize that it's only fair."

"That's extremely nice of you," I tell her.

"I know. But he's a good guy, and I know he really appreciates it."

"I'm going to miss you guys at Christmas!"

"How about you start stressing about that in six months instead of now?" She rolls her eyes. "I've gotta go. *Ciao, amore mio!*" She kisses Maude and is off like a shot.

✦ ✦ ✦

Maude and I have a busy morning going to her junior gym class and then Dunkin' Donuts for coffee and Munchkins. When we swing by my parents' place for a quick visit, I'm thrilled to see they're not at home. I call my mom on her cell.

"Sweetheart, I really can't talk right now. We're getting ready to serve lunch at the soup kitchen."

"Okay. Just wanted to let you know Max and I are back from Topeka. Is Dad with you?"

"Yes, but he's outside talking to Father Dugan about the plants around the rectory. I'll call you later."

I'm so happy my parents are in good health and acting like the young-at-heart midseventies couple they are. I still can't think of how they were slowly being poisoned without getting a sick feeling in my stomach. I'm just not ready for a world that doesn't have Kay and Ray in it. I doubt I ever will be.

✦ ✦ ✦

I decide to swing by Riverview Assisted Living to say hi to Laura and let Mr. Price know that we won't be needing Suite 100 anytime soon.

Shirley greets Maude and me as we walk through the front door. "Is that little girl here to see me?" she asks.

"She sure is, Shirley. Say hello to my granddaughter, Maude."

"My mother's name is Maude!" Shirley seems genuinely tickled by this fun fact. "Hello, Maude. Does anyone ever say 'Maude smells like a cod?'" She looks as though she's waiting for Maude to actually answer, and to my surprise, she does.

"Yes!" she says confidently.

Shirley nods knowingly. "Well, you don't smell like a cod," she informs my granddaughter. As she walks away, she continues, "Now, my mother is a different story. But she works at the cannery, so what can you expect?"

"Mom? Hi! Hi, Booboo!" Laura strolls toward us, looking official in her chef's uniform. "What are you guys doing here?"

"We just wanted to say a quick hello and tell Mr. Price he doesn't have to hold Suite 100 for us."

"Oh, he didn't. A couple from Lee's Summit moved in yesterday. He's diabetic and she's in a wheelchair."

"TMI, sweetie."

"I've got to run." She kisses Maude and then me and is gone as quickly as she came.

✦ ✦ ✦

While Maude is napping, I get a call from Nina. "How's life?" she asks me.

"Busy. Raffle Mania's tomorrow."

"That's kind of why I called. Yvette's guides have a message for you."

There was a time when this sentence would have left my eyes rolling and a smart-assed comment blurting out of my mouth. But since the pizza/Peetsa incident, I've learned to have an open mind.

"Really? What do they have to say?"

"Just that you need to prepare yourself for something big tomorrow."

"What do you mean, big? Good big or bad big?"

"They didn't say."

"Oh, jeez. Like I really need something else to worry about!" I practically yell into my phone.

"Don't shoot the messenger."

"Sorry."

"Okay, I've got a meeting. Let me know what happens. And don't worry. Big is probably good. At least they didn't say tragic."

"True. Way to look on the bright side."

"That's what I do."

I hang up wondering when was the last time something big passed my way. I'd say carbon monoxide poisoning counts. God, please don't let it be anything like that.

25

Raffle Mania is all set up in the field behind the school, and it looks incredible. The green Hyundai sits at the center of a huge display with tables on both sides of it. The seventy-inch television sits proudly on one table along with a large clear bag containing a yoga mat, block, strap, some yoga pants, and a tank top that has *Om Sweet Om* printed on the front. On the other table there's a big bag of KC Chiefs gear and blown-up copies of the tickets to the owner's box. Beside that is a huge spa basket and gift certificate and, finally, a beautiful red leather Prada wallet propped up in its box. Delia had a big banner printed, welcoming everyone to Raffle Mania, alongside a big archway of multicolored balloons. Across from the auction items, Grimaldi's has parked their portable pizza oven, and the smells coming from it are delicious. Music is pumping from the school's portable sound system, and what can I tell you? It looks like a great party.

My team and I are exhausted from the setup, but adrenaline is keeping me going, and as people arrive and react to what they're seeing, I start riding on a wave of back slaps and "Good job!"s from my fellow parents.

As I'm looking for my family—Ron is bringing Max and Maude—I see Asami making a beeline for me. *Shit.*

"Jennifer, a word, please."

"Hi, Asami!" I say brightly, and then I try to sidetrack her with a steady stream of questions. "Doesn't everything look great? Did you buy any raffle tickets? Guess how much money we made!"

"When were you planning to tell me?" she interrupts with her usual grace.

"Tell you what?" I'm trying to look innocent and relaxed, but I can feel my face getting red.

Asami gives me an arched eyebrow. I realize I'm busted, so I decide to just come clean and face the consequences of her wrath.

"Asami, it wasn't a big deal. They're kids. And I stopped it before anything bad happened."

"Stopped what? What are you talking about?"

"What are *you* talking about?"

"I'm talking about Suni almost missing the bus to dinner!"

"She did?" This is news to me.

"Yes! You told me you would keep an eye on her."

"I was! I did." My brain is playing catch-up with this conversation. "I had to go find Graydon during the head count. What happened to Suni?"

"Apparently, she and Lulu almost got on the wrong bus. Thank goodness Mr. Green saw them."

"You're kidding me! I didn't even hear about that. I'm sorry. Graydon went to the bathroom without telling anyone, so I had to find him." My heart rate is slowly regulating.

"So, what did you stop before anything happened?" she queries.

And up goes the heart rate again. Luckily, I'm a pretty good fibber when I have to be. "Someone brought, like, a Costco-sized box of Oreos, and the kids dove in like a pack of animals, but I stopped them before they could eat the whole thing in one sitting." I'm making it sound like I single-handedly prevented a smallpox outbreak.

"Oh, that. Well, I would've just let them go at it and learn their lesson."

"You're right, I probably should have done that."

"What time is the draw?"

"Six thirty sharp."

Asami looks at her watch and walks away. Bullet dodged!

"Principal Jackowski is looking for you," Alison Lody says from behind me. She's holding a plastic cup of white wine.

"Any idea why?"

She shrugs. "Maybe to congratulate you?"

"He should congratulate all of us." I look at her glass. "That looks good. I think I'll go get one."

She lifts her glass. "You've earned it."

On my way to the beverage table, I see Ron arriving with Max and Maude in tow, so I text him.

I'm over by the food and drinks

As I'm getting wine, I bump into all three Cathy Reids.

"Great minds think alike," says Red Nails.

"This job clearly drives you to drink," I tell them.

"At least no one got an eye twitch," No-Tech observes.

"There's still time," I inform her, then wave to Ron and the kids. Max scoots off before I can even talk to him.

"Hi, Gee Gee! I want a balloon."

"I don't have any balloons, Maudey."

"There." She points to the rainbow balloon archway.

"Sorry, sweetie. You can't have those."

"Noooo!" She starts to whine.

"I can't hear you when you talk to me like that," I tell her.

She stops and looks at me curiously. Then she yells at the top of her lungs, "I WANT A BALLOON!!"

"Well, you did tell her you couldn't hear her," Ron mumbles dryly.

"Maude. Stop that. You can't have those balloons. But we can look at them, and maybe touch them if you're a good girl," I tell her. She nods.

"Good girl."

My phone rings.

"Hello?"

"Jen, where are you? Why haven't you answered my texts?"

It's Sylvie Pike.

"I'm by the food. What's up?"

"Principal Jackowski is looking for you. He has some news."

"Is it *big* news?" I ask, thinking about Yvette's spirit guides.

"How would I know? Can you just find him before he drives me crazy?"

"Any idea where he is?" As I say it, I spot him standing by the auction items, gesturing toward the green Elantra to a woman I don't recognize. I tell Ron I'll be right back.

"You're looking for me?" I say as I approach him.

"Yes! Finally!"

Jeez, you could have called me, I think but don't say.

"Jen, this is Rochelle Reynolds, from the Blue Valley Schools Board of Education."

"Hi. Thanks for coming! That's so nice of you guys to support us."

"Well, I'm actually here because we got an anonymous donation to your fundraiser," Rochelle tells me.

"Really? That's random. Any idea who sent it?"

"Not a clue, but it's very generous."

"Who do we know that's rich?" I ask Jackowski, half kidding.

He shakes his head. "Maybe someone you asked to sponsor the event?"

"I only asked Grimaldi's to donate pizza." Could it be them, I wonder? Or Big Lou? But he already donated the car.

Rochelle Reynolds hands me a certified check made out to the William H. Taft Elementary School PTA for *HOLY SHIT* the entire amount we had been trying to raise! Ten thousand dollars.

"Oh my God! We have to find out who sent this!" I'm racking my brain. I'm also thinking that had I known someone was going to do this, I wouldn't have worried so much all year. What a waste of energy! I look at the check again and notice there's something in the memo line.

Three dimes, a hundred-dollar bill, and eighty-seven ones.

"What does that mean?"

They both shake their heads. "We thought you might know," Jackowski says.

"Does Sylvie Pike know about this?"

"Not yet. I wanted to tell you first. Great job, Jen. We've never raised this much money, ever."

"Well, I can hardly take credit for this." I hold up the check. "Oh my gosh, WeFUKCT is going to freak out!" I tell them.

"Who?" the Board of Education lady asks, proving yet again how unwise it is to say that name out loud.

"Nobody. Sorry. I need to go tell my team. This is big!"

Chalk up another one for Yvette's guides.

My team is over the moon when I tell them—except for Cathy Funfair, who surprises us all with her reaction.

"You just keep stepping in shit and coming up smelling like a rose, don't you?" Her incredulity is a bit off-putting.

"We also worked pretty hard," I remind her.

"Ya, but come on! A car drops in your lap, and now a donation? I mean, really?"

"This is a win for all of us, Funfair. Try to enjoy it," I suggest. I look at my watch. "Showtime, girls!"

We traipse over to the auction items and join Principal Jakowski, who's still standing there but now has a microphone in his hand.

"Do you have a final total?" he asks Alison Lody.

"Uh, yes." She consults her phone and shows him her screen. He writes the number down—old school, with a pen and paper—then signals for the music to be turned down.

"Good evening, everyone!" he booms into the microphone. "Welcome to Raffle Mania!" And then he does something completely unexpected. In his best (I'm guessing) wrestling-ring-announcer voice he says, "Let's get ready to raffle!"

The crowd loves it and gives him a big hand. We have an incredible turnout of students, teachers, and parents—there must be two hundred people. I hope Grimaldi's brought enough dough. I see Ron holding Maude, and Max standing with his buddies. The whole pickup crew is here with their families—even Peetsa, who is standing with a guy that I'm guessing is Brian because he really resembles Tour de France Jeff, but shorter. I'm surprised she's brought him to such a public outing so early in their relationship. Maybe she's hoping Buddy and the child bride will show up—and then I remember they have a newborn. They won't be going anywhere anytime soon. I turn my attention back to Principal Jackowski, who has been rambling on about end-of-school-year business.

"I want to acknowledge our PTA president, Sylvie Pike, who put together a dynamite group of ladies to raise money for our rising fourth and fifth graders to have top-of-the-line tablets."

Everyone applauds as Sylvie steps out from behind me and waves to the crowd. I look at my team and mouth, *Ladies?* They collectively roll their eyes.

"Thank you, Principal Jackowski. This has been one of the best team efforts I've ever seen from a fundraising group."

Really? I would have said "luckiest."

"Please give them a big hand!"

More applause, then Principal Jackowski takes back the mic.

"We've just finished tallying up the raffle ticket sales. Taking into consideration all the efforts the ladies made this year—selling candles and chocolates, receiving a very generous anonymous donation, and, finally, this raffle—I'm thrilled and proud to tell you we have raised"—he pauses for effect—"twenty-eight thousand six hundred and fourteen dollars!"

There is thunderous clapping and whistling at this announcement, no one's louder than mine. As I look out at the crowd, I see last year's committee head, Paulina Pruitt (PP). Her eye twitch is on full display.

"Let's pull these raffle tickets, shall we?" he yells over the still-cheering crowd. "First up"—he consults the paper he's holding—"a one-year membership to the Om Sweet Om yoga studio, plus a bag full of yoga gear. The winner will also receive six private yoga lessons and five spinning classes at Fusion Fitness, taught by this year's fundraising committee chairperson, Jen Dixon. Jen, would you like to come over and pick the winning ticket?"

This is a surprise. I step out front, then go over to the half-full jar of tickets. I stick my hand in and dig deep to pull out a name and then hand it to Jackowski.

"And the winner is . . ." There's that ring-ref voice again! "Jeremy's mommy!" He frowns. "That's a name?"

There is a squeal from the crowd and a woman I don't recognize runs up.

"Kindergarten moms are the worst," Red Nails mumbles beside me. I can't help but laugh. The crowd cheers, and Jeremy's mommy waves. I guess I'll be getting to know her soon.

And so it goes through all the auction items—Shirleen wins the TV, and some fourth-grade parents get the Chiefs tickets. A second-grade mom wins the Prada wallet, and one of the first-grade teachers gets the spa package. And then it's time for the big draw. The jar of tickets is twice the size of the other jars and completely full. Principal Jackowski makes a meal out of putting his hand in and moving around all the tickets until he picks one.

"And the winner of this bright and beautiful Hyundai Elantra is . . . Mark Crenshaw!"

I burst out laughing before I can stop myself. Vivs's lawyer won the car? I'm tempted to tell them to draw again—I mean, the man only bought the ticket because I guilted him into it. I take out my phone and call him while everyone wonders who the hell this person is.

"Mark Crenshaw."

"Hi, Mark, it's Jen Dixon."

"Hi, Mrs. Dixon. What can I do for you?"

"Remember the raffle ticket I sold you?"

"No."

"Really? Well, you bought one, and you've actually won."

"I did?" He doesn't sound too excited. "What did I win?"

"A bright green Hyundai Elantra."

"A car? I won a car?" I'm happy to hear he's a little more excited now.

"Yup. Congratulations."

"You said it's a Hyundai?"

"Yes, a very bright green Hyundai Elantra."

"How bright?" he asks skeptically.

"Bright enough that you'll want to paint it," I assure him.

26

To: All my friends in Mr. Green's Fifth-Grade Class
From: Jennifer Dixon
Re: Adios and vaya con Dios!
Date: June 20

My fellow parents,

And they said we'd never make it!

Congrats to all of us for surviving six years on the ever-bending road through William Taft Elementary. For those of you who have had me as class mom, I know my emails have sometimes seemed like they were written by a drunk birthday clown, but I hope you got one or two smiles from them.

Please remember to turn in all relevant materials to Mr. Green's classroom today. He is still looking for a few math books and, randomly, his copy of the 2012 federal tax guide.

After the graduation ceremony tomorrow, there will be a fancy party in the gym for all fifth-grade students, parents, and special friends that I'm pleased to tell you I had nothing to do with. I don't know about

> *you, but I'm bringing the whole* mishpocha *(that's Yiddish for the whole*
> *damned family), so I hope to see you there. Feel free to come introduce*
> *yourself to me if we've never met.*
>
> *And with that I bid you adios, au revoir, auf Wiedersehen, and,*
> *most important, thanks for the memories!*
>
> *Dixon out!*

Always my favorite email of the year to write. It's not even bitter-sweet that it's my final class mom email for ever and ever, amen. It's just sweet. I'm really getting out in the nick of time. One more year and you might have found me wandering a dirt road outside of KC looking for my mind.

As it is, I'm feeling great and grateful. I leave William Taft with my head held high and a fundraising record under my belt. I have a son who "met grade-level requirements," and I do believe I lost three pounds without even trying. What a year!

Kay and Ray surprised me the other day by announcing they're putting their house up for sale.

"It's just too big for us, sweetheart," my mom told me over lunch. "We don't need all this space. And your father doesn't want to be bothered with the lawn anymore."

"Really, Dad?" I asked him.

"I'd rather look after plants," he assured me.

"Where will you live?"

"We thought about Riverview. I mean, we met some nice people there, didn't we, Ray?"

He nodded as if he was barely listening and then said, "Too many old boyfriends hanging around."

"He's a little jealous," my mother whispered with a satisfied smile. "So, we thought maybe a two-bedroom condo in an over-fifty residence. There's a very nice one near our church."

I told them it sounded perfect, and I meant it. This will be a great transition for them. I'm just dreading all the crap I'll have to go through when they're downsizing. But hey, what else do I have to do with my summer?

Right now, I'm heading to my Friday 8:00 a.m. spin class. Tour de France Jeff and I are giddy with our success as matchmakers. Peetsa and Brian have been going steady for more than a month, so obviously we're planning what we'll wear as best man and maid of honor at the wedding.

I grab the rolling suitcase I'm lending Vivs as I head out the door. She and Raj are taking Maude to Disney World next week. I'm very bummed I can't go with them to enjoy all the cuteness, but I wasn't invited. They also have a trip to India planned for two weeks in December. I'm not invited on that one either.

Oh! And I think I solved the mystery of the anonymous donation! It's kind of a funny story. Recently, Laura has been on a tear to get Max to watch *classic* movies instead of the big action-hero movies he so loves. "Classics," according to Laura, are films like *Titanic*, *Scream*, *Austin Powers: International Man of Mystery*, *Speed*, and *There's Something About Mary* (I suggested we wait a few years on that one).

Last weekend she was over showing him the movie *Big*. I was in and out of the room, only half listening, when I heard something familiar. In the scene, the main character, played by Tom Hanks, is at the bank with his twelve-year-old friend, cashing his first paycheck from the toy company. When the teller asks how he wants it, he confers with his friend and then says, "Three dimes, a one-hundred-dollar bill, and eighty-seven ones." I made Laura back it up twice so I could be sure of what I heard.

Holy shit. Can it even be possible that *Tom Hanks* donated the money to us? That would be truly incredible, and, might I say, it would be just like Tom to do something so very nice. I can't prove my theory, so I won't spread it around, but I might share it with Delia so she can feel better about all her efforts. She was pretty down after the auction, even though I told her she contributed as much as everyone else with all the work she did. William Taft is going to need a new sucker—I mean volunteer—to shoulder the burden next year. This will make Delia think it's worth her time.

And as a gift to William Taft Elementary, I won't be the one to tell her it isn't.

Acknowledgments

Who to thank, who to thank, truthfully my mind is blank. And that's the only poetry you'll ever see from me.

I once again have to start by thanking you, the reader, who stuck by me through *You've Been Volunteered* and encouraged me to bring these characters back for a third novel. I love love love meeting you and hearing all your class-mom horror stories. Keep 'em coming.

Thanks to my editor, Serena Jones, who has the unfortunate job of telling me over and over again, "You can't say things like that anymore." I sometimes don't have the strongest sense of what is socially appropriate, so she has to put me on the straight and narrow more often than she'd like to. Other than that, she's a really nice person.

Thanks to the wonderful people at Henry Holt for all you do to save me from making bad decisions regarding things like book titles and cover art—Maggie, Pat, Marian, and the mighty Maddie. You guys are the best at what you do.

Pilar Queen, you are new to the party but already an invaluable voice in the mix. Thanks to you and UTA for all the support.

Nancy Frigand, you were so generous with your tales of woe from the over-fifty dating world. Even at my most imaginative, I could never have come up with a guy licking my nose, so thank you for sharing!

The legendary Sue Molnar, of Soul Cycle, helped give voice to Jen's woes as a spin instructor. Thank you for sharing all your new-instructor dramas with me and being the inspiration for Carmen. Thanks also to another Soul Cycle goddess, Mireya D'Angelo, for answering my endless questions and being such a strong supporter of my so-called work.

My early readers this time around included Jan Weiner, who has no problem telling me what she thinks; the great Paige Baldwin, who went above and beyond by rereading the first two books before she launched into this one; and Tom Bergeron (yes, *that* Tom Bergeron), who if you ask me really wasted his life in television when he could have been the world's greatest human spell-checker. All three of you gave me excellent, constructive notes. I want you to know I really listened to what you said.

I wrote this book during an interesting time in my life. I was recovering from spinal fusion surgery, and COVID-19 had just started ravaging the planet. I have to thank my sister Wendy for nursing me through the former, and my husband, Michael, and my daughters, Jamie and Misha, for quarantining with me through the latter. Neither could have been easy.

About the Author

Laurie Gelman was born and raised in Canada. She spent twenty-five years as a broadcaster both there and in the United States before trying her hand at writing novels. The author of *Class Mom* and *You've Been Volunteered*, Laurie has appeared on *Live with Ryan and Kelly*, *Watch What Happens Live*, and *The Talk*, among other shows. She lives in New York City with her husband, Michael Gelman, and two teenage daughters.

THE Class Mom SERIES
ON AUDIO

"I can't give Gelman enough credit for her performance. **She absolutely knocked it out of the park.**"
— *THE AUDIOBOOKWORM*

"Listeners will enjoy the story, which feels as if their favorite mom friend is regaling them with tales from her own life. . . . **Gelman's voice is energizing and her cadence confiding** in this debut novel."
— *AUDIOFILE*

AND DON'T MISS THE REST OF THE SERIES ON AUDIO
Including *You've Been Volunteered, Yoga Pant Nation,* and *Smells Like Tween Spirit*

"Author Laurie Gelman delivers her second in the Class Mom series in a style no less enthusiastic than her first narration. . . . Jen's emails to the third-grade parents remain her comedic stage— with **each one featuring deft sarcasm and perfect timing**."
— *AUDIOFILE* ON *YOU'VE BEEN VOLUNTEERED*